A Six-Letter Word for Death

THE HENRY TIBBETT MYSTERIES
BY PATRICIA MOYES

A Six-Letter Word for Word for DEATH

Patricia Moyes

An Owl Book
HOLT, RINEHART AND WINSTON
New York

Published by Holt, Rinehart and Winston,
383 Madison Avenue, New York, New York 10017.

Library of Congress Cataloging in Publication Data
Moyes, Patricia.
A six-letter word for death.
"An Owl book."
I. Title.
PR6063.O9S5   1983   823'.914   82-18738
ISBN: 0-03-005629-2 (pbk.)

First published in hardcover by Holt, Rinehart
and Winston in 1983.
First Owl Book Edition—1985

Designed by Debra Moloshok
Printed in the United States of America
1 3 5 7 9 10 8 6 4 2

ISBN 0-03-005629-2

This book is dedicated, with great affection, to the Isle of Wight, where I spent two unforgettable years in the Royal Air Force during World War II and many happy vacations subsequently. Carnworth is purely imaginary. However, Ryde, Ventnor, and St. Lawrence are real places, and I am assured that the clifftop path still exists as I remember it. I need hardly say that all the characters in this book are completely fictitious. I stress this particularly where it concerns the officers of the Ventnor Police Force and the Ryde Coroner's Court.

A Six-Letter Word for Death

1

London in August tends to be hot, sticky, and very dull. Some-times, of course, it may be wet and stormy, just to make a change. But almost invariably it is dull. And this applies as much to Scotland Yard as anywhere else.

In his office in the C (for Crime) Division on the fifth floor, Chief Superintendent Henry Tibbett sat at his desk, wishing that he were somewhere else—on holiday, out on a case, or just at home with his wife, Emmy, in their comfortable, slightly shabby Chelsea apartment. As it was, all he had to look forward to was the arrival of the morning mail, and he suspected that it would be as dull as the day.

Most of it was. But there was one intriguing envelope. It was marked PRIVATE, PERSONAL, AND CONFIDENTIAL, and was ad-dressed to Chief Superintendent Henry Tibbett in a fine italic hand in sepia ink.

Henry looked at it and sighed. He had, admittedly, been hop-ing for an interesting case to crop up, but he doubted that this would be it. The combination of the cheap mass-produced en-velope and the fancy handwriting added up in his mind to one word—crank.

He slit open the envelope and found his worst fears were justified. There were two sheets of paper inside, and the first that he unfolded bore the carefully drawn outline of a cross-word puzzle. The squares were neatly numbered in sepia ink, although the diagram itself had been traced in black, the solid squares meticulously filled in.

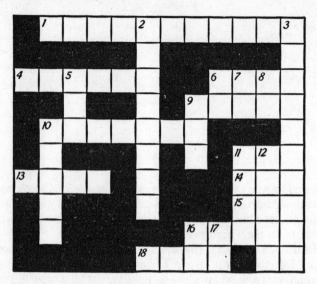

Underneath the diagram were two clues, also in italic script:

1 ACROSS: The lake's missing, to go by one Irish playwright, but another follows up the title. (Two words, 4 & 7)

3 DOWN: How's your hearing? Well? The first letter is misplaced, but it sounds all right, and initially is is all right. Just construct the vehicle. (Two words, 1 & 9)

On the second piece of paper, in the same hand, were the words "Chief Superintendent Tibbett. Keep this paper. More clues will follow." The signature was "A Lover of Justice."

Henry's first instinct was to crumple up both sheets and throw them into the wastepaper basket. However, he knew that even such apparent nonsense as this sometimes led to interesting results, and it happened that he was due to have lunch that day with an old acquaintance, Major George Manciple, whose brother was an expert in solving crossword puzzles. George Manciple was the eccentric Irish-born owner of Cregwell Grange in Fenshire, where Henry had once investigated a bizarre case. It was one of the few he looked back upon with affection, because of the people involved. George Manciple, predictably, hated London and came there only on the rare occasions when his wife, Violet, insisted. This time, his mission was to visit his tailor in Savile Row to be measured for a new suit.

Henry Tibbett and George Manciple met at the Major's club in St. James' Street. Henry noticed that Manciple had changed very little. He weighed a bit more, perhaps, but the iron-gray mustache was as neat as ever and the brown eyes as bright. For his part, George Manciple found himself amazed all over again that this slight, almost insignificant-looking man, with dark blue eyes and sandy hair now streaked with silver, should be one of the Yard's top detectives. Doesn't do to underestimate him, though, George remembered.

It was a pleasant lunch, filled with reminiscences. Over coffee, Henry remarked, "By the way, I'd like to get in touch with your brother, the Bishop of Bugolaland. The retired Bishop, that is."

"Edwin? Nothing easier, my dear fellow. Edwin lives with us at the Grange now. He's getting on, you know, and Violet thinks he needs looking after." George gave a snort of laughter.

Henry said, "I remember vividly that he gave me my first lesson in solving crossword puzzles."

"That's right. Trouble is, he has too much time on his hands these days, and he can't get enough of the really difficult sort—or so he says. Never did understand them myself," admitted George Manciple cheerfully.

Henry had had a photocopy made of his anonymous communication. He pulled it out of his pocket.

"I'd be grateful," he said, "if the Bishop would look this over and tell me what he thinks of it. He might even be able to solve the clues. You're going back to Cregwell this evening?"

"Sooner than that, old man. The three-fifty from Liverpool Street. Home before seven."

"Then if Edwin would cast his eyes over that puzzle to-night," Henry said, "I'd appreciate it if he'd call me at my office first thing tomorrow morning."

When Henry arrived for work the next day at half past nine, he was informed by a flustered switchboard operator that somebody had been trying to call him since . . . well, she had come on duty at eight, and found a message from the night operator that a Mr. Bishop had been trying to get through to Chief Superintendent Tibbett since six o'clock in the morning.

"It must have been an overseas call, Chief Superintendent," explained the operator. "Ivy said he kept saying he was from Bugolaland, in Africa, so that would explain the time difference, you see."

Henry grinned into the telephone. "It's more than a time difference," he said.

"You know this Mr. Bishop, then, Chief Superintendent?"

"Yes, I do. Please get me Cregwell 4789. Yes, Cregwell, in Fenshire."

"So there you are at last, Henry!" The voice of Edwin Manciple reverberated down the telephone line. "First thing in the morning, George told me, and here it is nearly ten o'clock. Where have you been?"

"I'm sorry, Bishop. I'm afraid I don't usually get to my office until—"

"Never mind, never mind." The Bishop was in high good humor. "Quite an ingenious little puzzle you sent me. Where are the rest of the clues?"

"I don't know," Henry said. "I'm told they will be sent in installments. Did you solve the first two?"

"Of course. Simple—but compiled by somebody who knows his trade. Why are they names?"

"I'm sorry—why are they what?"

"Names!" shouted the Bishop, causing Henry to hold the telephone away from his ear. "Both the clues you sent me. Names."

"I didn't know they were," said Henry. "What are the answers?"

"Got the puzzle in front of you?" asked Edwin Manciple, lowering his voice to a less earsplitting level.

4

"Yes."

"Very well, then. One Across is Lady Fanshaw."

"Is what?"

"Lady Fanshaw. I've never met her, but you must have heard of the family. Surely you see that the solution to the clue is obvious?"

"Obvious? I don't—"

Edwin was becoming impatient. His voice rose again. "The lake's missing!" he shouted. "Irish playwright! Two words, the first with four letters!"

"Yes, I know, but—"

Suddenly the Bishop lowered his voice to a near-whisper, with devastating effect. "*Lady Windermere's Fan*," he hissed. "By Oscar Wilde. Irish playwright. The lake—Windermere—is missing. So the first word, the four-letter one, is 'lady,' and the second word—omitting Lake Windermere—must begin with 'fan.' That leaves four letters at the end for another Irish playwright. The obvious answer is 'Shaw.' Fanshaw. The only other possibility would be 'Hyde,' author of *Casadh an tSugain* in modern Gaelic, and Fanhyde is not a name I have ever heard, whereas Fanshaw—"

"Yes," said Henry. "I've heard of the name."

"Well, there's your first clue," said the Bishop with satisfaction. "That means the second clue—Three Down—begins with a W. What does that tell you?"

"Not much," Henry admitted. He was writing the words "Lady Fanshaw" in the space along the top row of the puzzle.

"Look at the clue, man!" Edwin was getting exasperated again. Henry remembered that the Bishop never suffered fools gladly. He made an effort.

" 'How's your hearing?' " he read.

"Nothing the matter with my hearing, young man," retorted the Bishop, with spirit. "Ah, yes. The clue. Well."

"That's what it says," Henry remarked. "Well."

"And the first letter is misplaced. The first letter of 'well' is W. We know already from Lady Fanshaw that it's W."

"Yes. Yes, I see." Henry was trying to avoid sinking into the mental morass in which conversation with Edwin Manciple had always engulfed him. "And the first of the two words is just one letter."

"Aha!" said the Bishop approvingly. "Now you're getting somewhere. This second clue refers also to a name—W something. Constructor of a vehicle. The W, which is the initial, can be omitted from the name without changing the pronunciation. The answer—you have it?"

Henry was thinking. "Vehicle. Bus? Carriage? Car? *Cart!* Cartwright! Leave out the W, and it's still pronounced the same!"

"I told George the first time you came to Cregwell," said Edwin Manciple graciously, "that you were not as foolish as you looked. I am happy that my judgment has been vindicated. But Henry—why these names?"

"A silly joke, I suspect," said Henry. "Anyhow, I shall find out."

"And let me have the other clues as they come along," added the Bishop. "Very frustrating, a puzzle with only two clues."

"I'm assured," said Henry, "that there will be more."

Detective Inspector Derek Reynolds showed up in Henry's office a few minutes later, having been summoned from the canteen, where he was having a cup of coffee. Reynolds, too, was affected by the silly-season boredom of London in early August. He hoped against hope that this call to the office of the Chief might bring something interesting to break the tedium, but he had little real cause to think so. The only cases on his books at the moment were of the dreariest and most predictable sort, and nothing that had come through the Telex gave any prospect of more exciting happenings. The English criminal classes, apparently overcome by the heat and humidity, seemed to have given up.

Reynolds found Henry Tibbett sitting at his desk, with a piece of paper in his hand and a wry grin on his face.

Tibbett said, "Ah, Reynolds. Hot, isn't it?"

"Yes, sir. It certainly is."

"Well," said Henry, "we seem to have collected another of the weirdos who crawl out from the woodwork in the summer."

"Oh, yes, sir?"

"This one," Henry said, "is a crossword freak. He—or she, of course, we must be fair—has sent me a blank crossword puzzle with two clues. Here they are. What d'you make of them? You'd better sit down," Henry added.

Reynolds did so. He studied the squared diagram and the clues, and finally said, "I'd say we were dealing with somebody educated, sir."

"Why do you say that?"

"Well, sir—there's the fancy writing, for a start. Italics, I think they call it. And then, the crossword clues . . . I'm not a great one for puzzles, but when I do do one, like in the evening paper on the way home, it's the simple things like, well, 'domestic animal that purrs,' three letters, you'd be pretty sure that's 'cat,' wouldn't you? Unless, of course," added Reynolds, thinking hard, "it might be 'tom,' just to fool you. But you take your large Australian bird, three letters beginning with E—"

Henry was beaming. "You're perfectly right," he said. "I've had an expert working on this, and it's his opinion that the clues were constructed by somebody who knows the trade."

"On the other hand," Reynolds went on, looking at the second sheet, "this anonymous 'lover of justice' business smells like a crazy to me. Educated but weak-minded, I'd say."

"Or a practical joker," Henry said.

"Well," said Reynolds, "since I, for one, haven't an earthly idea about the answers to the clues, there's not much to be done, is there, sir?"

Henry said, "I told you I'd consulted an expert. The two clues have been solved."

"Blimey," said Derek Reynolds. "You must be joking, sir."

"No, I'm not. Both answers are the names of people. One Across is 'Lady Fanshaw,' and Three Down is 'W. Cartwright.' "

"Sounds potty to me, sir."

"I expect you're right, Reynolds. Nevertheless, having got that far, I think we should check up a little. Start with Lady Fanshaw, will you?"

Reynolds gave a wry grin. "Think I'll find her mug in the Criminal Records Office, sir?"

7

"I doubt it, but you'd better look anyway. I should think that *Who's Who* would be more useful, though. Also *Debrett's Peerage* and Burke's *Landed Gentry*."

Shortly after lunch, Inspector Reynolds was back in Henry's office with his report. Consulting his notebook, he began, "Fanshaw. Barony, created 1854 by Queen Victoria. Country seat: Fanshaw Castle, near Marksfield, Hampshire. Present title holder: George, 5th Baron Fanshaw, forty-eight years old, inherited seventeen years ago. Wife: Lady Fanshaw, née the Hon. Arabella Tewkhurst, second daughter of Lord Brentwood. Married twenty years ago, age now forty-five. Two sons, one daughter. Address: Fanshaw Castle and 601 Upper Pont Street, London W. Clubs: Junior Conservative, Whites, Royal Yacht Squadron. None of the family known to the police. There's Lady Fanshaw for you, sir."

"Distinctly unpromising," said Henry.

"That's what I thought, sir."

"Inherited seventeen years ago," Henry said thoughtfully. "That means his father's been dead since then. What about the Dowager Lady Fanshaw—the present Baron's mother?"

"Ah." Reynolds nodded approvingly. "That's right, sir. Much more to the point. She outlived her old man by fourteen years. Died just over three years ago, aged eighty-nine."

"Was she another sprig of the aristocracy?" Henry asked.

"I doubt it, sir. I haven't had time to do much research, but I did find an old copy of *Debrett* in the library, and it seems she was a Miss Clarissa Vandermeer of New York City before she married."

"Rich," said Henry.

"That'd be my guess, sir. In her own right."

"The epoch fits," said Henry.

"I beg your pardon, sir?"

"Edwardian England," Henry explained, "was the heyday of marriages between American heiresses who wanted titles and impoverished English noblemen."

Inspector Reynolds stood up. "I'll go and look into it right away, sir," he said.

"Look into it?"

8

"The Dowager Lady Fanshaw's will, sir. That was what you were going to suggest, wasn't it, sir?"

"Of course."

"No sense in wasting time, then, is there, sir?"

Under British law, a will, once probated, becomes public property, and anybody may request a copy of it. In fact, however, this is a fairly lengthy proceeding, and even Inspector Reynolds's standing as a police officer did not enable him to lay hands on Lady Fanshaw's will until nearly a week later; and by then there had been new developments.

For a start, Henry had submitted the original note and clues to his handwriting experts, with no results. The paper and envelope were of the cheapest quality, obtainable anywhere. As for the writing—well, said the experts, stylized italic writing was a much more clever device for anonymity than the usual badly written capital letters. The whole point of the script was to iron out individualism, and while it might be possible to distinguish between the writing of one expert and another if samples of both were available, the fine italic hand would bear no resemblance to a person's ordinary scrawl. All Henry could be sure of was that his correspondent was a skilled calligrapher and had access to a bottle of sepia ink. If there was a reasonably short list of suspects, these facts would surely . . . Henry replied that there was no list, and went back to his normal duties.

Then, six days after the first letter, the second set of clues arrived.

"Solved the first two?" asked the elegant sepia flourishes. "One Across will help you to get going."

2 DOWN: They say no man achieves this while alive— but it's allowable in one about to die.

4 ACROSS: Ill? The only alternative is the river.

10 ACROSS: He's lit up on the port, followed by a small group of fellows. Then he begins economizing—as indeed he should. (Two words, 4 & 3)

12 DOWN: Her one lace blue gown is in disarray.

Henry reached for the telephone, and was soon in contact with Edwin Manciple. He could almost hear the Bishop rubbing his hands with glee at the other end of the line.

"Wait while I get a pencil . . . Yes, yes, of course I have the puzzle . . . was beginning to think the fellow would never send any more . . . Two Down, did you say? Yes, I have that . . . yes . . . yes . . . I'll call you back in about a quarter of an hour . . ."

Seventeen minutes later, Henry's telephone rang, and the operator informed him that Bishop Manciple was on the line.

"Sorry to have taken so long, Tibbett. I had to check one word in the dictionary." Edwin Manciple sounded almost disbelieving. "Did you know that the word 'fey' in Scottish means 'doomed to die'?"

"No," said Henry. "I didn't."

"Well, it does. Had to, of course, but I had to doublecheck it. Well, now I've given it away, haven't I?"

"Given what away?"

"Two Down. Begins with *F*, from Lady Fanshaw—"

Henry thought for a moment. Then he said, "Call no man happy until he is dead."

"Correct. Herodotus."

"What does he have to—?"

"The original Greek author, that's all. Go on, Tibbett. You're doing well."

Henry went on. "Happiness . . . fey . . . licit means allowed . . . Felicity!"

"Absolutely right. Got it in one. Now for Four Across. You will see that when you write in 'Felicity,' you get a final *L* in Four Across."

"Yes, I see."

"What's the alternative to 'ill'?"

" 'Well,' I suppose."

"Right. Ill or well."

Enlightenment dawned. "The River Orwell!" Henry cried. "I've sailed there."

"Now," said the Bishop, "if we are to presume—and I think we must—that all the clues we have been sent so far refer to the names of people, then you should start searching for a lady named Felicity Orwell."

"Orwell might mean the river itself," Henry objected.

"It might, it might. But Ten Across is also a name."

"It is?"

"Yes. An ingenious clue. However, being a sailor, you should be able to solve it. You see that the second word, with three letters, begins with a *C?*"

"What has that to do with sailing?"

"Nothing, Tibbett. Nothing at all. But the first word has."

Henry studied the clue. " 'He's lit up on the port,' " he read.

"Now, relate that to sailing. What's lit up on the port?"

"I don't know. A bibulous Portuguese . . . oh, I see what you mean. A port-hand navigation buoy with a light on it."

"And what does a lighted buoy do?"

"Flashes at certain intervals," answered Henry promptly.

"And on your chart, it would be marked—"

"Flashing red! F. Red. Fred!"

At the other end of the line, Henry heard the Bishop chuckle. "I do believe you're beginning to enjoy yourself, Tibbett."

"I'm beginning to find out how to solve crossword puzzles," Henry said, "but as for enjoying myself . . . well, let's get on with the second word in the clue. Three letters, beginning with *C.*"

"Right," said Manciple, becoming businesslike. " 'Lit up on the port'—we have that. Followed by a small group of fellows. What is a group of fellows?"

"A band? A fraternity?"

"Begins with *C,*" repeated Manciple.

"Oh—'company.' But that's too long, seven letters."

Patiently, Edwin Manciple said, "There's a well-known abbreviation for the word 'company,' Tibbett. And the clue says 'small.' "

"Co. *C-O.* But that's too short."

"Ah, but the clue hasn't finished yet. Put in the *CO.* Leaves you one space to fill. 'Begins economizing.' The first letter of 'economizing.' *E.* Get it?"

Slowly, Henry said, "Fred Coe. The name rings a bell."

"Of course it does. Frederick Coe is a well-known economist—which explains the rest of the clue. I told you it was ingenious." The Bishop chuckled. "As for Twelve Down, that's childishly simple. Alice."

"Why Alice?"

"Never heard the song 'In her dear little Alice-blue gown'?" The Bishop made a hideous sound, which Henry interpreted as humming. "In crosswords, the word 'one' can mean the letter *I*. Lace in disarray. Scramble those letters, and they make 'Alice.' "

"I suppose so," said Henry. "Okay. We have five names: Lady Fanshaw, W. Cartwright, Felicity Orwell, Fred Coe, and Alice. But what on earth does it mean?"

"Aha," said the Bishop. "You're the detective, Tibbett."

"I'm beginning to think," Henry said, "that I'm the patsy."

"Patsy? That's a woman's name—"

"I was talking American," Henry explained. "What I mean is that I am being made a fool of."

"Difficult," said Edwin Manciple.

"I know it is, but—"

" 'It is I of whom a fool is being made.' "

"Not you—me."

"No, no. Not 'me.' 'I.' But it doesn't help. 'Me, of whom they are making a fool.' No, it seems impossible."

"Well, it depends. We don't know—"

"Impossible," repeated the Bishop decisively. "It seems to me quite impossible to avoid ending your sentence with a preposition. Never mind. What was good enough for Winston Churchill is good enough for—what's that? Yes, yes, Violet, I'm just coming. You remember Violet, Henry? George's wife. She's running me down to Cregwell for some shopping . . . must be off . . . good-bye for now . . . keep the clues coming."

Henry hung up, and looked at the puzzle with its new penciled-in entries. Lady Fanshaw, W. Cartwright, Fred Coe, Felicity Orwell, and Alice. Two of them undoubtedly real people, even distinguished ones: Lady Fanshaw, the deceased American heiress who married into an aristocratic English family, and the

12

celebrated Professor Frederick Coe. Henry had to admit that the name was unfamiliar to him, but Bishop Manciple had identified him at once. What about the others, W. Cartwright and Felicity Orwell? Real people too? It seemed likely.

And then came a call from the dock area of East London, where a seaman off a Liberian-registered ship, long suspected of drug running, had been found stabbed to death in a sleazy rooming house, and the unpleasant facts of real life closed in on Henry and Inspector Reynolds.

Fortunately the dockside murder turned out to be the work of greedy amateurs rather than of their highly professional masters, and Henry was able to make an arrest within the week. It was the following day that he found time to look at his "Crossword Crazy" file, and to his surprise it contained a new document. This was a photocopy of the will of the late Dowager Lady Fanshaw, and one bequest was heavily circled in the green ink Inspector Reynolds always used to emphasize passages in documents for his Chief's special attention:

> To Dr. William Cartwright of 698B Harley Street, who has contributed so much to the happiness of my later years by restoring to me the inestimable gift of hearing, I give and bequeath the sum of one hundred thousand pounds.

Although impressive enough, this bequest was insignificant when compared to others in Lady Fanshaw's will. Five hundred thousand had been left to the doctor who finally had the unpleasant task of helping her as easily and ethically as he could out from the burden of an incurable cancer and into another and, let us hope, happier world. A hundred thousand each went to her personal maid and her butler, while lesser but still considerable amounts were left to her chauffeur, her hairdresser, and her cook. The residue of the estate, which ran many millions of pounds even after death duties, went to her son and daughter-in-law, the present Lord and Lady Fanshaw. Nevertheless—a motive for murder?

13

"Forget it," Henry said to Derek Reynolds. "A motive for a little spitefulness against Dr. Cartwright."

"All the same, sir—"

"I said forget it."

"Well—Frederick Coe is a well-known figure. I could inquire if a Felicity Orwell had ever—"

"Derek," said Henry, "you're an incurable reader of mysteries. All right, as long as you don't waste the Yard's time, do as you like."

Two days later, Derek Reynolds was back with the answer. "It's like this, sir. Professor Coe is a famous economist."

"I know that."

"His wife's name is Alice."

"Oh?" Henry tried not to sound surprised. "So what?"

Reynolds cleared his throat impressively. "Mrs. Coe—Alice, that is—was born a Miss Orwell. She had a maiden aunt of great age called Felicity. When Miss Felicity Orwell came down with chronic bronchitis, the Coes refused to allow her to go into a hospital, but took her into their own home. They—Mrs. Coe in particular, as I understand—"

"You understand? From whom?"

Reynolds went slightly pink. "I have become on good terms with Professor Coe's secretary, sir. A very charming young lady."

Henry grinned. "All right. Not on the Yard's time, I hope?"

"Oh, no, sir."

"Very well. Go on."

"Well, as I was saying, sir, Professor Coe and his wife nursed Miss Felicity Orwell with great devotion all through her last illness, according to . . . to my source of information. Miss Orwell died last year, leaving the Professor and Mrs. Coe all she possessed, which amounted to a matter of some hundreds of thousands of pounds. I understand that certain other members of the family were bitter over this, Miss Orwell having changed her will only a few weeks before her death. However, what Tracey—that is, my source of information—says is that most of the family thought the Coes deserved all they inherited. After all, they had put up with the old . . . uh . . . lady for several months, when nobody else wanted to do anything but shove her into a nursing home." There was a moment of silence. Then Reynolds said, "Well, that's two, sir. They tend to go in threes, as you know. I reckon we'll get another set of clues, which will lead to the same thing."

"You mean, living people who have gained by the deaths of certain other people?"

"Exactly, sir. And this joker—the one with the crossword puzzle—is trying to plant it in your mind that some or all of these people could have been murdered for gain."

Henry sighed. "Medical murders are two a penny," he said, "and just about impossible to prove. If Lady Fanshaw was dying in agony from incurable cancer—"

"Ah, but the allegation isn't being made against that doctor, sir. Just against the one who helped her with her deafness."

"That's true."

"And Miss Felicity Orwell—well, I had an aunt myself, come to think of it—"

"Oh, God, Derek," said Henry. "Spare me your aunts. I always said you were as bad as Jeeves."

"All I meant, sir, was that my father and mother took care of this aunt of mine—Sibyl, her name was—for a matter of ten years. It wasn't that easy. My Aunt Sibyl was what you might call a testy old lady, which is just what Tracey—that is, my source of information—tells me about Miss Orwell. All the same, sir, people can live for a long time with chronic bronchitis. It's funny that my Aunt Sibyl lived for ten years—a pest to one and all, if you'll excuse the expression—whereas Miss Coe expired in a matter of three months. Much easier all round, if you follow me."

"I follow you like a bloodhound, Derek," said Henry. "Now go away and write me a report on the Limehouse stabbing incident."

"Very well, sir." Reynolds was poker-faced, but he noticed the small smile that hovered on Henry's lips.

The next day, the third set of clues arrived.

2

"How is the great expert doing?" inquired the fine italic hand in its sepia ink. "Here we go, then."

13 ACROSS: *Though singular, she was certainly blue. (See 16 ACROSS) (4)*

5 DOWN: *Disorganized raid flew over this frequently in W.W. II.*

10 DOWN: *(8)*

16 ACROSS: *Each b . . . (though confused) succeeded in putting an end to unlucky number here.*

11 ACROSS, 6 ACROSS: *The savage has lost Ian, but she's still retained his heart at the end. (11)*

11 DOWN: *Let's hope this little black sheep has 14 and 16.*

14 ACROSS, 16 DOWN: *First he's champion, then he loses the end of a bid—but don't worry—with this he's out of trouble. (5)*

9 ACROSS: *He holds the keys to everything, of course.*

After these clues, a firm line was drawn across the paper, and under it the italic hand had written: "I won't worry you with the rest of the clues to unimportant words. You are dealing with something 15 Across (3). The 9 Down is mighty, but don't underestimate the sword (3). 17 Down: This measure is only half the size of your wife (2). 18 Across: Another of your profession got the affirmative wrong, after this fantasy (4). 19 Across: Tu, you brute (2)?"

Henry was on the telephone to Cregwell in a matter of minutes. The Bishop sounded quite excited. "That's the last of them, then. Wait while I get a . . . Violet! . . . get me a . . . you know . . . a pen or something . . . and paper . . ." There was a long silence from the Cregwell end as Henry read out the list of clues. As he finished, Bishop Manciple said, "This is very interesting, Henry. I think I shall run into town."

"To Cregwell, you mean?" The Bishop, a well-known eccentric, was often to be seen jogging along the road to Cregwell, dressed in sneakers, running shorts, and a clerical collar. "A man should take sufficient exercise, wear clothing suitable to the activity, but never lose sight of his vocation," as the Bishop frequently explained to surprised passersby.

Now, however, he sounded impatient. "No, no. I said Town. London."

"I'm sorry," Henry said. "I misheard the capital *T*."

Edwin Manciple chuckled. "You're a good fellow, Henry," he said. "Mausoleum Club, one o'clock tomorrow. Wish you could bring your charming wife, but club rules, you know. Anyhow, the food is inferior in the ladies' dining room. I look forward to renewing our acquaintanceship in person. Good-bye for now."

Henry was careful to be slightly late for his appointment the next day, because, not being a member of the august club to which he had been invited, he wanted to make sure that Manciple arrived ahead of him, and would therefore be able to authorize his immediate entry. He might have known that Edwin Manciple would be censorious.

"Delighted to see you, Henry," he said, as Henry entered the lobby. To the porter he added, "This is my guest, Pelham. Mr. Tibbett. He is six minutes late."

17

"Yes, Your Lordship," replied Pelham dutifully. A lesser man, uncertain whether only an archbishop is entitled to be called "Your Grace" or whether a retired bishop should be referred to as "Your Reverence," might have dodged the issue with a mere "sir." But the porter at the Mausoleum knows these things as surely as Charon on his boat on the Styx—and is just as careful about whom he admits, and to where.

"Well, come in then, no sense dallying about." The Bishop led the way into the big, comfortable club room. "You'll take a whisky, I trust? Two whiskies, Harvey, with water and no ice." To Henry, Manciple added, "Can't stand these newfangled American ideas. Do you know, you actually have to *specify* no ice these days?"

The drinks arrived, and were consumed, accompanied by gossip of Cregwell and the Bishop's family. Then came an excellent lunch in the dining room, which is still barred to women—even the wives of members. Have to have some privacy, what? Important things to discuss among men. The Prime Minister? Well, that's rather a different case . . . a great pity, if you ask me. The Queen? My dear fellow, she is *much* too well bred to make such a request, which, of course, could hardly be refused. Now how did we get on to this topic? Oh, yes. The crossword puzzle. And abruptly, over the sherry trifle, the Bishop got down to business.

He produced a very creased piece of paper from his pocket, set his pince-nez firmly on his nose, spread the paper on the table, and said proudly, "There you have it."

The puzzle had been meticulously filled in, in the Bishop's slightly shaky hand.

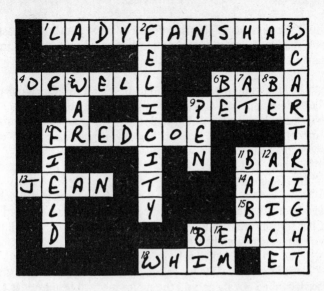

The crossword grid reads:

¹L	A	D	Y	²F	A	N	S	H	A	³W
				E						C
⁴O	R	⁵W	E	L	L		⁶B	⁷A	⁸B	A
		A		I		⁹P	E	T	E	R
¹⁰F	R	E	D	C	O	E	N			T
I				I		N		¹¹B	¹²A	R
¹³J	E	A	N		T		¹⁴A	L	I	
E				Y			¹⁵B	I	G	
L						¹⁶B	¹⁷E	A	C	H
D				¹⁸W	H	I	M		E	T

"Quite ingenious," Edwin Manciple remarked generously. "I won't bore you with the details of all the clues. You see he hasn't even bothered to give clues for Six, Seven, and Eight Down. The others, I daresay, you've worked out for yourself."

"I did get Nine Across—Peter—and Eighteen Across—Whim," said Henry. "Referring to Lord Peter Wimsey, of course. I thought the *H* was a bit of a cheat," he added.

"Well," said the Bishop indulgently, "he had a difficult task."

"He or she," said Henry. "There's no sex discrimination when it comes to crossword puzzles."

"But—" Manciple began. For once, Henry cut him short.

"Just what do you mean by difficult?"

"All those names." Edwin gestured with his dessert spoon. "The whole gist of the thing consists of names, even you must see that. Any other words formed are incidental—and yet I feel that any of them to which he provided clues probably have some bearing on something."

"Go on," Henry said.

"My dear Henry, you're the detective." Edwin Manciple

wiped the remains of sherry trifle off his lips with his damask table napkin. "Nevertheless, certain things are obvious. For instance, the clues came in groups."

"That's true."

"The first couple were Lady Fanshaw and W. Cartwright. The surname spelled with a W, I presume, since the clue talked about its being displaced, but making no difference to the pronunciation. Now, may I ask if you have made any effort to establish a connection between those two people?"

"You may, and I have."

"Aha. Go on, Henry."

"He is a famous ear doctor. She was an extremely rich woman of American origin who died a few years ago. The bulk of her fortune went to the present Lord Fanshaw, her son. But she also remembered her doctors in her will."

"What did she die of?" asked the Bishop.

"Not of deafness." Henry grinned. "Few people do. No, the poor lady died of cancer, and the major medical bequest was to the doctor who helped her to leave the world as painlessly as possible. Nevertheless, Dr. William Cartwright does seem to have given her great relief in her later years from her deafness—which is a disability nobody ever seems to take very seriously until they have suffered from it, or had to live with someone who does."

The Bishop nodded sympathetically. "I think you met my late sister Dora."

"I certainly did."

"Tragic affair. We don't discuss it in the family anymore—no point, is there? But you may remember what a great trial her deafness was—not only to herself, but to all of us."

"I do."

"I think she—or for that matter, any of us—would have been prepared to reward a doctor who helped her in that way, if we could have afforded it. You will take some coffee? Or better, a plate of Stilton with some of the club's excellent port. That's the thing. Waiter!"

When negotiations over cheese and port had been concluded,

20

the Bishop leaned forward across the table to Henry, and said in a hissing whisper, "How much?"

"Oh, just a small piece, please," said Henry. "I've never been a great one for blue cheese," he added, watching in fascination as the tiny cheese mites, just visible to the naked eye, writhed on the blue and white creamy surface.

"No, no, no," said Edwin testily. "I meant—*how much?*"

Comprehension dawned, as it always did sooner or later, when one was dealing with Edwin Manciple. "A hundred thousand," said Henry.

Edwin whistled. "A hundred? And this was a comparatively minor bequest?"

"The will isn't secret," Henry said. "Her personal maid and her butler got the same, and the cancer specialist got half a million."

"Nevertheless, a strong motive," pronounced Edwin, digging heartily into the Stilton, mites and all. "Motive enough for many men. And as a doctor—well, let's say no more about that one. Proceed." He took a sip of port. "My word, this is good, is it not? Best in London, if you ask me. What did Professor Frederick Coe have to do with a lady named Felicity Orwell, and who is Alice?"

"Felicity Orwell was Alice's aunt," Henry said. "Alice is Mrs. Coe."

"Is she indeed?" Edwin's eyes lit up. "You begin to interest me. Alice in her little blue gown, Twelve Down, if I remember rightly."

"But there's not the slightest suspicion of—"

"Of what?"

"Well," Henry admitted, "when Miss Orwell became very ill and couldn't live on her own anymore, Professor and Mrs. Coe took her into their house and gave her the most devoted care."

"For what ailment?"

"Chronic bronchitis. She only lived a few months, as a matter of fact. But during that time, she changed her will and left all she had to the Coes. Not an enormous fortune, like the Fanshaw affair, but certainly a useful addition to anybody's savings."

"Ha," said Edwin. "So there we have two. I suspected from the beginning that there would be three."

"Who are the others?" Henry asked. "You haven't explained the latest clues to me yet."

Edwin picked up the puzzle, adjusting his pince-nez. He said, "There is a lady called Jean Warfield, who appears to have suffered a misfortune of some sort on a beach. Or at the hands of a character called Beach. This is not clear. Her connection is with two people—both identified by Christian names only. Barbara and Peter, who is said to 'hold the keys'—but this may be a mere punning reference to Saint Peter and the keys of heaven. I would say, knowing him—"

"Knowing whom?"

"The compiler of this crossword," said Edwin. "Knowing him, I think that Jean Warfield died—or maybe was drowned—near a beach. 'Put an end to an unlucky number,' the clue says, and 'Jean' is Thirteen Across. The little black sheep in Eleven Down is 'Baba'—you know the ditty, 'Baba, black sheep, have you any wool?' " sang the Bishop in a cracked tenor, causing several members to suspend their meals and look austerely at the Manciple table.

"I know it," said Henry hastily.

"Well, Baba sounds to me very much like a nickname for Barbara," said Edwin, relapsing into normal speech. "And the compiler hopes she has an alibi. As to the others, you—Henry Tibbett, I mean—are warned that you are dealing with something big. That's Fifteen Across. You are told that the pen is mighty, but not to underestimate the sword. I take this to mean that the whole farrago has something to do with writing, and could turn violent. Lord Peter Wimsey you got of your own accord, as you told me—but I still believe that another Peter figures somewhere here. Of course, Peter could be a surname. Barbara Peter. Worth investigating. 'Em'—a standard printers' measure—makes up half the name of your charming wife. How is Emmy?"

"Very well, thanks," said Henry. He was beginning to feel slightly dazed.

"The final and inevitable 'et,' " the Bishop went on with relish, "of course refers to the last words of Julius Caesar, 'Et tu, Brute?' I need hardly tell you that it means, in Latin, 'You too, Brutus?'—but to translate it as 'And you, you brute?' is probably the oldest schoolboy howler in the book.

"Still, I have a feeling that everything clued means something in this extraordinary puzzle. I think that somebody was involved in a murder, or a supposed murder, who might have been presumed to be perfectly innocent, a friend of the victim's. Have some port, dear fellow. You notice that I am passing the decanter with the sun, even though there are only two of us. A curious superstition—but one tends to stay with the old ways."

Henry did not pick up the decanter. Instead he slapped his forehead and exclaimed, "Of course! I'm an idiot. I should have seen it sooner."

"Seen what, my dear fellow?"

"The pen is mightier than the sword," said Henry.

The Bishop looked puzzled. "That's right. That's one of the clues."

"It's *the* clue," said Henry. "You see, in a few weeks I'm due to address a group of writers—they call themselves the Guess Who club, because they all use pen names. This crossword is obviously something they've thought up to tease me with." He poured himself a glass of port. "I suspect," he added, "that my leg is being pulled out of its socket. I can't thank you enough, Bishop."

"Call me Edwin, please, my dear Tibbett. Edwin. And may I call you Henry?"

"I thought you always had."

"Have I? Ah, well, one grows forgetful, Mr. Tibbett. I am happy to have been of assistance."

"You're probably the only person in the world," said Henry, "who could have helped me out of this one."

"Helped you out?"

"As well," Henry added, "as giving me a most excellent lunch." He was trying not to look at the cheese, whose mites now seemed to be semaphoring for assistance. "Many, many thanks, Edwin."

23

As the two men rose to leave, Henry said, "Just one more question, if I may?"

"Certainly, Tibbett—or may I call you Henry?"

"You are a great expert at solving crossword puzzles, Bishop. Is there such a thing as a—well, a signature that one can come to recognize?"

Edwin shook his head. "They're not signed," he said. "Not in this country. I believe in America—"

"I didn't mean an actual signature," said Henry. "I meant—can you tell me who composed this crossword that we've been dealing with?"

"With which we have been dealing," murmured Edwin automatically. "My dear fellow—of course. I have been trying to tell you all through lunch, but you seemed to think it was compiled by a woman."

"I'm sorry. I—"

"You would like to know his name?"

"I certainly would."

"This puzzle," said Edwin, with some solemnity, "was compiled by Harold Vandike of Oxford University. I happen to know that he also compiles the only Sunday crossword worth doing, and I would know his style anywhere."

Back at the Yard, Henry consulted with C.R.O., with Inspector Reynolds, and with other colleagues, but as far as Barbara and Peter were concerned, he got nowhere. There were, of course, a number of Warfields in the Births, Marriages, and Deaths record office—some dead, some still living. None appeared to have been christened Jean.

Inspector Reynolds, a meticulous note-taker, did jot down the names of all the Warfields who had died in the fairly recent past. His first entry was Francis Arthur Warfield, of natural causes at the age of sixty-two, in London, twenty-four years ago. Then came Letitia Warfield, of natural causes, aged ninety-two, in Brighton, twenty years ago. Herbert and his wife, Agnes Warfield, had both been killed in an aircraft accident eighteen years earlier. The following year, Eugenia Warfield had died accidentally at the age of eighteen. Subsequently, Joan Warfield had committed suicide at the age of twenty-four, and a few days later Teresa Warfield, aged seventy-eight, had succumbed to natural causes. Both came from the same town in the north of England. Coincidence? Or was Teresa, Joan's grandmother or great-aunt, already ill and shattered by the young woman's suicide?

In Derek Reynolds's careful report, however, the name of Eugenia Warfield was circled. In the margin, he wrote, "Eugenia—Jean?" The finding of accidental death had been given by a coroner's jury at Ryde, Isle of Wight. The cause of death was drowning.

3

Several weeks earlier, Henry had received an invitation, on impressively embossed notepaper, from Sir Robert Oppenshaw of Oppenshaw and Trilby, the publishers. Sir Robert informed Henry of the existence of a very small private club called the Guess Who. It consisted of a group of successful writers (all published by Oppenshaw and Trilby, of course) who for one reason or another wrote under pen names, and carefully guarded their real identities.

The club was purely social, Sir Robert explained, and met four times a year for a private dinner in a London club. They also held a week-long meeting each summer at Sir Robert's country place, Carnworth Manor, on the Isle of Wight. During this week, a guest speaker was invited to address the club on some topic of interest to the members, who wrote in the field of crime or mystery fiction. He named several previous speakers: a world-famous pathologist, a top American literary agent with wide knowledge of world markets, a representative of a renowned public relations firm in London. This year Sir Robert, his wife, and the members of the club would feel honored if Chief Superintendent Tibbett of the C.I.D. would be good enough to consent to speak to the members about police procedure. Henry and his wife were cordially invited to be the guests of Sir Robert and Lady Oppenshaw at Carnworth Manor for the final weekend of the meeting. The Oppenshaws hoped that the

Tibbetts would be able to arrive on Friday evening. Henry could give his talk on Saturday morning, and then, Sir Robert hoped, enjoy the rest of the weekend at Carnworth. With Emmy's enthusiastic approval (August is dull even in Chelsea) he had accepted the invitation.

Back in his office, Henry thought about the group of writers, all working in the field of crime and mystery and all under assumed names. They clearly knew who the guest speaker at Carnworth was going to be. This crossword and its clues, so like the improbabilities of a "classic" detective story of the thirties, must be a joke thought up by the Guess Who club, and Professor Harold Vandike must be a member. A little test to see if a real-life C.I.D. man could solve mysteries as efficiently as the sleuths of fiction. Henry was a little annoyed at the waste of time involved, but thanks to Inspector Reynolds and Edwin Manciple, he felt that he had done fairly well in coming up with the solution, and he could not deny that he had enjoyed himself.

Just to check, he put through a call to Sir Robert Oppenshaw at Carnworth Manor. Without surprise, curiosity, or hesitation, Sir Robert told him the name of the London club where the Guess Who members held their dinners, and the date of the most recent one. As Henry had suspected, it was just four days before he had received the crossword and the first set of clues.

Each of the five members of the Guess Who club had a different reason for using a nom de plume and keeping his or her true identity strictly under wraps. For instance, admirers of Tex Lawrie, that tough and casually amorous private eye of fiction, would undoubtedly have been disillusioned to know that his creator, Jack Harvey (a character, the publisher's blurbs subtly suggested, that much resembled a real-life Tex), was actually Mrs. Myrtle Waterford. Myrtle was a highly respectable, still pretty woman in her late fifties, married to the branch manager of a well-known bank in a small country town. Apart from the publicity image, the fact that she was Gerald Waterford's wife had a great deal to do with Myrtle's decision to build a wall between herself and Jack Harvey. The Waterfords were respected in their local community, and Myrtle sat on several ladies' committees under the banners of various charitable enterprises. Jack Harvey (and, for that matter, the lusty Tex Lawrie) was entirely a matter between Myrtle and her typewriter.

Quite different was the perspective of Harold Vandike, a brilliant lawyer, athlete, Oxford don, writer of literary criticism, and compiler of the most erudite crosswords for a Sunday newspaper. In fact, under his own name he was currently at work on a history of Oppenshaw and Trilby, the venerable publishing house that brought out all his works and that had been founded in the eighteenth century by Richard Trilby. Harry Vandike was considered by many sighing ladies to be England's most eligible bachelor (except that his biting, satiric wit might have been a little hard to live with).

However, everyone enjoys at least one activity against which every predictable personal instinct should rebel. In Harold's case it was the writing of sentimental Gothic mysteries about heroines in chiffon nighties, gaunt houses looming out of the mist, and enigmatic lovers with haunted faces and strong, sensitive hands. This he did, with great success, under the name of Elaine Summerfield. The reaction of the Senior Common Room alone, not to mention the serious literary world, would have been devastating, had Harold's secret been revealed.

The case of Dr. William Cartwright and Professor Fred Coe was something else again. Both in their forties, William and Fred were much respected in their professions. William practiced as a successful otologist in the Harley Street area of London, contributed brilliantly original papers to medical journals, and was esteemed by his colleagues. Fred was an economist, a prominent left-winger who dabbled in politics and lectured at the London School of Economics. His articles on the interrelation of recession and inflation had caused a sensation among the readers of learned economic journals. Only a handful of people, apart from their wives, knew that Bill and Fred were, jointly, Freda Wright, whose lovable, myopic, silver-haired Miss Twinkley was the favorite private detective of countless ladies in countless public libraries.

Barbara Oppenshaw—at twenty-five, by far the youngest member of Guess Who—had an entirely different problem. She was a talented writer who had the misfortune to be the daughter of Sir Robert Oppenshaw, now the sole proprietor of the publishing house, since the last Trilby had left for Australia many years earlier, when the business seemed on the verge of collapse. The name Trilby had been retained both for sentiment and prestige.

The truth was that Oppenshaw and Trilby published Barbara's books for no reason other than their excellence; Sir Robert was much too shrewd to risk money in the cause of nepotism. But, Barbara reasoned, whoever would believe that, if her name appeared on the title page? So she wrote as Lydia Drake, and Oppenshaw and Trilby was much gratified by the success of her bluff, pipe-smoking Scotland Yard detective, Superintendent Burrows.

The idea of the Guess Who club had originated with Sir Robert Oppenshaw, who was not eligible for membership himself but happened to publish all the authors concerned. He was a very wealthy man—thanks to a private fortune, for publishers seldom make millions, whatever authors may think—and naturally it was to his house, Carnworth Manor, that the club members were invited for their annual Literary Week.

The event was really no more than a pleasant social occasion, enriched by the famous hospitality of Sir Robert and his wife, Pamela. There was excellent food and drink; tennis, golf, and horseback riding (the Oppenshaws kept a small stable); and swimming and sailing, for the gardens of Carnworth led down to the English Channel, on the southern side of the island. However, to give the semblance of a literary seminar—and to make his expenses tax-deductible—Sir Robert always invited for the final weekend an expert in some field of crime.

Barbara Oppenshaw had brought the news of Henry's acceptance to the Guess Who dinner in London. Inevitably, the table talk turned to the differences between real-life policemen of the C.I.D. and the heroes and heroines created by the diners.

Cartwright and Coe maintained that Miss Twinkley's great strength lay in the fact that she was an amateur, unhampered by police procedure. This, they said—quoting Sherlock Holmes, Lord Peter Wimsey, and others—was the reason that most great fictional detectives were not policemen. Myrtle pointed out that

Tex Lawrie was not really a detective at all, but an adventurer whose career inevitably involved him in criminal circles. Harold Vandike said sardonically that none of his featherbrained heroines would be able to detect a fox in a chicken coop, let alone a murderer.

"You, my dear Barbara," he went on, "are the only one of us who purports to portray an actual Scotland Yard detective. And I cannot remember that Chief Superintendent Tibbett's cases have ever remotely resembled those so brilliantly solved by Superintendent Burrows."

"There's no need to be sarcastic, Harry," said Barbara. "I write in what is known as the great classic tradition, and my books sell better than yours."

"That may or may not be true," said Harry, who knew very well that it was. "The fact remains that your plots are ridiculously elaborate and fanciful. First of all, you maroon a small group of people on an island or in a snowstorm or some such artificial situation. Then you produce clues of whimsical erudition—for instance, all your victims may be ladies named after Shakespearean heroines, so that after the demise of Juliet Jones and Miranda Brown, we may be fairly sure that Portia Smith is in for trouble. And—"

"I've never used that one," said Barbara thoughtfully.

"And finally," Harry went on, "your detective assembles all the suspects and arranges a reenactment of the crime, which unmasks the villain. Can you imagine that happening in real life?"

"It would be interesting to know," remarked Bill Cartwright, "how a real detective would react if he found himself faced with a so-called classic fictional crime."

At this point the conversation became confused, and somebody suggested that it might be amusing to put Henry Tibbett to the test. In no time the whole table was buzzing with laughter, and suggestions were pouring in.

"Let's see if he's as good as Burrows," Vandike said.

Fred Coe remarked, "I met him once, at a party at the Cobhams'."

"Lord and Lady Cobham, do you mean?" asked Myrtle, much impressed.

"What was a staunch old Marxist like you doing there, Fred?" asked Barbara.

"Never mind," said Fred Coe. "The point is that he does know the most unexpected people. He struck me as having a sense of humor. I think he'll see through us."

"More important," said Cartwright, "will he recognize you?"

The identities of the Guess Who members were not revealed to the visiting experts at Carnworth Manor. They were introduced, by their Christian names, as authors who used pseudonyms, and while the lecturer was given the names of the authors whom he was to meet, he was given no clue as to which was which.

As a matter of fact, most of the visitors imagined that Dr. Cartwright, working with Harry Vandike—a couple of obviously brilliant minds—must jointly write as Lydia Drake. (After all, everyone knows that English ladies writing in the Agatha Christie tradition are extremely popular. The combination of a couple of clearly clever gentlemen would not produce the same cozy effect.) Fred Coe, with his bluff manner, was generally assumed to be Jack Harvey, creator of the tough Scot, Tex Lawrie. Myrtle Waterford was obviously the Gothic writer, Elaine Summerfield, while Barbara Oppenshaw, whose identity as Sir Robert's daughter was never concealed at Carnworth, was presumed to have dreamed up the homely Miss Twinkley under the pen name of Freda Wright.

Professor Coe was able to reassure his collaborator. "We were never actually introduced," he said. "It was a big cocktail affair. I just hovered around a group of people who were talking to Tibbett, and listened from the fringes, as it were. If he has a phenomenal memory, he may recognize my face—but if he does, he'll put me down as Jack Harvey or one-half of Lydia Drake. No worry."

So it was agreed, and the conspirators went to work, becoming quite giggly with mischief and champagne. Within the week, it was decided, Chief Superintendent Henry Tibbett would have a really classic case on his hands. He would have just a month to solve it before the practical jokers at Carnworth, having extracted every ounce of fun from the situation, would reveal themselves and make him look as silly as a chief superintendent of the C.I.D. has ever looked. Harry Vandike warned them that if Henry Tibbett was at all bright, their true identities might stand revealed—but nobody minded. They urged Harry to get to work. They could hardly wait.

4

Carnworth Manor, as Sir Robert himself often laughingly remarked, was just the sort of place where an English murder mystery of the 1930s would feel at home. A compact but beautiful house, it dated from the mid-eighteenth century. A spiral staircase ascended from its circular marble entrance hall, in the center of which a small fountain boasted a bronze dolphin that incessantly vomited water toward the domed roof some eighty feet above.

From this circular foyer, doors opened into a drawing room of comfortable elegance and into the library, decorated floor to ceiling with leatherbound books and fitted out with a leather-topped desk, an eighteenth-century library ladder of leather and mahogany, and some ingenious modern electric light fittings, which enabled the seeker after knowledge to find what he wanted on the shelves and to read it at the desk or lectern. This was the original library, Sir Robert would chortle to his guests, where the Baronet should be found by the butler, stabbed through the heart by a dagger of oriental design. Other doors led to a pretty dining room, and to a curious chamber called the morning room officially, but always known as the old nursery.

Here an ancient, balding teddy bear sat dangling his legs from the mantelpiece, a couple of well-worn rag dolls were draped over a chintzy sofa, and a big, scarred nursery table held a half-completed and complicated jigsaw puzzle. In fact, the most important thing in the room was barely noticeable. It was a typewriter with a tape recorder beside it, which stood on a simple wooden desk under the window. Barbara Oppenshaw's typewriter. For this was Barbara's old nursery, now her study, which she used on the rare occasions when she worked at Carnworth.

The final door leading from the circular hallway—apart from one to a cloakroom—was a modern version of a green baize door, cunningly disguised with plastic marble, which swung to and fro as the domestic staff made their way—metaphorically—from downstairs to upstairs.

Truly upstairs—up the spiral staircase, that is—were the bedrooms, on two floors. Once again, the equivalent of a green baize door hid the servants' quarters from the sleeping area of the gentry. Originally, there had been twelve bedrooms—six on each floor. Now Carnworth had only eight, four to each landing, the others having been turned into private bathrooms.

The master suite on the first floor was, naturally, given over to Sir Robert and Lady Oppenshaw. On the same floor was Barbara's room, which was seldom occupied, for Barbara had a small apartment in London where she spent most of her time. Nonetheless, she did come to Carnworth for weekends, especially in the summer, for she was an accomplished horsewoman and had her own chestnut mare in the stables. However, the Oppenshaws were hospitable and enjoyed company, so the guest rooms were rarely empty. Authors, agents, actors, and politicians all spent pleasant days at Carnworth. Sir Robert himself traveled by car ferry in his chauffeured Bentley to London twice a week to make sure that all was well in his office; otherwise, he conducted his business via a private telephone with an unlisted number at Carnworth Manor.

The Bentley was waiting at Fishbourne Pier when Henry and Emmy descended from the Portsmouth ferry. The young chauffeur, smart in his dark green uniform, picked up the Tibbetts' well-worn suitcases with a faintly supercilious sneer and loaded them into the car. Twenty minutes later, the Bentley was winding its way up the drive, between rows of stately trees, into the graveled forecourt of the house.

Sir Robert and Lady Oppenshaw were both on the front terrace to greet the Tibbetts in a typically warm and thoughtful welcome. A handsome couple, both seemed to be in their fifties—although a closer inspection convinced Emmy that Pamela Oppenshaw, despite expert cosmetic surgery and makeup, was a good many years older than her husband.

"My dear Chief Superintendent, this is indeed a pleasure. And Mrs. Tibbett. May I introduce my wife, Pamela? We are both flattered that you took time from your busy life to come and talk to our little group."

Polite murmurs of greeting and introduction fluttered among the four as Henry and Emmy were led into the entrance hall. There was no sign of their suitcases, which must have been whisked off to the back door.

Pamela Oppenshaw said, "I expect you would both like to freshen up after your journey. We have put you in the Blue Room on the first floor. When you are ready, you will find us in the drawing room." She indicated one of the doors off the marble hallway. "Then we shall be able to have a little chat and tell you something about the members of our group."

They climbed up the circular staircase, and Lady Oppenshaw ushered them into a large, elegant bedroom, blue-carpeted and blue-draped, with a large window commanding a view of parkland sweeping down to the woods, and the sea beyond. Glancing through the window, Henry caught a glimpse of a couple on horseback—a girl on a chestnut and a man on a gray—disappearing at a brisk trot into a spinney of trees.

Pamela Oppenshaw was saying to Emmy, "This is your bathroom. Annie will be up with your suitcases in just a moment. She will unpack for you. We'll see you downstairs in a few minutes." She smiled—a social smile—and went out, closing the door softly behind her.

Feeling a little overwhelmed, Henry and Emmy explored their domain. The very modern bathroom—also blue—was furnished with blue towels of every dimension from huge bath sheets to small linen hand towels. The medicine cabinet was thoughtfully stocked with tissues, aspirin, Band-Aids, toothpaste, and new toothbrushes in plastic cases, as well as eau de cologne and a most expensive make of blue soap, bath essence, and talcum powder. There were even disposable razors, new hairbrushes and combs, and terry bathrobes hung on the door.

In the bedroom, the Queen Anne writing desk was equipped with postcards, envelopes, writing paper, stamps, and pens, while the inlaid walnut chest contained sewing materials. A visitor, arriving with no more than a handbag or a briefcase, would be completely fitted out. Henry and Emmy washed, combed their hair, and went downstairs.

It was just after three o'clock, the time when country house-guests are traditionally off on their own particular devices, ready to assemble later for tea, or, more likely in these days, cocktails. So it was only Sir Robert and Lady Oppenshaw who were in the drawing room when the Tibbetts came in. To their relief, it was not like a museum of priceless antiques; while beautifully furnished, it had a comfortable, lived-in feeling. Sir Robert was engulfed in a huge armchair, reading *Country Life*. Lady Oppenshaw sat on a low sofa, playing solitaire on a glass-topped coffee table. These pursuits were at once abandoned. Pamela Oppenshaw excused herself on the pretext of some domestic task, and Sir Robert began his exposition.

"As I explained to you in my letter, Tibbett, the people here are all writers of crime fiction—all on my list, I'm proud to say. However, for various reasons they all use pen names. The writers you will be meeting are Lydia Drake, Freda Wright, Jack Harvey, and Elaine Summerfield. They will be introduced by their first names only—Fred, Bill, Harry, and Myrtle. You will have observed, of course, that while there will be three male guests and only one lady, at least two of the men use a woman's name as a nom de plume. However, you are not being asked here to solve a mystery—just to be your entertaining and informative self."

"Thank you," said Henry.

"As far as the other guests are concerned, there will be just my daughter, Barbara, and her fiancé, Peter Turnberry. Barbara is . . . well, she dabbles a little in writing, so she always comes to our little gatherings. This will be Peter's first time. I think you will find him a delightful young man. Their engagement has not been formally announced, but it will be appearing in *The Times* in a couple of weeks. So, with Pamela and myself, that completes the party. We have arranged for you to give your talk on police procedure at eleven o'clock tomorrow morning, if that is convenient for you. After that, we hope you will simply enjoy yourselves. Do you sail?"

"Yes," said Emmy with enthusiasm.

Sir Robert beamed. "Good, good. You will find our eighteen-foot day boat at your disposal. Now, is there anything else you would like to know?"

"Just one thing," said Henry. "Does the name Warfield mean anything to you?"

Sir Robert's face stiffened into the molded smile that had accompanied his last banality. For a moment he seemed frozen. Then he said, "Why do you ask?"

Henry smiled warmly. "I see it does," he said. "Please don't be alarmed or upset. It's just that these people—your Guess Who club—have been playing a rather pretty trick on me."

"A trick? On you?"

"Yes. There's no need to go into details. I'll do that tomorrow morning when I give my talk. Meanwhile, they have . . . well, you could say that they have given me a problem to solve. The last piece of the jigsaw, or rather the crossword—"

"My dear Tibbett, what on earth are you talking about?"

"They have been sending me crossword clues to solve," Henry explained. "Fortunately, I've been able to do so, and I hope to enhance the reputation of Scotland Yard a little bit tomorrow. However, as I was saying, the last clue concerned Jean Warfield. Eugenia Warfield, I think, to be more exact. A young girl who died accidentally by drowning not very far from here. All this goes back many years, of course. Almost twenty, I believe."

Sir Robert was looking fixedly at Henry. At last he said, "If you have checked the facts so far, you must know the truth. I don't know why you bother to ask me."

"Because I'd like to hear it from you, Sir Robert."

"Well, Jeannie Warfield was Pamela's stepdaughter. That's to say, before she married me, Pamela was the second wife of a man named Francis Warfield. By his first wife, he had a daughter Eugenia—known as Jean or Jeannie. She was fifteen when her father died, and eighteen when Pamela married me. Naturally, Pamela brought Jeannie to live with us. A sweet girl. She treated Barbara just like a younger sister. She used to call her Baba, which is still our family nickname for her."

Henry began, "Then the arrival of a new baby didn't—"

Sir Robert interrupted him. "No, no. Barbara was five when Pamela and I married. She's my daughter by my first wife, who died in childbirth. I'm afraid we're a rather complicated family." He smiled. "And yet—not really. Pamela and I had both been widowed, and were each left with a child to bring up—except, of course, that Jeannie was many years older than Barbara. The combining of the two half-families seemed an obvious and sensible solution for all of us. Yes, Jeannie's death was a great tragedy."

"What actually happened?" Emmy asked.

"Nobody knows for sure. Jeannie was an adequate if not very strong swimmer, and she was teaching Baba. We felt perfectly happy about the two of them going off to the beach together on their own.

"It was a lovely morning in August, I remember—just the perfect time for an early-morning dip. I remember looking out of the window and seeing the two of them in their swimsuits going down through the park to the beach. About eight in the morning, it must have been. Jeannie was walking ahead with that long stride of hers, and Baba was skipping after her.

"We didn't worry when they didn't show up for breakfast at half past eight—we thought they were just enjoying themselves. But by nine Pamela was very uneasy, so I said I'd go down and make sure they were all right." Sir Robert paused. "At first I couldn't see anybody on the beach. Then I heard a sort of wailing, and there was Baba on her own, among the trees that lead down to the sea. She seemed—well, completely stunned, poor little mite. 'Where's Jeannie?' I said. All that I could make out between her sobs were the words 'In the sea.' "

"Are there currents around these waters?" Henry asked.

Sir Robert nodded. "There are. Very strong and treacherous

ones. But as a rule, Jeannie never went out of her depth—I told you she was teaching Baba to swim, so she would just stand waist-deep, supporting the child. I suppose that morning she sent Baba ashore and decided to go for a proper swim herself. She must have been caught by the current. Her body was washed up a couple of miles down the coast the next day." Sir Robert paused. "Can you keep a secret, Tibbett?"

"Certainly."

"Well, the coroner's jury naturally brought in a verdict of accidental death—but Pamela and I have always been haunted by the idea that the real cause might have been different."

"Different? You don't mean—?"

"Shortly after we got married," said Sir Robert, "Pamela told me—this is in strict confidence, of course—that Jeannie was suffering from multiple sclerosis. It was in its very early stages, and as far as we knew, the girl herself had no idea of her condition. However, as you know, there's no cure, and the doctors thought it was unlikely that she'd live much beyond her twenty-first birthday—or if she did, it would be as a helpless cripple. Now, if she had somehow found out . . . well, young people are often less afraid of death than of chronic disability. I just don't know."

Emmy said, "In a way, I suppose you can get some sort of comfort from the fact that she would have died anyway. But what a terrible experience for little Barbara. How old was she then?"

"Just six. Yes, it was traumatic, I'm afraid. She doesn't consciously remember anything about it now, but she's hated the sea ever since, and she's never been down to that beach again. We bought her a pony to try to take her mind off it all—and we certainly succeeded, she's horse-crazy now. Of course, Pamela was utterly shattered. She had been so determined to make Jeannie's last years happy. But it was a blessing that she had Baba to care for. She looks on her completely as her own daughter." Sir Robert sighed. "I suppose there's a tragedy in everybody's life somewhere, but it's no less true for being a cliché that time is a great healer. We're a very happy family."

Henry said, "You must forgive me for raking up these sad

memories, Sir Robert. It seems to me that it was very unkind of . . . whoever is playing this practical joke to mention Jean's death. The other cases referred to are quite different."

"Other cases?"

"Two other cases that seem to bear a resemblance to each other, but have nothing in common with this one." Henry paused. "You've hinted at suicide, and the verdict was accident. There's no possible suggestion of foul play?"

"Certainly not!" Sir Robert was shocked. "The only other person there was a child of six who couldn't swim."

"One more question, and I'm through," said Henry. "Did anybody stand to gain financially by Jeannie's death?"

"What an extraordinary—"

Apologetically, Henry said, "It's because of the other cases. I just wondered—"

"Well, the answer is no. Oh, I believe her father, old Warfield, left her a bit of money that was to come to her when she was twenty-one. I suppose it went to Pamela, such as it was. We were all far too upset to worry about that sort of thing."

"Of course," said Henry.

There was a slightly awkward pause, which Emmy broke tactfully by saying, with a complete switch of subject, "You must be very happy about Barbara's engagement."

Sir Robert instantly became genial. "Indeed we are." He beamed. "Peter is a most charming young man. You'll meet him this evening. He shares Barbara's love of horses. In fact, they're out riding now."

"I think I saw them from our bedroom," Henry said.

"Very likely. But Peter's not just your hunting-and-fishing type. Dear me, no. He did extremely well at Oxford, and is now completing his law studies. A remarkable blend of sportsman and intellectual. An ideal son-in-law." Sir Robert glanced at his watch. "Four-fifteen. My wife has given up serving tea, I fear. It always used to be one of my favorite moments of the day. However, she finds that it bores the young people, and the older ones all seem to be watching their waistlines. So generally we assemble here for drinks at half past six. Perhaps you and Mrs. Tibbett would care for a stroll in the gardens before you change for dinner?"

It was a clear dismissal. Henry and Emmy agreed politely, and Sir Robert escorted them to the French windows, pointing out the yew walk and the way to the rose garden.

Out of earshot of the house, Emmy looked at Henry and said, "Well?"

"Well, what?"

"D'you think you've got a murderer in the house?"

"No. I think I've got a rather cruel practical joker, whom I intend to deflate tomorrow, if I can. Meanwhile, I didn't much like the sound of that 'changing for dinner' bit. If he thinks I've brought a dinner jacket, he's mistaken."

"Oh, surely he just meant—"

"My dark gray suit is the most he's going to get," said Henry.

Emmy said rather wistfully, "I could wear my long black skirt."

"Wear what you like, darling."

"I mean . . . changing for dinner is . . . well . . ."

"Is something that most women enjoy and most men detest," said Henry, with a grin. "Anyhow, if there ever was a change-for-dinner house, this is it. So why don't you wear your long skirt and that pink chiffon blouse thing?"

"Yes," said Emmy. "I will."

As it turned out, the Tibbetts found themselves quite correctly dressed when the company assembled at half past six. There were no dinner jackets or black ties, but Sir Robert had changed his tweeds for a dark suit, as had the other men in the party. The exception was a man who wore, with a certain air of defiance, black dress trousers, a maroon velvet smoking jacket, an elaborately pleated shirt, and a green bow tie. Henry realized that this must be Harold Vandike. As for the women, their attire varied from long skirts and shirts, like Emmy, to shorter but distinctly dressy creations that tended to float or shimmer. Lady Oppenshaw herself was in coffee-colored chiffon, with a huge sapphire brooch and a sapphire-and-diamond ring like a knuckle-duster. As drinks were discreetly served by the chauffeur—

41

now transformed into a white-coated bartender—the Tibbetts were invited to meet their fellow guests.

Henry studied each of them with interest. Myrtle was middle-aged, long-skirted, eminently respectable, with blue-rinsed hair. Barbara had blonde, fashionably frizzy hair, and wore a costume that seemed to have been influenced by both India and the Cossacks, and certainly came from a way-out London boutique—the sort of outfit that only the young and skeletal can get away with. Peter Turnberry, her fiancé, was as proper and as unmemorable as a handsome young man can be. Harry—the man Henry thought must be Vandike—was clearly aiming at the outrageous and only missing the bull's-eye by an inch. He was dark, with a small goatee and satanic eyebrows. Fred, a large man in his forties, had a straggly brown beard and looked disheveled in spite of an obvious effort to smarten up. Henry guessed he missed his wife's civilizing influence. Bill, dapper and correct, was a neat little man with small, deft, very white hands. Among this group were the creators of Miss Twinkley, Tex Lawrie, Superintendent Burrows, and the wide-eyed heroines of Elaine Summerfield's works. Here also was the practical joker with the barbed wit. Henry was thoughtful as the company trooped into the candlelit dining room.

The conversation at the dinner table was lively but hardly remarkable. Sir Robert had made it clear that, owing to the anonymous circumstances of the club, the subject of literature in any form was taboo. So Barbara and Peter talked of horses, Fred and Harry described their day's sailing—Harry with enthusiasm and Fred with a shuddering loathing. It had, he said, been his first experience of small sailing boats, and he fervently hoped that it would be his last.

Myrtle and Pamela talked of committees and charity events. Bill, who was sitting next to Emmy, was inclined to be silent and almost morose, until Emmy, trying desperately for a conversational opening, first of all complimented her hostess on the excellence of the dinner, and then revealed that she herself was an enthusiastic if not expert cook. Bill came to life at once, and soon he and Emmy were deep in the best way to make a hollandaise sauce and the superiority of fresh herbs over the dried variety.

Henry noticed that he and Sir Robert Oppenshaw were playing the same game: joining this or that conversation, inserting a remark or two, but basically listening. Judging. Summing up. He wondered how much Sir Robert knew about the practical joker.

5

The entire party, including Sir Robert and Lady Oppenshaw, who seated themselves unobtrusively at the back of the room, assembled next morning in the drawing room to listen to Henry's talk on police procedure.

A semicircle of chairs had been arranged around a small Georgian table with a glass of water on it, which identified it as the speaker's podium. Emmy sat at the farthest end of the semi-circle, where she found herself joined by Peter Turnberry and Barbara Oppenshaw. Myrtle and Harry sat together, separated by an empty chair from Fred and Bill. Emmy could not help noticing the atmosphere of expectancy—of mischief almost— that ran like a string of Chinese firecrackers through the group. She sensed at once that it had not been a single joker but a concerted effort that had produced the crossword puzzle. She wished that she had time to convey this to Henry, but he was already standing at the table, sorting out what looked like notes, although Emmy knew he had brought none.

Henry started with deadpan solemnity. He first congratulated the assembled writers on their accuracy in describing police procedure.

"I am familiar with the work of all of you," he said, "with the exception of Miss Summerfield. I gather that her books are romantic rather than investigational, and you must know that there is no such thing as a romantic policeman. However, each time Miss Twinkley or Tex Lawrie comes up against the law, as they are bound to do in the course of their adventures, the police side of things seems to me to be well and discreetly handled. As for Superintendent Burrows, Miss Drake has obviously researched the ways of Scotland Yard, for I can relate to him as a colleague. Just one small point, Miss Drake. Murder investigations nowadays are never entrusted to an officer below the rank of chief superintendent. So I think our friend Burrows is due for promotion." He regarded the company with a smile, which was carefully not directed at any particular member of it.

"Now, when a murder is first reported . . ." So the talk went on—accurate, amusing, and informative. The audience began to get a little restive. This was not what they had come for. Was it possible that Henry Tibbett had just ignored the crossword puzzle and the clues? Glances, which Emmy did not miss, passed among the writers. She smiled, a small inward smile, reflecting that these people did not know Henry.

"As I'm sure you're aware," Henry was saying, "most of the murder cases we have to deal with are boring beyond description and are pure routine. The killer almost always turns out to be a family member or else a rejected lover. Most murders are committed in hot blood, as the culmination of a quarrel, probably inflamed by alcohol or drugs. Others, colder and more calculating, are committed for financial gain. In either case, the problem of identifying the murderer is not often difficult. What is much more difficult is supplying enough evidence, in proper legal form, to convince a judge and jury, and get a conviction.

"There is another type of case which is almost equally uninteresting from your point of view, ladies and gentlemen, because it is virtually unsolvable. Anybody who takes it into his or her head to kill a complete stranger, just for the fun of it, will nearly always get away with it. You only have to look at the Moors Murder cases. If Brady hadn't decided to bring David Smith in on the murder of Edward Evans, he and Myra Hindley might well have gone on for years, killing a young stranger every six months and burying the bodies on the moors, while

45

outwardly remaining a bright, friendly young couple. It is almost as though the sheer boredom of too-easy success made Brady deliberately court danger by involving an outsider.

"Now, since no writer wishes to bore a reader, there seems little to be made of this kind of murder in fiction. If it bores the killer himself, what will it do to the reader?

"So we are left with the murder which is found almost exclusively in fiction—the puzzle. Who did it? How? Why? Clues are scattered and suspects paraded. For this purpose, the setting must be confined and the group of people reduced to manageable numbers. Then there should be a bizarre element, either in the manner of the murders or the presentation of the clues. This type of mystery reached its height in the 1930s, in the hands of such masters—or should I say mistresses?—as Christie, Sayers, Allingham, and Marsh. The form is still widely used, and has remained popular with readers."

Henry looked at his audience. Each was leaning forward, charged with expectation. He went on, "There have been many devices for the presentation of clues—one remembers *The ABC Murders*, *Ten Little Indians*—the more recent *Chelsea Murders*, and so on. But I don't think I have ever read a book in which clues were forwarded to the detective in the form of a crossword puzzle."

In the dead silence, Henry picked up a page of his ostensible notes. It was a copy of the crossword, with all its spaces filled in. He displayed it to the audience.

"You may recognize this. The crossword and the first two clues were sent to me a month ago. Further clues arrived at intervals." He grinned. "Ladies and gentlemen, you have been very ingenious. Do you send these puzzles to all your guest speakers, or am I specially honored? In any case, I am delighted to be able to tell you that I have solved the puzzle, the clues, your identities, and . . . well, something more. We'll leave that for the moment."

Again, dead silence. With a smile, Henry said, "Shall I go on now? Is there anybody here who doesn't know what I'm talking about?"

Emmy wished she had eyes in the back of her head, to watch

46

the reactions of her host and hostess, but remembered that Henry was facing them and presumably registering their reactions. For the rest, the semicircle gazed fixedly at Henry in silence.

Henry said, "Good. I have done a little checking up, and I find that the crossword and its first clues arrived only a few days after the Guess Who members had met for dinner at their usual London club. So it took no great power of deduction to work out that it was at this dinner that the scheme evolved. The crossword and the clues were composed, of course, by Harry—Mr. Harold Vandike—among whose many gifts is the composition of erudite crossword puzzles for *The London Sunday Star*."

Here there was a little ripple of surprised reaction. With a smile, Henry said, "I have already told you, ladies and gentlemen, that we at Scotland Yard rely a great deal on expert witnesses. In this case I referred your mysterious crossword to Edwin Manciple, retired Bishop of Bugolaland, who is among the most astute solvers in the country. He had no difficulty, not only in solving the clues, but in identifying the compiler. He explained that he could recognize the style instantly, just as I am told that Morse radio operators can detect the sender of a message by his special touch on the seemingly impersonal key. As soon as I was told that one of your number would be known as Harry, I identified him as Professor Vandike, known to his many readers as Elaine Summerfield."

Harold Vandike stood up and made a little bow. "Full marks, Mr. Tibbett. But why should you accuse me of being Elaine Summerfield?"

"Accuse? You think it an accusation? I should have thought it would be a compliment. After all, your books must sell very well, judging by the number I see in paperback. As for my reasoning, it goes like this. I eliminated Myrtle at once, because she would have no reason to deny her work as Elaine Summerfield. I eliminated Fred and Bill for reasons I'll explain later on. I knew that you fulfilled your love of mental gymnastics in your crossword puzzles, and in any case, if you were Lydia Drake or Freda Wright, I don't think you would go to such lengths to

47

disguise the fact. You are a man who enjoys public acclaim, Mr. Vandike, and Oxford has produced a number of excellent detective writers who are not at all ashamed of the fact. On the other hand, if your students and colleagues discovered that you were Elaine Summerfield, you could be exposed to ridicule, for which not even hefty royalty payments could compensate. Ergo, you are Elaine Summerfield."

Harry Vandike had sat down again. He said, "This is pure conjecture."

"I don't agree," said Henry amiably. "In any case, since you have given me this puzzle, you must in fairness allow me to solve it."

Heads nodded. Expectancy mounted. Henry went on, "The puzzle itself, apart from a few odd and apparently unrelated snippets of words, referred to three incidents—in none of which Mr. Vandike himself was concerned. The clues came in sets, linking certain names with certain other names. In the first case, a W. Cartwright was somehow associated with a Lady Fanshaw." He grinned at Bill. "Dr. Cartwright, I presume?"

"Guilty," said Bill, with a prim little smile.

"You are an otologist, and a very good one," Henry went on. "The Dowager Lady Fanshaw, now deceased, consulted you about her hearing. She was very grateful for the help that you gave her, and in gratitude left you a substantial sum in her will. Correct?"

"Correct."

"The puzzle appeared to hint that you might have speeded her death in order to inherit. It took very little research to find that she had not consulted you within six months of her death. She died in a hospital, of cancer. The doctor who attended her during her last illness, and who benefited a lot more than you did, might possibly have been suspected of hastening her death. But you were clearly innocent. So the first case was just a test of my ingenuity, and easily disposed of."

"I'm very glad to hear it," said Dr. Cartwright. "May one ask if you have also established my pen name?"

"One may," said Henry. "You and Professor Coe were not very subtle in your choice of pseudonym. Once I knew from the

48

crossword that your name was Cartwright, and I was introduced to him as Fred, it became obvious that the two of you collaborate under the name of Freda Wright. Miss Twinkley, if I may say so, does you credit. She gives an enormous amount of pleasure to many people.

"I should say that you and the professor form an ideal team. I have taken the trouble to reread some of your books, and Miss Twinkley always seems to have a local doctor at hand to supply medical details. I suspect that you, Doctor, think up the plots and look after the medical end, while Professor Coe amuses himself by doing the actual writing. In any case, the second series of clues concerned Fred Coe and two ladies—Felicity Orwell and Alice.

"It was not difficult to establish that Alice is Professor Coe's wife, and that Miss Orwell was her aunt. You, sir"—he gave a little bow in Fred's direction—"and your wife were good enough to take Miss Orwell into your home and nurse her through her last illness. A task, I understand, which no other member of the family was prepared to undertake, owing to her somewhat abrasive disposition. She died a few months later, having changed her will to leave everything to you and your wife. Mr. Vandike, in his capacity as a lover of justice, appeared to imply that her death, too, might have been accelerated. I think this very unlikely, although if events warrant it, I shall of course investigate further."

It was Pamela Oppenshaw, surprisingly, who said in her clear voice from the back of the room, "Mr. Tibbett, if you are right, and Fred and Bill are collaborators, where is your fourth author?"

"Where indeed?" said Henry. He looked straight at Barbara. "Your father told me you dabbled in writing, Miss Oppenshaw. It is perfectly obvious that you do much more than dabble. You also have the best of reasons for adopting a false name, for fear of being accused of nepotism. The question remains—who is Jack Harvey and who is Lydia Drake? I don't think it's hard to decide. Myrtle—I don't know your surname—Myrtle would, I'm sure, be perfectly happy to be known as the creator of Superintendent Burrows, soon to be promoted. The writing of classic detective fiction by eminently respectable English ladies is a venerable tradition. So—Myrtle must be Jack Harvey, and Tex Lawrie the surprising emanation of her subconscious mind."

Myrtle had gone very pink, concentrating on a small white handkerchief that she was twisting between her hands as they lay on her lap.

Henry said cheerfully, "Don't worry, Myrtle. Your secret is safe. I regard myself as an honorary member of the Guess Who club, and bound by its rules. In any case, you were not even mentioned in the crossword puzzle, which presumably means that nothing even vaguely reprehensible has ever occurred in your past."

Once again there was silence. Henry went on, "This brings me to the last and most interesting set of clues. It refers to the death by drowning of Eugenia—or Jean—Warfield, which occurred here at Carnworth some twenty years ago. It links both the name of Barbara and the childhood nickname of Baba to the incident."

The silence in the room was absolute. Henry said, "I have, simply by asking Sir Robert, discovered what this refers to. When Miss Oppenshaw—known then as Baba—was only six years old, she went to the beach for a swimming lesson with her stepsister, eighteen-year-old Jean Warfield. Somehow, during the swim, Jean got carried out to sea by the strong current, and was drowned. It was a terrible and tragic experience for the whole family—especially for little Barbara." Henry turned suddenly on Vandike, and said almost fiercely, "It was a very cruel thing to bring this matter up, Mr. Vandike. Will you kindly tell us why you did it?"

Harry Vandike was looking thoroughly upset. "I . . . well . . . we all agreed, didn't we, Barbara . . . ?" His voice trailed away.

Barbara Oppenshaw said, coldly and sharply, "Yes, Chief Superintendent. We all agreed. As you so rightly guessed, at that dinner. We had the idea of giving you this . . . this lighthearted test. We felt the need of three possible murders. Bill and Fred willingly volunteered as guinea pigs, since they had both inherited from elderly ladies. I seemed to be the only other person with any sort of unnatural death in my background."

"So the idea of raking up the past in this way didn't upset you?"

"Not in the least, Mr. Tibbett."

"I'm very glad to hear it," Henry said. "To be quite frank, Miss Oppenshaw, the only reason I wasn't looking forward to this morning's meeting with relish was the fear of distressing you. As it is—"

"As it is," said Barbara, with a slight smile, "please go ahead and enjoy yourself." She sounded perfectly calm and self-possessed. Only Emmy, sitting beside her, noticed that her hands, which appeared to be resting quietly on her lap, were in fact tense and gripping each other for support.

Henry smiled. "Very well. Then I'll go on. The name Peter is also mentioned. I imagine this to refer to Mr. Turnberry. The clue mentions that he holds the keys."

"To heaven," Harry Vandike said loudly.

"Yes, that explanation of the clue did occur both to myself and the Bishop," said Henry. "Actually, I suspect that his name was brought in simply because it fitted the puzzle. There are other enigmatic words—'big,' 'alibi,' 'pen,' 'whim,' and a few more. My ingenious expert, combining the clues with the answers, tells me that I am being told by Mr. Vandike that I am onto something big, that the pen is mightier than the sword—or even the blunt instrument—and that 'Et tu, Brute' refers to one of the most famous murders in all history—that of Julius Caesar. He also connects 'whim' with a misspelling of Lord Peter Wimsey, thereby dragging in the detective motif. Personally, I think this is all a little farfetched. The clue to 'alibi' interests me, however. It says that it hopes Barbara has a good one." Again he wheeled on Vandike. "Wasn't that an unnecessary piece of spite against a six-year-old? Or was it put in to score off an author whose books sell better than yours do?"

Harold Vandike had turned red under his goatee and flurry of side-whiskers. "I really don't know why you're picking on me all the time, Tibbett. I simply did as I was asked, and composed the crossword. It wasn't easy, I assure you, with all those names to fit in. Naturally a few odd words emerged."

"I was talking about the clues," said Henry. "However, far be

51

it from me to pry into professional rivalries." He paused. Then, with a change of tone, he said, "Well, ladies and gentlemen, have I passed your test?"

At once the atmosphere lightened. There was a burst of applause and laughter, and everybody seemed to be talking at once.

Sir Robert got up from his chair and came over to Henry. He shook him warmly by the hand, and then indicated that he wanted silence.

"Ladies and gentlemen," he said, "I think we owe a vote of thanks to Chief Superintendent Tibbett—or, as we shall now always think of him—to Henry." Loud applause. "He has not only educated and entertained us by his expertise in his own field, but he has shown us that real-life detectives can be as cunningly ingenious as those of fiction. I confess that your little game of Guess Who was quite unknown to me until Henry told me about it yesterday afternoon—but I think we must give him full credit for solving every mystery you gave him, and we can all feel relieved that he has found the whole thing to be nothing but a game." Applause and laughter. "And now, dear friends, Pamela will get you drinks to see you through until luncheon."

At this signal, the meeting formally broke up. Drinks were served, the semicircle of chairs was disarranged, and conversation became general. Myrtle insisted on telling Henry that her name was Waterford, and became quite tipsy over sherry. Fred and Bill soon had Henry laughing over the way they concocted their impossibilities for Miss Twinkley, and Barbara circulated coolly, refilling glasses and confessing that it was a relief to be able to confess to being Lydia Drake for a while.

Only two of the party seemed less than genial: Harry Vandike and Peter Turnberry. In the case of Vandike, Henry put it down to the fact that he had been publicly attacked for his unkindness. And of course Elaine Summerfield was an embarrassment.

The case of Peter Turnberry, however, puzzled Henry. The whole matter would appear to have nothing to do with him, and yet he stood looking out of the window, alone and morose. When Barbara went up to speak to him, he seemed—Henry was out of earshot—to dismiss her with an abrupt remark, for she turned away quickly and went to talk to Sir Robert.

It was shortly before the gong sounded to announce the serving of lunch that Peter seemed to come to a decision. He elbowed his way through a group that had formed around Henry and, interrupting the general flow of conversation, said loudly, "Chief Superintendent, may I have a word with you?"

It was at this moment that the gong temporarily put an end to all talk. As its reverberating notes died away, Henry became aware that Peter Turnberry was still speaking. In the momentary silence that followed the sounding of the gong, he was saying ". . . this afternoon. I'll come to your room at five."

"Just as you like, my dear chap," said Henry. He was aware, with a slight prickling of alarm, that everyone in the room must have heard Peter's words.

Then conversation started up again, and Sir Robert, taking over easy command, said, "Well, my friends, shall we go in to luncheon?"

6

Lady Oppenshaw led the way into the dining room, followed by her chattering crowd of guests. Henry was one of the last, having been buttonholed by Fred Coe, who had some questions on exact police procedure bearing on the novel he and Bill were completing. Consequently, Henry arrived only just in time to see the butler discreetly whisking away a place setting and rearranging the others so that no gap was noticeable. As the company took their seats, Henry glanced around the table and saw that Peter Turnberry was missing.

Henry, who was sitting next to Barbara, remarked, "I see that your fiancé is lunching elsewhere."

"Oh, I doubt it." Barbara sounded bored. "He often skips meals. As a matter of fact, he told me in the drawing room that he was riding over to see his parents."

"To St. Lawrence?" said Pamela Oppenshaw, surprised.

"That's where they live, Mother," said Barbara.

"What a curious thing to do." Lady Oppenshaw sounded puzzled. "He'll barely have time to get there and back, if he really intends to see you at five, Mr. Tibbett."

"Oh, he said something about fetching something." Barbara seemed to lose interest in the subject, and turned to talk to Professor Coe, who sat on her other side. Nobody else mentioned Peter Turnberry's absence.

When lunch was over and coffee had been drunk in the drawing room, the members of the party dispersed to their chosen afternoon activities.

Barbara, predictably, was off for a ride. "Nothing strenuous, just a gentle hack. Might meet Peter on the way home." She went off to change.

Sir Robert and Lady Oppenshaw were engaged for tea with a dowager countess who lived some twenty miles away. They apologized for neglecting their guests. "The old darling is over ninety," Pamela explained, "and she gives these teas on the first Saturday of every month. It's her only form of social activity, and we didn't feel we could disappoint her. Don't worry, we'll be back for cocktails. Tea with Lucy is strictly tea, and no more!" As it was such a beautiful day, they had decided to drive themselves in the Jaguar, taking the longer road over the downs to enjoy the scenery.

Henry and Emmy opted for the beach, looking forward to a lazy afternoon with a couple of good books and a leisurely swim. Harry Vandike asked his host's permission to take out the day-sailing boat alone—"The man must be mad," remarked Fred Coe—and this was given, as Vandike was known to be a first-class sailor. However, Sir Robert spoke earnestly of the strength of the tides and the unpredictability of the wind, and Harry smilingly agreed not to venture beyond the protective arms of the little bay.

Professor Coe, still smarting from his boating experience of the previous day, announced that while the others might be on holiday, he had an article to finish for *The Economist* with a Tuesday deadline, and that he would work on it in the library. He might possibly take a short walk on the grounds as a break.

Bill Cartwright also announced his intention of taking a walk—but his was with an object. He wished to search the surrounding woods for rare species of edible fungi. Remembering her culinary conversation with him the previous evening, Emmy was not surprised. There was quite a bit of good-natured chaffing about not trying them out on the guests for dinner, which seemed to rile Cartwright. He was an expert, as he pointed out with a certain amount of pique, and knew as well as any man in England what was poisonous and what was not.

As for Myrtle, the last member of the party, Emmy found something a little sad about her decision to spend the afternoon in her room, writing letters. It seemed as though she had waited until last, hoping against hope that somebody would ask her to join in his activity. In fact, kindhearted Emmy had been about to suggest that she come with them to the beach, when a warning look from Henry stopped her.

"I live such a *busy* life normally," Myrtle remarked bravely, "that I'm afraid my correspondence gets terribly neglected. It will be a splendid opportunity to catch up."

And so the afternoon was planned, and the house party dispersed, leaving Carnworth Manor to the maids, who were cleaning up; the cook, taking her afternoon nap; the butler, sipping port and languidly polishing silver in his pantry; the chauffeur, washing the Bentley; Myrtle Waterford, writing to an old schoolfriend, who was the only person she could think of to whom she owed a letter; and Harry Vandike, checking on the exact meaning of the word "piffero" in Sir Robert's big dictionary and finding to his delight that one of the definitions of it was "a rude oboe." Should be able to get a good clue out of that one, he thought, as he closed the dictionary and went to change into blue jeans for sailing.

At the library desk, Frederick Coe was putting the finishing touches to his *Economist* article. "Please close the door quietly," he said, not being able to think of anything more cutting. He had always disliked Harry Vandike. A very peaceful, very English summer afternoon.

Henry and Emmy felt that they had made a good choice. Of course, the beach was not private to Carnworth Manor; every English beach below the high-water line belongs to the Crown and is therefore public property. Although the Carnworth estate ran right down to the water's edge, there was an ancient right-of-way (an overgrown footpath) that enabled outsiders to reach and enjoy the sandy bay. However, the right-of-way from the road was little known and few holiday-makers ever found their way to what was always known as Carnworth Beach, so that it was as nearly private as it could be. Consequently, the Tibbetts had it to themselves.

Sir Robert's day-sailer—a pretty clinker-built eighteen-footer —was bobbing at her mooring a little way offshore, and her dinghy was hauled up on the beach. The Tibbetts helped Harry Vandike carry the dinghy to the water and watched approvingly as he set sail, dropping the mooring neatly and heading out into the bay, with the dinghy bobbing behind him like a chick following a mother hen. Henry and Emmy were not surprised when after a couple of turns across the mouth of the bay—the offshore wind giving a delightful reach in both directions—the sailboat disappeared around the point and into more adventurous waters, strictly against Sir Robert's rules. The Tibbetts were sailors themselves, and could recognize expertise when they saw it. Harry Vandike would come to no harm on this lovely afternoon, currents or no currents.

After a sunbath and a swim, Henry and Emmy settled down on their beach towels, heads in the shade. Emmy said, "I thought you did marvelously this morning, darling."

"Did you?" Henry sounded abstracted. "I wonder."

"They set you a problem, and you solved it beautifully," said Emmy. She laughed. "I've never seen a lot of people more surprised."

"And not very pleased," said Henry.

"What do you mean?"

"I don't quite know. Some of them hoped that I wouldn't have made any sense of it—or even solved the clues—so that they could make a fool of me. That's understandable. What is stranger is that others—somebody else, at least—was annoyed because I hadn't solved enough. There's something else about that puzzle that I was supposed to have grasped, and didn't."

Sleepy with sunshine, Emmy said, "Peter holds the keys."

"That's just what I mean. Peter holds the keys to more than the pearly gates, if you ask me."

"Well," said Emmy, "you'll see him at five. That's what he said, wasn't it? Five o'clock in our room."

By five o'clock, most of the visitors to Carnworth Manor had had enough of their afternoon activities and were back in their rooms, taking a bath, putting their feet up for a leisurely read, preparing to change for dinner, and—in a few cases—fortifying themselves with a drink from a private bottle. Sir Robert and Lady Oppenshaw's Jaguar turned back into the drive at a quarter to six. They had not with any decency been able to leave poor old Lucy before a quarter past five, and the drive back took a good half hour. They were surprised to be met in the hall by Barbara, still wearing her jodhpurs and riding shirt.

"Hello, darling," said Pamela Oppenshaw. "Have a good ride? Our tea was gruesome, as you can imagine, but at least our consciences are clear."

Barbara said bluntly, "Mother, I'm worried. Peter hasn't come back."

"What d'you mean, not come back?" Sir Robert asked brusquely. He found Lady Lucy's teas even more irksome than Pamela did, and was in no mood for any worrisome matters. "Why should he have come back? He often stays out later than this."

"That's not the point." Barbara almost stamped with impatience. "Didn't you hear him say to Henry Tibbett that he'd see him in his room at five?"

"Yes, but—"

"I got back just after five, and Timmond told me there was no sign of Peter or Melly."

Timmond was the Oppenshaws' groom, and Melly—short for Melisande (by Pelleas out of Lost Love)—was Peter's favorite mare, whom he had taken out at one o'clock, when the rest of the party was sitting down to lunch. Timmond, like Sir Robert, was not unduly worried. Barbara had waited until half past five, then telephoned the Tibbetts' room. No, Henry had said, there had been no sign of Peter. He, too, did not sound alarmed. No, he had no idea of what Turnberry wanted to see him about, but surely it could wait.

Barbara was just back from visiting the stables again, but there was no sign of either horse or rider.

"My dear girl, you do get worked up over nothing at all," said Sir Robert, not unkindly. "He'll be back for a drink before dinner. Plenty of time yet."

Pamela Oppenshaw, however, was worried by Barbara's obvious distress. She said, "Why don't we call the Turnberrys and see if Peter did ride over there, and if so, what time he left? Would that set your mind at rest?"

"Oh, thank you, Mother. That's a splendid idea. I was afraid you'd think I was just fussing."

"Now, you go up and have a bath and change, Robert," said Pamela in a voice that brooked no contradiction. "Barbara and I will telephone."

Mrs. Turnberry sounded like reassurance itself. Yes, indeed, Peter had ridden over on Melly to see them. Arrived at . . . what time would you say Peter arrived, dear? . . . That's right, I'd just gone down to pick some roses from the garden, so it must have been a little before three . . . Didn't stay long, though. A flying visit, you might say . . . Pamela.

It still took an effort for Nora Turnberry to call Lady Oppenshaw "Pamela." The Turnberrys were not and had never claimed, nor wanted to be, what the English describe as upper-class, or "county," or (if one of them) "one of us." James and Nora Turnberry were business people, self-made and proud of it. The son of a butcher, James Turnberry had made a comfortable amount of money in the business, opening half a dozen shops in the West London suburbs. Tiring of London and wanting semiretirement, James had sold these shops to a chain store, making a good profit. He had moved to the Isle of Wight and bought a small farm, and now he owned the two best butcher shops on the island. This could hardly be called "a chain of stores"—but it was as a chain that Lady Oppenshaw described the ownership of her future in-laws' stores to her friends.

However, she often thought, who could afford the luxury of being a snob these days? In fact, was it a luxury at all, rather than a shortsighted and unpleasant trait? Only to herself had Lady Oppenshaw ever admitted that Peter's parentage had come as something of a shock to her. Naturally, she had met Peter first through Barbara, and had considered him a very desirable young man. However, shock or no shock, there it was. She had insisted at their first meeting—an awkward and stilted tea party at Carnworth Manor—that Mrs. Turnberry should call her Pamela, and hoped she might return the compliment by referring to Barbara's future mother-in-law as Nora.

59

"I don't feel easy with it, Father," Nora Turnberry had said to her husband.

To which James had replied sensibly, "Look, old girl, Peter's doing well for himself, so don't you go letting him down."

Peter had proved his worth at the local grammar school, from which he had just scraped a scholarship to Oxford. There, while taking a second-class degree in law, he had contrived to become first-class himself. He had been careful to make friends at Oxford who would be socially useful later on, and had turned himself into an excellent horseman. He was about to become a lawyer. His parents considered him brilliant.

"Besides," James continued, "what's so special about Lady Oppenshaw? She's only a human being, isn't she?"

Unable to deny this, Nora Turnberry had made a big effort to call Lady Oppenshaw by her first name, and had to admit to herself that it was becoming a bit easier. To her many friends on the island, however, Nora always referred to her as Lady Oppenshaw.

Now, as the women spoke on the telephone, Nora had come out with the "Pamela" almost naturally. "Yes, a very short visit, just to collect something," she explained.

"Collect something? What?"

"Well, to tell the truth, Pamela, I don't know. He simply said hello to Father and me, and then went up to his room. I went to the bottom of the stairs and called up to him wouldn't he like a cup of tea, but he came out almost at once and said, 'No, thanks, got to be going, got an appointment at five.' "

"And you've no idea what he'd come to collect?"

"Well, it couldn't have been very big, could it? Stands to reason, I mean. Something like a paper or an envelope he could put in his pocket, I'd say. He certainly didn't have anything in his hands when he came downstairs, if you follow me."

"So he left very soon after three?" Pamela's voice was brisk.

"That's right, Pamela." Funny, it gets easier as you go on with it, she thought. "About a quarter past, I should think, wouldn't you, Father?"

There was a mumbled assent somewhere offstage.

"That's right," said Mrs. Turnberry. "About a quarter past

60

three, so he should have been back with you at about a quarter to six—unless he took the cliff path, of course, which I've always said is dangerous, but you know young people, don't you? If he'd taken the cliff path and hurried, he'd have been back for this appointment at five, whatever it was."

Pamela Oppenshaw said quite sharply, "Well, he's not back, nor is Melly. Barbara is beginning to worry."

"Oh, I wouldn't do that," said Mrs. Turnberry. "He probably decided to take the ride back slowly, and go by the North Downs. Pity he couldn't have taken the car."

"Nora, dear," said Lady Oppenshaw, "we agreed not to mention that, didn't we?"

"Oh, sorry, Pamela. Anyhow, he'll be along in a minute, you'll see. Give our love to Barbara, won't you, Pamela? It seems a long time since she was over here."

Pamela made suitable noises of farewell, and turned to her stepdaughter, who had listened in on an extension.

"Well, you heard that."

"Why isn't he back?"

"I have no idea. Perhaps he didn't want to meet Mr. Tibbett at five after all."

"That's an idea," said Barbara.

Lady Oppenshaw looked at her stepdaughter for a moment. Then she said, "Sometimes you baffle me, Baba. You really do. Here you are, all worked up because Peter's a little late back from a ride, and on the other hand . . ."

"On the other hand, what?" said Barbara sharply.

"Darling, forgive me . . . I don't mean to pry . . . but I've had a feeling lately that there's been some sort of trouble between you and Peter. Of course, it's perfectly natural that when two people—"

"Oh, for God's sake, stop hedging, Mother," said Barbara. "Peter and I are no longer engaged. I broke it off last night, and you know it very well. We're just keeping up a pretense until this ghastly weekend is over."

Lady Oppenshaw opened her eyes very wide. "Now, my dear, this sort of thing happens all the time. I'm sure everything will sort itself out—"

"Oh, stop," said Barbara. "I'm going to change. I can do with a drink." She turned and ran upstairs.

It was unfortunate that it should have been just before half past six, when the Carnworth guests had assembled for their pre-dinner drinks, that Melisande should have returned, alone and in obvious distress, with no saddle and no rider. Covered in sweat and froth, she galloped into the stables, where she found Timmond, who loved her dearly and had no intention of going off duty until some sort of news had reached him about the mare.

Tending the mare, Timmond summoned the under-gardener, who was just going off duty, to fetch somebody from the kitchen. And so, by a long series of connecting links, the story reached Mr. Sowerby, the butler.

Sowerby was well trained in his profession. He served drinks to the assembled company, his final assignment being Sir Robert's inevitable whisky and soda. As he served this, he whispered into his employer's ear, "If I might have a word with you, sir."

"Of course, Sowerby. Go along to the pantry, and I'll be with you in a minute."

Several people in the drawing room remarked on Peter Turnberry's absence, but both Barbara and Lady Oppenshaw smiled unconcernedly and explained it by saying that he was visiting his parents, who lived on the island, and might stay there to have dinner. Only Henry Tibbett noticed the brief exchange between Sir Robert and Sowerby, and the former's unobtrusive exit a moment or so after the butler had withdrawn.

Ten minutes later, Sir Robert was back, looking grave. He had a quiet word with his wife, who spoke equally quietly to Barbara. Barbara and Pamela Oppenshaw then went out onto the terrace, and Sir Robert said in a loud voice, "Ladies and gentlemen. If you please." He sounded like a toastmaster at a banquet. Conversations dwindled into silence.

Sir Robert went on, "I'm afraid I have some rather disquieting news. As you all probably know by now, Peter rode over to see his parents at St. Lawrence this afternoon and has not returned. We were not at all worried. However, his mare has just arrived home, without her saddle and in a state of great distress, according to my groom. Peter's parents have told us over the telephone that he left them before half past three. It would seem as though he has met with an accident of some sort."

There was a general murmur of dismay and sympathy. Sir Robert went on, "His mother is of the opinion that he may have taken the cliff path in order to make the return journey in a hurry, as I believe he had an appointment with Mr. Tibbett at five o'clock. Is that not so, Henry?"

"Yes," said Henry. He added, "I've no idea what he wanted to see me about, and frankly I wasn't alarmed when he didn't show up."

"Quite. Well, I very much hope that there is no cause for alarm. The most obvious explanation is that he broke a girth, lost his saddle, and was thrown. The mare obviously bolted in panic and, not being used to the cliff path, has taken a long time to get back here. Poor Peter is therefore probably trudging it on foot. However, there is always the possibility that he was injured in the fall and is unable to walk. Consequently, Barbara and I are going to ride the cliff path in search of him. Barbara will take the big bay gelding, which is quite capable of supporting both of them if Peter should need a lift home. This is the only way we can provide a search party. The track is quite impassable by any sort of vehicle. Now, do please carry on with your dinner as usual—Peter will probably be back long before we are, but it's better to be safe than sorry, and we should leave now to take advantage of the daylight." He paused. "Now, please excuse me while I go and change."

It was only a few minutes later that the company in the drawing room saw the riders setting out across the park—Barbara looking ridiculously small perched on the big bay.

Henry said to Emmy, "Back in a moment. Forgot my handkerchief." He slipped out into the circular hall.

From there he made his way quickly through the disguised green baize door. Behind it, a flagstone-paved corridor led to the kitchen, which had doors that gave access to the butler's pantry, the staff sitting room, and the flight of stairs leading down to the cellar. The kitchen itself was a hive of activity, with a buxom cook chiding two kitchen maids to get on with their work and stop gossiping. Sowerby, who looked more shaken than any other member of the staff or family, was morosely sipping a glass of port. From him, Henry got directions to the back door and the stables.

Timmond was still rubbing down the mare when Henry reached the stables, with their aromatic horsy smell and general air of restlessness as the other two mounts fidgeted in their stalls, obviously sensing something wrong.

Timmond was talking gently to Melisande, and he looked up resentfully as Henry came in. This was, after all, his domain. Henry, however, was suitably humble, and Timmond soon relaxed and began to talk freely as he groomed his charge, who grew steadily quieter under his familiar ministrations.

"I just don't understand it, sir," said Timmond, his voice distorted by the inevitable piece of straw that he was chewing.

"What don't you understand, Mr. Timmond?" Henry asked.

"Well, several things, to tell you the truth, sir. First of all, where's her saddle?"

"Sir Robert said the girth might have broken," Henry suggested.

Timmond's reply was to spit eloquently onto the ground. "I saddled up Melly for Mr. Turnberry at lunchtime," he said. "In a great rush to be off, he was. I tell you, sir, that girth didn't break. That were a new saddle, and the girth as sound as . . . well, as sound as I ever seen. That's the first thing I don't understand. Second is, if he left St. Lawrence before half past three, as his mother says, according to Sir Robert, how come Melly took so long to get herself home? Answer me that, eh?"

"If he came by the shortcut, and she's not accustomed—"

"They know," said Timmond, with a countryman's unassailable wisdom. "They know the way home. It's not as if Melly's never been on the cliff path before."

Henry said, "I'm afraid I don't know enough about horses to—"

"Well, I do," said Timmond flatly. "Take it from me."

"Then the answer must be that he wasn't riding straight back here," said Henry. "He must have gone out of his way on some—"

"Sir Robert says he told his mother he had to hurry for an appointment at five. Here at Carnworth."

Henry said, "People don't always mean what they say, you know."

Grudgingly, Timmond said, "Well, I suppose it's possible, but it don't account for the saddle, do it?"

Henry had to admit that it did not.

"And there's another thing."

"What's that?"

"See this?" Timmond picked up a piece of old frayed rope from the stable floor, which abounded in such bits and pieces.

"What about it?"

" 'Twas attached to her bridle, that's what. I pointed it out to Sowerby, but he don't know a horse from a pig, let alone a curb from a snaffle. I tell you, sir, that mare was tethered to something."

"Well," said Henry, "she'd have to be, wouldn't she, while Mr. Turnberry was in his parents' house?"

"Yes, but normal you'd use the reins, wouldn't you? Why use a bit of rotten old rope? And what's more, it weren't untied. It broke, like it was bound to in the end, with her plunging and rearing to get away."

"I see," said Henry slowly. Then, "Did you tell Sir Robert about this?"

"Didn't have the chance, sir. He comes in here, takes one look at Melly, and he's off, saying to saddle up the chestnut and the bay, as he and Miss Barbara's off to look for Mr. Peter."

"But will you tell him?"

"I'll do that, sir, unless Mr. Peter comes back safe and sound, and with a proper explanation of what happened."

By the time Henry got back to the house—this time by the more orthodox route through the garden and up the terrace—Sowerby was announcing that dinner was served.

This was a depressing meal, punctuated by long, embarrassed silences, despite Lady Oppenshaw's attempts to keep a conversational ball rolling.

At one point, trying to help out, Henry remarked, "Wouldn't it have been quicker and easier for Sir Robert to have taken one of the cars to look for Peter?"

To this, Pamela Oppenshaw replied, "Of course not. The road doesn't go anywhere near the path. Didn't you hear him say that the only way was on horseback?" Then, in a tone that aimed at being lighthearted and missed by a mile, she turned to Fred Coe and said, "Now that we have no more identity secrets, thanks to Henry's brilliance, won't you tell us something about the new Miss Twinkley book?"

Fred muttered something about the plot not being worked out yet, and the gloomy silence descended once more.

The diners had finished their dessert and were helping themselves to cheese when the dining room door opened, and Sir Robert came in. One look at his face showed that the news was not good.

He said, "Dr. Cartwright?"

"Yes, Sir Robert?"

"Please come with me."

As the two men left the room, Henry quietly pushed back his chair, got up, and followed them. After that, there was nothing that even Pamela Oppenshaw could do to restore any semblance of normality. Cheese plates were pushed away, untasted. Lady Oppenshaw gave the signal to rise and, anticipating bad news, everyone went into the drawing room for coffee and liqueurs.

7

In the hallway, Sir Robert said to Cartwright, "Please come into the library, Bill." Then he turned, saw Henry, and seemed far from pleased. "This is a medical matter, Mr. Tibbett. I don't think—"

"Peter Turnberry has had an accident," said Henry.

"Yes."

"Is he dead?"

Sir Robert hesitated. Then he said, "I'm afraid it seems likely."

"Then the police will have to be informed," said Henry. "I think you'd better let me in on this, Sir Robert."

"Oh, very well." Grudgingly, Oppenshaw opened the library door and stood back to let the other two precede him into the room. Then he shut the door behind him and said, "I've sent Barbara up to bed with a strong sedative. There is nothing she can do."

"Where is Peter?" Henry asked.

"At the foot of the cliffs, below the path," said Oppenshaw. "We could see him quite clearly, sprawled on the rocks. It's a long fall—several hundred feet. There seemed to be no sign of life at all. The only thing to do was to hurry back and get help."

"How can you get to him?" Dr. Cartwright demanded.

"I've called the coast guard," said Sir Robert. "The local lifeboat is turning out. However, as luck would have it, Carn-

67

worth's only doctor is out on an emergency case, which is why I've called you in, Bill. I know you're an ear specialist—"

Cartwright said dryly, "I think I can remember enough general medicine to know whether a man is alive or not, Robert."

Henry said, "If Turnberry is lying on the rocks, how are the lifeboat men going to reach him?"

"They can beach their boat in a nearby cove, and there's a footpath from there," said Oppenshaw. "Now come along, Bill, we should get going. Do you have any sort of medical kit with you?"

"I'm afraid not," said Bill Cartwright, "but the lifeboat is sure to be equipped with the basics. Not, I fear, that anything will be needed except a stretcher and some strong men."

"I'll go with you," said Henry.

"Now, Tibbett—really, that's exceeding your authority . . . you are a guest here . . . naturally, if police advice is needed . . ."

Sir Robert was plainly flustered. Henry said quietly, "I think I should be on that lifeboat. I can help carry the stretcher."

"Oh, well, I suppose I can't stop you. Come along, then. No time to lose."

The Carnworth lifeboat was already on its launching ramp, and the crew aboard, when the Bentley pulled up at the small quayside. In the car, it had been arranged that Sir Robert should notify the nearest hospital and have an ambulance waiting for the return of the boat and the victim.

Henry's presence was accepted without question by the skipper, a strong, grizzled man with a weatherbeaten face. The lifeboat was a far cry from the frail-looking open vessel, manned by stalwarts with oars, that the word generally conjures up. It was a sturdy diesel-driven craft with a roomy cabin, and with such tumble home as to make it virtually unsinkable. Dr. Cartwright nodded his approval as he inspected the medical supplies. Henry noticed that it was also equipped with a breeches buoy, stretchers, inflatable dinghies, and radar, together with a powerful searchlight. A reassuring boat.

The crew, all local volunteers, were mostly in blue jeans and sweaters, since the calm sea and warm August evening seemed unsuitable for oilskins and sou'westers, but the latter were all there, supplemented by thigh-length sea boots.

At a signal from the skipper, the launching mechanism was set in operation, and the craft moved slowly down the sloping ramp to hit the water. Engines and searchlight went on, and the boat turned west, heading for that part of the coast where gently sloping meadows and sandy beaches gave way to white cliffs towering above cruel rocks, culminating in the chalky pillars of the Needles.

The skipper took the wheel, his eyes on the echo-sounder to check depth, keeping the boat as near the shore as he could. By now it was that time between twilight and night when ordinary visibility is difficult, yet is not greatly helped by artificial light. Nevertheless, the searchlight was swiveled to scan the rocky shore, probing for the small crescent beach where the boat could nose ashore. A shout went up as the first man spotted it. With infinite caution and skill, aided by charts and echo-sounder, the skipper maneuvered his vessel between the rocks and the shoals, up the unmarked channel that was the only way to the beach.

As the lifeboat neared the sand, the skipper gave an order and an anchor was thrown out astern, with several men paying out the line. As the prow touched bottom, other men in tall sea boots jumped overboard and waded ashore to plant a second anchor firmly in the sand. Thus held fore and aft, the craft could remain steady where she was for the time being, and then back out—and what a feat *that* would be, Henry thought— through the sinuous channel to open water.

Meanwhile, there was plenty of activity. Henry and Dr. Cartwright had both been provided with sea boots, in which they jumped off the prow into a few feet of water and waded ashore. Other men followed with the collapsible stretcher and powerful torches. The ship's searchlight probed anxiously to port, and a few moments later found its target: a body, like a broken doll, sprawled awkwardly on the hard gray rocks.

"There he is!" cried a voice.

"Come on, lads, we can get to him from the path!" shouted another.

With the help of the torches, it was now possible to see that a rather steep track had been hacked out among the rocks and eventually up the cliffside. Never used now and extremely dangerous, it had originally been made by smugglers for landing cargo on the beach and conveying it to the clifftop, where horsemen would be waiting for it. But that was long ago. Now, holiday-makers in small dinghies would find the little beach and explore a few yards up the rocks. Once in a while, a foolhardy adventurer would attempt the climb down. But there had been accidents, and a notice at the clifftop announced that any such attempt was formally forbidden. As for the climb up, an expert, or preferably two, with proper equipment, could do it quite easily, and sometimes did, but there was no longer any question of simply backpacking contraband up the cliff as had been done a couple of centuries ago.

However, the job of reaching Peter Turnberry from the beach path was comparatively uncomplicated. The gang of men with the stretcher stood at a respectful distance as Dr. Cartwright and Henry approached the body, armed with powerful torches. Dr. Cartwright knelt on the sharply uncomfortable rocks to make his examination. It was not long before he stood up, shaking his head.

"He's dead," said Henry. It was a statement, not a question.

"No doubt about that," said Bill Cartwright. There was a still moment, as if invisible caps were being removed in silent homage. Then Cartwright, wiping his small white hands on a handkerchief, said, "All right, then. Two of you set up the stretcher, and the other two come and help us get him onto it. Be very careful. The doctors at the hospital will want to do a complete examination to establish the exact cause of death."

So, with infinite care, Peter Turnberry was eased onto the stretcher and carried back to the boat, where the stretcher was laid on the cabin floor and covered with a sheet. Then the engines started up and the forward anchor was released from the sand. As the crewmembers who had done this jumped aboard, others hauled away on the stern line, helped by engines ticking gently in reverse, until the after anchor was also free and could

70

be winched aboard. With the aid of a second searchlight mounted aft, the skipper negotiated the twisting channel backward with an easy nonchalance that could only have come from years of experience and an encyclopedic knowledge of local conditions. Within minutes the lifeboat was in open water again.

Sir Robert had been as good as his word. An ambulance was standing beside the Bentley at the Carnworth jetty as the lifeboat pulled in alongside. Sir Robert was there, helping to take a line from a crewman. There was no need for words. The lifeboatman simply shook his head sadly. Oppenshaw nodded, and turned away as the stretcher was brought ashore and taken over by the ambulance attendants. The ambulance doors closed.

Sir Robert said with a deep sigh, "Well, there's nothing useful we can do. Best get back and break the news. Come along, Cartwright . . . Tibbett . . . where are you?"

The ambulance was reversing now, preparing to head back to its base. Henry rolled down the window opposite the driver, stuck his head out of it, and said, "Dr. Cartwright and I are going to the hospital, Sir Robert. We'll find our own way back to the Manor."

"But—"

"Dr. Cartwright," said Henry, "was the first to examine Peter and pronounce him dead. Obviously he must go."

"That's no reason for—"

Sir Robert's voice was lost in the roar of the engine as the ambulance turned off the quayside and toward the main road. Thoughtfully, Oppenshaw got back into the driver's seat of the Bentley, and headed toward Carnworth Manor.

The hospital had, of course, been alerted and was also in radio communication with the ambulance. Consequently the driver was able to inform the operator that a doctor, who was traveling with him, had pronounced the victim dead. So, when they arrived, the ambulance drove past the hospital's emergency entrance and straight to the mortuary at the back, where a pathologist was waiting to give his formal verdict and conduct a postmortem examination.

As the body was carried in on its stretcher, the three men introduced themselves: Dr. Cartwright, Dr. Spenceley, and Chief Superintendent Tibbett of the C.I.D.

"C.I.D.?" echoed Dr. Spenceley, surprised. "The police have already been called in, then? But I understood this was an accident."

Henry explained the coincidence of his presence, hesitated a moment, and then said, "All the same, the local police will have to be informed, and an inquest held. There are a few things about this accident that . . . well, that I'm not entirely happy with."

Spenceley gave Henry a sharp look. "What do you mean by that?"

Henry hesitated. Then he said, "I'd like to be absolutely sure that Turnberry wasn't either already dead or at least unconscious when he fell from the cliff."

"That's not going to be easy to establish," said the pathologist. "However, you'd better come in and take a look before I start the autopsy, and I'll do what I can for you."

"What on earth is all this about, Tibbett?" demanded Dr. Cartwright querulously. "There's not the slightest doubt what happened."

Dr. Spenceley said, "I think there are some formalities you have to go through concerning the death certificate, Dr. Cartwright. Perhaps you should go to the administrative office." He beckoned an aide. "Show Dr. Cartwright to the administration wing, will you please, Jones?"

With a suspicious look at Henry, Dr. Cartwright followed the aide toward the main building. Dr. Spenceley said, "Well, let's go in and view the remains, as they say. I warn you, it won't be a pretty sight—but then, you must be used to this sort of thing."

The doctor was right. Peter Turnberry was not a pretty sight. He had fallen on his face, which, although recognizable, was badly smashed. One of his legs and both arms had been broken, and lay at grotesque angles.

Spenceley nodded to himself. "About what you'd expect from a fall like that onto the rocks. Not the first one we've had, I'm afraid—these young daredevils trying to climb down with no

72

proper equipment. I daresay his spine is broken too, but we'll soon find out. By the way, do you recognize him?"

"Oh, yes," Henry said. "It's Peter Turnberry, all right."

"Nevertheless, we'll have to get a member of his family to identify him formally. Are his parents living, do you know?"

"Yes. He'd been visiting them at St. Lawrence, and was riding back to Carnworth along the cliff when it happened."

"Then we'd best tell the police to get his father," said Spenceley. "Once we've got him tidied up a bit. It's enough of an ordeal for the parents, without . . ." He stopped, realizing that Henry was not listening. He was, in fact, closely examining Peter Turnberry's hands.

"What are you doing?" the doctor demanded.

"Looking for something," said Henry.

"For what?"

"For something that's not there."

"Could you be a little clearer?"

Henry straightened up. He said, "His hands are quite untouched."

"Well, that's a chance that—"

"What I'm driving at," Henry said, "is that if he'd been thrown from his horse and plunged over the cliff, he would surely have tried to use his hands to save himself. Wouldn't you expect lacerations?"

Dr. Spenceley was suddenly interested. "I see what you mean."

"Of course," said Henry, "he might have taken such a toss that he fell clear of the cliffside—"

Spenceley shook his head. "You don't know that path, do you?"

"No. I intend to take a look at it tomorrow morning."

"Well, I know it well. It's a favorite walk of mine. It never comes near enough to the cliff edge for anyone to be thrown clear into nothingness. In fact, I'm wondering if his horse was on the track at all, and not on the grass between it and the precipice. You say he lived in St. Lawrence, so he must know the path well. I suppose if he was an inexperienced horseman—"

"On the contrary," Henry said. "He was an expert."

73

"Then what do you suppose happened?"

Henry said, "His horse arrived home on her own and without a saddle. The theory is that the girth broke. We know that Peter was hurrying back to Carnworth, because he had an appointment. If he'd been cantering, and the girth suddenly broke, he'd have been thrown, expert or no."

"Yes," said Spenceley thoughtfully, "and he might have rolled to the cliff edge before he could stop himself. But in that case, as you pointed out, his hands— Well, it's none of my business. I'd better get on with what is my business—to find the exact cause of death, if I can pinpoint it. You'd better go and join Dr. Cartwright in the office. I imagine someone has already informed the local police."

"There's one more thing I'd like to know," Henry said.

"What's that?"

"What did he have in his pockets?"

"Well, now, the contents of the pockets and the clothing must be turned over to the local police and then returned to the next of kin."

"Please," said Henry.

"Oh, very well. Wait in the anteroom outside. Don't say anything. One of my chaps will be bringing the things out as we get them off him."

A few minutes later a young assistant came out of the autopsy room, carrying Peter Turnberry's clothes—blue jeans, rubber-soled shoes, socks, a green shirt, and a loose tweed jacket. He went through the pockets of the jeans, apparently oblivious to Henry's presence, and found nothing. Shoes and socks were examined. Nothing. The shirt had no pocket.

The jacket revealed very little. In the inside breast pocket was a slim wallet containing a bank credit card and ten pounds in notes. In the capacious side pockets were a handkerchief, a key ring with two keys on it, a squashed pack of cigarettes, and a book of matches. Nothing else. Henry quietly left the mortuary building and made his way to the administrative section.

At this late hour the office was manned only by a couple of secretaries. Here Henry found Dr. Cartwright filling in forms he had probably not seen for years. Ear trouble can be acute and agonizing, but it is seldom fatal. One of the secretaries told Henry that the local police station had been informed of the death, but that no action was being taken until the results of the autopsy were known. The duty sergeant had confirmed that there would have to be an inquest. The police would notify the coroner's office on Monday, and a date would be set. The usual machinery of medicine and law was moving smoothly, but without haste, into action.

Henry asked the name of the duty sergeant who had taken the message, and was told that it was Robinson. Then, as Dr. Cartwright finally completed the form to the hospital's approval, he and Henry asked that a taxi should be called to drive them back to Carnworth Manor.

The mood at the Manor was subdued, to say the least. There was no sign of Barbara. Pamela Oppenshaw had volunteered to drive over to the Turnberrys to break the news to them in person, as she did not feel that it would be suitable to telephone. A brave decision, Henry thought. Even telephoning would have been bad enough.

The other members of the Guess Who club were nursing drinks provided by Sir Robert, and wondering how soon they could decently say good night and go to bed. It had been suggested by Myrtle that since the meeting was due to end on Monday morning anyhow, it would be fitting for the members to go home tomorrow, Sunday, rather than impose themselves on a household bereaved by a tragic accident. This idea had won general acceptance, and while Sir Robert protested that his hospitality was completely at their service, he predictably allowed himself to be persuaded. The Guess Who club would be dissolving into its constituent parts in the morning, not to meet again until the next dinner in London in three months' time—far enough away for Peter Turnberry's death not to cast gloom over the proceedings.

One by one, drinks were finished, sad good nights were said, and only Henry and Emmy remained with Sir Robert Oppenshaw. Dr. Cartwright, Henry noticed, had been one of the first to leave the drawing room.

Oppenshaw said, "If you and your wife want to get off to bed, Tibbett, please don't worry about me. Naturally, I'll wait up until Pamela gets back."

"There are just a few things—" Henry began.

"Surely nothing that can't wait," said Oppenshaw, passing a hand over his eyes.

"No, not really," said Henry. "I just thought I'd warn you that both Dr. Cartwright and I will have to give evidence at the inquest, and the date won't be set until Monday. Naturally, we'd both like to know the result of the autopsy, which won't be available until tomorrow. So if you can bear with us until the hospital telephones . . ."

"My dear fellow, of course. Stay over until Monday—and when you know the date of the inquest, you must naturally come here if you're needed to stay overnight."

Henry shook his head. "You're very kind, Sir Robert," he said, "but I can easily find out the date of the inquest by telephone, and since I presume it will be held in Ryde, which is quite a way from here, I really think it would be best if we put up at a hotel. If we have to stay the night, that is."

"As you wish, Henry. But you know you're always welcome."

Henry hesitated before asking, "You didn't find Peter's saddle?"

"We didn't stop to look, once we'd spotted him. I'm planning to go back and look first thing in the morning, as I was telling the others while you were at the hospital. We'll surely find it then."

"Well, that's that. Come along, Emmy, let's get to bed." Henry and Emmy both rose, and Emmy said, "I can't tell you how sorry we are that such a beautiful weekend had to turn out like this, Sir Robert."

"Very kind of you, my dear. But at least let's be thankful that there's no suggestion of foul play. A tragic but straightforward accident. No, no, don't worry about me. I'll just wait up until Pamela gets home."

Inside their bedroom, Emmy said, with a question in her voice, " 'A tragic but straightforward accident'?"

Henry rubbed the back of his neck with his hand. "I'd like to think so," he said. "But—"

"I knew there was a 'but.' "

"How did you know?"

"Just watching you, darling, I can always tell."

"In that case," said Henry, "don't be surprised to wake up tomorrow morning and find I'm not here. I'm going for an early-morning walk."

"I'll come with you," said Emmy at once.

Henry shook his head. "No, better not. I should be back in time for breakfast, but in case I'm not, just tell everyone that I was making the most of my last day in the country with an early stroll. You can say I left before seven, and that you were too lazy to come along with me. Okay?"

Emmy sighed. "All right. But won't they all think it a bit odd?"

"If I'm back for breakfast," Henry said, "nobody will think it odd. If I'm not, they'd think it much odder to find us both missing."

"Missing?"

"Missing for breakfast," said Henry blandly.

8

Actually, Emmy did wake up when Henry got out of bed at half past four in the morning, but she feigned sleep. When Henry gave instructions, it was always wise to follow them. Noiselessly he dressed in lightweight trousers, a T-shirt, and a sweater, and left the room, closing the door behind him without a sound. Emmy often thought that if he had taken to the other side of the legal fence, he would have made a first-rate burglar. She turned over and tried to go to sleep again.

Meanwhile, Henry had gone downstairs, undone the chain and lock on the front door, and disappeared silently into the misty dawn, which promised another day of brilliant sunshine. Carnworth Manor slept on, undisturbed.

Down the winding driveway, out of the big wrought-iron gates, turn left—and, walking briskly, by five o'clock Henry was in the small town of Ventnor. The police station was small but unmistakable, with its familiar blue lamp glowing in the fast-increasing light. Henry walked in.

A tired-looking sergeant sat at the desk, reading a magazine. He looked up, surprised. Ventnor is not used to such early callers.

"Yes, sir. Can I help you?"

"Sergeant Robinson?"

"Yes, sir." The sergeant looked even more puzzled.

"My name is Tibbett. Detective Chief Superintendent of Scotland Yard. Here are my credentials."

Henry fished his wallet out of his pants pocket and laid the relevant identity documents on the desk. Robinson took one look at them and struggled to his feet, trying to hide the magazine behind his back.

"Sir. What can we do for you, sir? I had no idea—"

Henry grinned. "Of course you didn't, Sergeant. I'm here on a purely personal visit. But . . . you got a phone call from the hospital at about ten o'clock last night, didn't you?"

"That's right, sir." With a great display of efficiency, Sergeant Robinson produced a large ledger in which such items were noted. "Ten-oh-three P.M. Body of a young man, not yet formally identified but thought to be Mr. Peter Turnberry of St. Lawrence, recovered from rocks at foot of cliffs near Smuggler's Bay, by lifeboat team accompanied by Dr. William Cartwright of London. Pronounced dead by Dr. Cartwright. Thought to have fallen from clifftop. Autopsy being performed at hospital by Dr. Spenceley. Inquest to be arranged Monday. Mr. James Turnberry contacted by telephone to go to hospital for formal identification. Detective Sergeant Hemming will view remains and report tomorrow—that's today, of course, sir."

"All quite correct," said Henry. "As a matter of fact, I was with the lifeboat crew as well as Dr. Cartwright. We are fellow guests at Carnworth Manor."

"Yes, sir." Sergeant Robinson sounded wooden, in order to mask his lack of comprehension. An obvious accident, and everything proceeding according to the rules. Why on earth should a chief superintendent from Scotland Yard turn up at five in the morning?

Answering the unspoken question, Henry said, "I want to see where Turnberry fell from, and I want to do it before anybody else gets there. Do you know that clifftop path?"

"Yes, sir. Since I was a boy."

"What's the best way to reach it?"

"Well, sir, I usually walk, myself—but it'd take a good hour on foot. If you're not on horseback, the quickest way is to drive

79

to the nearest point on the road, and then cut across the fields."

"You have a police car?"

"Yes, sir."

"I'd like to borrow it."

"I'd have to call out one of the drivers, sir—"

"No, I'd prefer to drive myself, if you'll just give me directions."

The sergeant looked dubious, as well he might. Then he looked at Henry's identification again.

Henry said, "If you're in any doubt, telephone the Yard. They'll give you a full description of me, and tell you where I'm spending the weekend."

Sergeant Robinson turned red. "Oh, no, sir, that won't be necessary." He took a bunch of keys off a hook on the wall behind his desk. "Here are the car keys, sir. She's in the yard at the back. How long do you—?"

"I'll have her back by seven, with any luck," said Henry. "Thank you, Sergeant."

Following Robinson's admirably clear instructions, Henry swung the black police car out of the little town and along a steeply rising road that wound its way upward until it flattened out on the clifftop, giving breathtaking views out to sea through the left-hand window, while to the inland side wooded copses and green fields stretched peacefully away toward the island's hilly center.

Henry began to look out for landmarks. A turn to the right, with a signpost reading GODSHILL 3. A sign indicating a sharp bend in the road.

"About a hundred yards farther on," Robinson had said. "You can pull the car off the road under some bushy-topped trees. Then walk across the fields towards the sea. You can't miss the path."

It was really getting light now. Henry glanced at his watch. Ten to six. The mist was rolling up in the heat of the rising sun, revealing a calm, shining sea. About ten minutes' walk, and there was the footpath. It ran some fifteen feet from the grassy cliff edge. The path was well worn, with foot and hoofmarks and the tracks of bicycle tires visible on its sandy surface.

Henry had a poor head for heights, and had to steel himself to cross the path and look down over the precipitous edge of the cliff. He found himself gazing down onto a gray jumble of rocks several hundred feet below. To his right he could make out the small sandy crescent of Smuggler's Bay, where the lifeboat had landed. So, back to the path, a little farther along, and he would be at the right spot.

It was a few minutes later, at a point where the path was about ten feet from the edge and a straggle of windblown trees made a small copse to the right of the path, that Henry saw the saddle. It was lying on its back under the trees, just off the path. Henry went over, squatted down beside it, and took a careful look, making sure not to touch anything.

It was a handsome saddle, made of the finest leather, and the girth looked, as Timmond had said, almost new. Nevertheless, it was undoubtedly broken. Still without touching anything, Henry examined the break. It seemed to be a straight tear in the tough canvas, with the ragged ends of fibers lying limply, wet with morning dew. Henry gave it his full attention, with the aid of a pocket magnifying glass. It would be difficult to prove in a court of law, but it seemed to him that both edges of the girth had been cut to a depth of a few millimeters. Once the edges had been cut, of course, any slightly abnormal strain would cause the girth to rip.

And another thing. If Peter Turnberry had been thrown from his horse in such a way as to roll over the cliffside, why was the saddle on the other side of the path, under the trees? There was an obvious answer. Had the saddle been lying openly on the grass between the path and the precipice, Sir Robert and Barbara—or whoever composed the search party—would certainly have seen it. Either somebody had been up here and moved it, or . . . Henry reviewed the various possibilities in his mind.

He went back to the grass verge and took another look at the ground and the cliff edge. But the path was too scuffed with comings and goings for any single footprint to be decipherable, and the heavy morning dew had obliterated any traces that might have been left on the grass. Only one thing seemed certain. There was no sign in the tufty grass that overhung the precipice of anybody scrabbling for his life, tearing at fragile and useless supports to stop his fall. Nor, as far as Henry had been able to see in the torchlit darkness the night before, had there been handfuls of grass and soil on the rocks below. Too late to hope for any more clues down there, of course. The tide had been on the rise as the lifeboat came in, and the skipper had explained to Henry that in another few hours the rocks where the body was found would be underwater.

Henry's next move was to inspect the trees in the little copse with meticulous care. It took him ten minutes to find what he was looking for. A piece of old rope with a frayed and broken end, still attached to a stout tree branch by a bowline knot—the sort of small expertise that you would expect from a sailor or a mountain climber. Henry hesitated for a moment. Then he took out his pocketknife and cut a small incision around the bight of the rope, some two inches from the end and a few millimeters deep. A hard pull, and the rope parted. He did a little artistic fraying to make the rope-end look as naturally worn as before and pocketed the small piece that he had detached. Then he went back to the car and drove down to Ventnor again. By a quarter to seven, he was back at the police station.

Sergeant Robinson was undoubtedly relieved to see him. He had not been at all sure whether or not he had exceeded his authority in allowing someone to drive off in Ventnor's one available police vehicle—Chief Superintendent or not.

Henry said, "I'll be going back to London later today, Sergeant, but I shall probably have to appear at the inquest. And, Sergeant—"

"Yes, sir?"

"Don't mention to anybody—and I mean *anybody*—that I came here this morning." Henry reached for his wallet and brought out two one-pound notes. An expression of horror began to dawn on Sergeant Robinson's honest face. Henry grinned. "I'm not trying to bribe you, Sergeant. Just use this to replace the petrol I've used, and give what's left over to the Police Benevolent Fund."

Sergeant Robinson began to smile, slowly. Then suddenly he said, "That's no good, sir."

"What do you mean, Sergeant?"

"The odometer, sir. The mileage has to be logged every time the car goes out."

"Don't worry. I've turned it back to where it was."

Robinson gaped. "You've *what*, sir?"

With a smile, Henry said, "One of the few good things about mixing with criminals is that you learn a lot of their tricks. It's not very difficult to do. Ask any used-car salesman."

Leaving Sergeant Robinson gazing after him with a mixture of admiration, incredulity, and shock, Henry walked out of the police station and back down the road toward Carnworth Manor. It was just before ten past seven. As he approached the big gates, he heard the sound of horses' hooves on the gravel driveway.

Henry stepped behind the protective cover of a large oak tree beside the road, just in time to see the Manor gates opened from inside by Timmond, the groom. Sir Robert then rode through on the same chestnut gelding that he had taken the evening before to look for Turnberry. Timmond led the big bay through the gates and closed them. He mounted expertly, and the two horsemen trotted off down the road away from Henry, the direction that would bring them fastest to the start of the cliff path. It seemed that Sir Robert was fulfilling his promise to return to the scene of the accident early in the morning. Henry felt relieved that he had taken the precaution of getting there earlier, before Sir Robert and Timmond—doubtless with the best intentions—could destroy or move the evidence.

Once inside the Manor grounds, Henry went straight to the stables. They were deserted except for the remaining horses stirring in their stalls, and a small lad whistling through a straw as he piled hay into the mangers. He did not pause in his work as Henry came in.

"Mr. Timmond about?" Henry asked.

The lad took the straw out of his mouth for long enough to say, "No. 'E's gorn orf wiv the master," before turning his back on Henry to pitch another forkful of hay into Melisande's manger.

Near the stable door, several rusty hooks protruded from the ancient black woodwork, and on one of them Henry recognized the piece of rope that Timmond had shown him the evening before. It had been thrown carelessly over the hook, and would never have been noticed in the general clutter of the stable. Henry took the frayed end from the tree out of his pocket. It certainly looked like a piece of the same line—but one piece of old rope is very like another. Again, what sort of evidence would that be, if it came to convincing a jury? Henry put the rope back into his pocket and made his way into the house.

Breakfast was a somber meal. Neither Lady Oppenshaw nor Barbara appeared at all. The other guests talked little, and then only about their various arrangements for getting home.

Professor Coe, who had driven to Carnworth in his own car, offered a ride to Myrtle Waterford, as he had to pass through the small Surrey town where she lived on his way back to London. He warned her that he must catch the car ferry from Fishbourne to Portsmouth at ten-thirty, which would mean leaving Carnworth at half past nine. Myrtle assured him almost inaudibly that she had already packed and would be waiting for him in the hall.

Harold Vandike planned to take the same ferry, and grudgingly accepted a lift as far as Fishbourne. As he breakfasted, Vandike had an open railway timetable beside him, and was working out by what circuitous route he could get from Portsmouth to Oxford without going all the way to London, across town, and out again from a different station. Only the Tibbetts and Dr. Cartwright were making no plans, as they were staying on to hear the result of the autopsy.

At nine o'clock, from his bedroom window, Henry saw Sir Robert and Timmond returning on horseback. Astride the bay gelding, Timmond carried in front of him the saddle that Henry had seen under the trees on the clifftop, with its broken girth dangling. They rode straight to the stables, and Sir Robert did not reappear.

However, Pamela Oppenshaw—as composed as ever, and wearing a black silk dress—was in the hall at half past nine to say good-bye to her departing guests. Hands were shaken sadly, thanks mumbled together with condolences—and then the three members of the Guess Who club went thankfully out through the front door and clambered into Fred Coe's waiting car—Myrtle sitting beside the driver, and Harry climbing with neat agility into the back seat.

The hospital was prompt and efficient. At precisely ten o'clock, a telephone call came through from Dr. Spenceley in person, asking to speak to either Dr. Cartwright or Chief Superintendent Tibbett, perhaps to both of them at the same time. Dr. Cartwright took the call in the drawing room, while Henry listened in from his bedroom.

First came a spate of medicalese, which Henry could not entirely follow, despite the fact that he had been listening to this sort of thing for years. However, the words "multiple fractures" and "internal hemorrhage" were familiar enough. When the two doctors had concluded their specialized conversation, Dr. Spenceley said, "Are you there, Chief Superintendent?"

Henry said that he was.

"Well," the doctor went on, "I don't know how much of that you understood, but what it boils down to is that Turnberry's injuries are entirely consistent with the accident he appears to have suffered."

"What about his hands?" Henry asked.

The doctor gave an impatient little sigh. "They prove nothing, one way or the other. I agree, I might have expected to find marks indicating that he had tried to save himself, but it's perfectly possible that he was stunned by his fall from the horse, and simply rolled over the precipice, unconscious."

Henry pounced on this. "You mean he *was* hit on the head before he fell?"

"Now don't put words into my mouth, please, Chief Superintendent. I'm merely suggesting a possible explanation to cover the facts. As you know, his skull was virtually smashed up—to use layman's language. It's impossible to tell at what point the various injuries occurred." A little pause. "Well, I'll see you at the inquest, no doubt. No, no date fixed yet. Well, good-bye to you both."

Henry came downstairs to the hall, passing Dr. Cartwright on his way up. The doctor nodded briefly. "Just what we expected, eh? I can tell you'd like to make a mystery out of it. So would I, come to that, might be able to use it in a book. But it was an accident, and that's what the coroner's jury will find. I'm off to pack." He continued on his way upstairs.

As Henry reached the hall, Sir Robert Oppenshaw came out from the door leading to the kitchen quarters. He was still wearing the old jodhpurs and hacking jacket that he had used for his early-morning expedition with Timmond.

"I heard the telephone," he said. "Was it—?"

"Yes," said Henry. "The autopsy results. Very much what we expected, of course." He paused. Then, "I see you found the saddle."

"How did you—?"

"I noticed you from our bedroom window." Another pause. "You'll be handing it over to the police, I suppose?"

"The police?"

"Certainly. It'll be one of the chief exhibits at the inquest. Proving how the accident happened."

"Oh, yes. Yes, of course. No news of when the inquest will be, I suppose?"

Henry shook his head. "Not until tomorrow."

"Well," said Sir Robert, "it'll be a simple affair, no doubt about that."

"I hope so," said Henry. Then he added, "Did Timmond tell you about the rope-end?"

"Oh, that." Sir Robert sounded impatient. "Apparently, Timmond found a bit of old frayed rope attached to Melly's bridle, that's all. Presumably, Peter tethered her to the gatepost or somewhere when he was visiting his parents, and the rope must have snapped."

"Timmond seemed to think she might have been tethered to a tree at the clifftop," Henry said.

"What a ridiculous idea. Why would Peter have done a thing like that?"

"I don't know," said Henry. "It was just a thought. I don't suppose you found any rope near the scene of the accident?"

"We did not, although Timmond insisted on looking. There was just the saddle, girth broken, as we guessed." Sir Robert sighed deeply. "Poor little Baba She's taking it very hard, I'm afraid." A pause. "Well . . . now that the autopsy results are in . . ." The phrase hung in the air.

Henry said, "Yes, Emmy and I should be getting off. I left her doing our packing. Shouldn't be long now. I daresay Dr. Cartwright will be leaving too."

"There's a car ferry at midday," said Sir Robert, with what sounded like relief. "Cartwright drove down, so he'll be able to give you a lift. You should leave by a quarter past eleven. That will give you plenty of time."

Henry glanced at his watch. "In that case, I've nearly an hour. If you've no objection, I'll take a last walk in your beautiful park."

"Of course, dear fellow. Anything you like." Sir Robert cleared his throat and then said hesitantly, "Pam and I . . . we're . . . we're extremely sorry that what started as such a pleasant weekend should have turned out so . . . so . . ."

"You mustn't feel sorry for us," said Henry quickly. "It's your family and the Turnberrys who have suffered from this terrible accident."

"Well." Oppenshaw seemed to perk up a little. "I hope it won't leave such depressing memories that you won't come and see us again. Anytime. And my invitation to stay here over the inquest still stands, should you change your mind."

Out in the clear, crisp sunshine, Henry walked briskly across the rolling green meadows beyond the formal gardens, until he was sure that he was out of sight of the house. Then he doubled back and made his way to the stables. The boy to whom he had spoken earlier told him that Mr. Timmond was in the kitchen, having a cup of tea with Cook.

Henry knocked on the back door, which was opened by a stout woman in a white apron—the formidable figure who had been chivvying the kitchen maids the day before. She stared at Henry and said, "Yes?" It was clear that she had not noticed Henry's quick progress through the kitchen the evening before, for she gave no sign of recognition.

"I'm sorry to disturb you," Henry said meekly. "I was looking for Mr. Timmond."

"I'll send him out to you, and welcome," said the cook. "He's had three cups already, and I've got lunch to see to."

A minute later, Henry and Timmond were in the stableyard, with the kitchen door closed firmly behind them.

Henry said, "So you found the saddle."

"That we did, sir. And with the girth broken. I don't understand it, and that's a fact."

"Sir Robert tells me that you did tell him about the frayed rope-end—"

"I tried, sir, but he wouldn't listen. Just said that Mr. Peter must have tethered Melly at his parents home, and I suppose that's the truth of it, because there wasn't no rope-end where we found the saddle, even though there's trees on the other side of the track. I had a good look myself."

"The other side?" said Henry.

"The side away from the sea, sir. On the far side of the path, there's quite a little spinney. But no rope on any of the trees."

Henry said, "So the saddle was on the cliff side of the path."

"Right at the edge, sir. 'Twas a wonder it didn't go over with poor Mr. Peter. Well, you wouldn't have expected to find it anywhere else, would you, sir?"

"No," said Henry thoughtfully. "No, I wouldn't. Well, Mr. Timmond, my wife and I are off home soon. By the way, if the cook mentions that somebody called to see you—"

Timmond winked. "I'll say you was a gentleman from the feed company, sir. I quite understand."

"Thank you," said Henry. Then, "What do you quite understand, Mr. Timmond?"

"Well, sir . . ." Timmond hesitated. "I know who you are, sir, and I know you think there was something odd about Mr. Peter's death, just as I do, sir, even though everything seems to fit so nice and proper. And if there was any hanky-panky . . . well, you never know, do you, sir, with all them strangers in the house—writers and so on. I'm glad you was here, sir, and if there's anything I can do to help—"

"Thank you, Mr. Timmond," said Henry.

By the time Henry got back to the house, Dr. Cartwright's gray Lancia was already at the front door, and the butler was loading the suitcases into the trunk. Emmy and Cartwright were in the drawing room with Lady Oppenshaw.

"Ah, there you are, Mr. Tibbett." Pamela Oppenshaw's voice was muted with grief. "You should be off if you're to make the ferry in good time." She paused. "Barbara has asked me to say good-bye for her. She doesn't feel able to—"

"Of course, we quite understand." Henry's voice, equally hushed, was joined by an assenting mumble from Dr. Cartwright.

A couple of minutes later, the Lancia, with its driver and passengers, was purring down the drive to the main road.

9

The route to the car ferry at Fishbourne went through Ventnor, up the coast road through Shanklin and Sandown, and then to the island's main town, Ryde. It was as Dr. Cartwright was negotiating Ryde's narrow streets that Henry suddenly said, "Just a moment. I've had an idea. There are other ferries this afternoon, aren't there?"

Surprised, the doctor said, "Of course. Or you can fly if you like, or take the hovercraft. It's only five miles over the water to the mainland."

"Then," said Henry, "I think we'll leave you here, have some lunch, and do a bit of exploring. You've always wanted to see something of the island, haven't you, darling?" he added, to Emmy.

"Yes, I have," said Emmy, who had never given a thought to the Isle of Wight before their invitation to Carnworth. "What a good idea."

"But . . . I can give you a lift all the way to London," protested Cartwright.

"Please, Doctor. It's very good of you, but—"

"Oh, very well, if that's what you want," said Cartwright. He pulled the car to a halt beside the curb, and Henry jumped out and began taking suitcases from the trunk. Quickly, Emmy followed him. Cartwright shrugged, waved, and drove off toward

Fishbourne, leaving the Tibbetts and their luggage on the pavement.

Emmy said, "So I've always wanted to see the Isle of Wight, have I?"

Henry grinned at her. "Sorry, darling. I have a lot of explaining to do to you, but I didn't dare do it at Carnworth."

"Where on earth did you go at half past four in the morning?"

"Oh, you were awake, were you?"

"Of course I was."

"I went where we're going now, as soon as I've made a phone call and we've had something to eat."

"And where is that?"

"Ventnor Police Station."

From a nearby public call box, Henry got in touch with the police station and asked for Detective Sergeant Hemming. He was in luck. Hemming had just returned from the hospital morgue, where he had spoken to Dr. Spenceley and viewed the remains. He proposed to visit Carnworth Manor after lunch, for a talk with the Oppenshaws, and later he would go and see Peter Turnberry's parents.

Meanwhile, Hemming was in his office at the station, where he took Henry's call. Naturally he mentioned neither his previous activities nor his future plans to his anonymous caller, who said that he wished to see the detective sergeant concerning the Turnberry case. He merely said that he would be at the station until one o'clock, after which he would be out for the whole afternoon.

"I'll be along at once," said Henry. "I'm speaking from Ryde. Please don't go until I get to you."

Outside, he hailed a cab and said to Emmy, "No lunch for the moment, I'm afraid." To the cabby, "Ventnor Police Station, as fast as you can. And please wait for us there. We shan't be very long."

Detective Sergeant Hemming was mildly—but only mildly—intrigued by his mysterious caller. In his mind, Peter Turnberry's death had been a pure and simple accident, and the inquest would be a formality. However, any sort of violent death aroused a few crackpots with theories to propound. Certainly the very last thing he expected was a visit from a detective chief superintendent from Scotland Yard, and accompanied by his wife, of all things. Sergeant Robinson, true to his word, had written nothing in his log about Henry's early-morning visit before he went off duty.

Hemming was a smallish, stout man with shrewd little eyes. He sat behind his desk and scrutinized Henry's credentials with an amazement that was not apparent, for his face had the bland unexpressiveness of an undercooked suet pudding.

At last he said, with patent untruth, "Well, Chief Superintendent, I'm delighted to see you. Delighted and honored. But I don't believe the Chief Constable has requested any assistance from the Yard in this matter."

"You're quite right, Sergeant." Henry smiled hopefully, but got no response. "I came into this simply because I was a fellow guest at Carnworth Manor, and . . . well, I'm naturally inquisitive, as I'm sure you are."

"I do my job, I hope, sir," said Hemming woodenly. "It'll be up to the coroner's court to decide what happened to the poor gentleman, won't it?"

"Of course it will," said Henry. "But I thought you ought to know that certain evidence was tampered with."

"Tampered with?" There was a faint reaction in the suet pudding. "What makes you say that . . . sir?"

Henry said, "I've a confession to make to you, Sergeant."

"A confession?"

"I visited this station in the early hours of this morning, spoke to your sergeant, and borrowed your police car."

"Well, I'll be— Sorry, sir. Yes, of course, sir, if you considered it proper."

"I didn't consider it at all proper," said Henry. "But it was the only thing to do. I paid for the petrol and turned the odometer back eight-point-six miles, which was the distance I traveled. So long as I suspected that there was a murderer in the vicinity, I didn't want to leave any traces. Now, however, the

Carnworth house party has dispersed, and apart from Dr. Cartwright, I don't suppose any of them will be called to give evidence at the inquest. I shall, however, give evidence, and it may well overturn the verdict of accidental death. That's why I came to see you."

"I really don't understand what all this is about, sir," said Hemming. "All I've been able to gather to date is that you and Sergeant Robinson conspired to misuse Her Majesty's property, to wit, one police vehicle—"

"Please let me explain," said Henry.

"Very well." Hemming had by now dropped the "sir." He could foresee trouble, and trouble was what he didn't want, not here on the island.

Henry said, "When Peter Turnberry didn't come back to Carnworth last evening, nobody worried very much. They naturally thought he had stayed on with his parents. However, when his mare arrived home in a sweat, with no saddle, at about half past six, there was very natural alarm. Sir Robert Oppenshaw and his daughter, Barbara, set out at once on horseback to explore the cliff path."

"Why the cliff path?"

"Because Mr. Turnberry had arranged to meet me privately at five o'clock at Carnworth Manor, and the only way he could have been back in time was to take the cliff path."

"I see, sir." Hemming, Henry was delighted to realize, was intrigued at last. "What was this meeting to be about?"

"I've no idea," said Henry. "At least—well, we'll talk about that later. For the moment, something else is puzzling me, and I hope you can throw some light on it. It's obvious that Peter Turnberry wanted to go to St. Lawrence for some reason before he came to see me. Why didn't he go by car, instead of on horseback? Didn't he drive? There was no driving license in his wallet."

A slow smile spread over Hemming's face. "I can tell you that all right, sir. He didn't have a license because the magistrate took it away from him last sessions. Three convictions for speeding in six months. We'd been after him for some time."

"Thank you, Sergeant," said Henry. "That explains why he had to go on horseback. Anyhow, you can see the logic of the Oppenshaws' setting out to ride along the cliff path to look for him. Sure enough, they spotted the poor chap—on the rocks below the cliff. The lifeboat was called out, and Dr. Cartwright and I went with it. Turnberry was already dead—but you know all this."

"Yes, sir. Not the first time such an accident has happened. I spoke to Sir Robert this morning, as a matter of fact. I'll be going along to Carnworth Manor later, and I intend to pick up the saddle."

"Yes," said Henry. "The saddle. That's just the point."

"What's the point?"

Henry said, "If Turnberry had fallen as he was supposed to have done, due to a broken girth while cantering at full speed, both he and the saddle would have rolled to the cliff edge, and either fallen over or stopped at the brink of the precipice."

"That's just what did happen, according to Sir Robert," said Hemming.

"No." Henry was quiet and very serious. "That's why I borrowed your car this morning. There was the saddle and the rope-end." He explained what Timmond had found on Melisande's bridle.

"Tethered at the Turnberry house—"

"No," said Henry again. "Please let me tell you this my own way, Sergeant. Everybody in the Manor knew that Sir Robert was going out early this morning to look for the missing saddle. So somebody got there first, moved the saddle, and cut the rope-end off the tree."

"How do you know, sir?"

"Because I was up even earlier, Sergeant, and I borrowed your car to get as close as I could to the spot where Turnberry fell. The saddle was on the inland side of the path, under the trees, and the rope-end was still tied to a branch nearby. Naturally, I didn't move or touch anything. I was on the spot at half past five, and left about a quarter after six. By the time I had delivered the car back here and spoken to Sergeant Robinson—who, by the way, is not in the least to blame for any of this—and then walked back to the Manor, I was just in time to see Sir Robert setting out, a little after seven. I suppose he found the saddle at eight, or thereabouts. By that time, somebody had moved the saddle to the seaward side of the path, where you would expect to find it, and the rope-end had gone. That's what I mean by tampering with evidence."

Hemming sat for a moment in silence. Then, reluctantly, he said, "We've only Sir Robert's word that he found the saddle where he said he did."

"No, we haven't," Henry said. "Mr. Timmond, his groom, was with him. He confirms that they found the saddle on the seaward side of the path. He also made a special search for the rope-end, and found nothing. He seems to me to be a reliable person."

"Yes, sir. I know him well."

"At the hospital last night," Henry said, "I saw an orderly laying out the contents of Mr. Turnberry's pockets."

"That's right, sir. I've got them here now. Nothing at all unusual. The keys were to the Turnberry house. Just what you'd expect."

"I know," said Henry. "That's what puzzles me."

"Puzzles you, sir?"

"Yes." Henry rubbed the back of his neck with his left hand—an unconscious gesture that always meant a problem. "Why did he ride over to see his parents?"

"Well . . ." Hemming was growing stodgier again. "Why did the chicken cross the road, sir? If you'll forgive me. The chicken wanted to get to the other side, and Mr. Turnberry wanted to go to his parents' home."

"To talk to them?"

"One must presume so, sir."

"Then why didn't he telephone? Why did he set out on a long ride that involved missing his lunch?"

"Missing his lunch?" At last, a responsive chord seemed to have been struck in Sergeant Hemming. Clearly, for him, lunch was something with which only the gravest emergency could interfere.

"Yes. And then he could only have stayed a very short time,

and was riding back as hard as he could, by the shortcut over the cliffs." There was a heavy pause. Henry said, "You must see it, Sergeant. Peter Turnberry went to St. Lawrence to collect something."

"What, sir?"

"I don't know. Something small, that he could put in his pocket. Something that he didn't want anybody to know about. And yet, when he was found, that object wasn't there."

"I see what you're driving at, sir," said Hemming, with no enthusiasm. More and more, he felt, this case might have nasty and unsettling repercussions. Why couldn't people mind their own business? A simple riding accident. Now, with this Chief Superintendent shoving his nose in, there could be all sorts of awkward complications.

Henry went on, "What time were you thinking of visiting the Turnberrys, Sergeant?"

Thankful to be on what seemed a safer topic, Hemming said, "Well, sir, I'm off for my lunch now." The sergeant obviously had no intention whatsoever of emulating Peter Turnberry and missing a meal. "Then I thought I'd go to the Manor to see Sir Robert and get the saddle. I'll have a word with Joe Timmond while I'm there, too, in view of your information. Then on to the Turnberrys."

"That's very good," said Henry, a little enigmatically. "And when you get the saddle, I do advise you to examine the broken girth very thoroughly. Well, my wife and I will get ourselves something to eat, too, and then we have to get back to London."

Hemming stood up. Awkwardly he said, "As a matter of procedure, sir . . ."

"Yes?"

"Well, what I mean . . . you're not taking this case over, are you, sir?"

Henry looked shocked. "Of course not, Sergeant. It's entirely your case—unless and until your Chief Constable decides to call in the Yard, which would surprise me. I'm here just as a member of the public, giving information."

"Thank you very much, sir," said Hemming.

The cab was waiting outside the police station in the sunshine. Henry asked the driver to take them back to Ryde, and sought his advice on a good place to have lunch. Apart from a few friendly remarks from the driver—"You'll be down on holiday from London, I wouldn't wonder?" and "Lovely weather for once—last summer was terrible"—to which Henry replied monosyllabically in the affirmative, the ride was made in silence. Once Emmy said, "Henry, there's something I—" but he gave her a warning look, and she shut up.

After a pleasant but hurried lunch, Henry said, "Now we must hire a self-drive car. I noticed an office when Cartwright dropped us off."

Formalities were soon concluded, and Henry was behind the wheel of a lively little sedan, headed once more down the coast road toward Ventnor, and beyond it to Carnworth and St. Lawrence.

Emmy said, "What are you being so mysterious for? I only—"

"I don't want anybody at Carnworth Manor to know that we didn't go back to London this morning," Henry said.

"Why?"

"Because it might be dangerous. Because somebody might repeat it to one of our fellow guests, for example."

"Dr. Cartwright knows," Emmy said.

Henry frowned. "I know," he said. "I didn't see how it could be done without his knowing. Anyhow, I just hope . . . well, it'll be a while before Cartwright reaches London, anyhow."

"So where are we going now?" Emmy asked. "Isn't this the way back to Carnworth?"

"Yes, but we're not stopping there. We're going to see the Turnberrys. Before Sergeant Hemming gets there."

"Well," Emmy remarked, "the Turnberrys are almost certain to tell somebody at the Manor that we've visited them."

"Maybe. Maybe not. In any case, it won't matter so much then."

"I give up," said Emmy. "Anyhow, can I finish what I was going to say in the taxi?"

Henry took his eyes off the road long enough to give her a big smile. "Of course, darling."

"Well, I just remembered. After you went sneaking out at that ungodly hour, I drifted off to sleep again. I can't possibly tell what time it was . . . but I had the impression that I heard a car engine, somewhere in the distance. I thought it must be on the road."

"You couldn't possibly have heard a car on the road." Henry was very interested. "The Carnworth cars are kept at the back, by the stables. The Bentley and the Jaguar are in garages, but there's a big parking area for visiting cars."

"Dr. Cartwright's and Fred Coe's."

"Exactly. Our room was toward the back of the house. You could have heard if one of the cars from the Manor had started up."

"But wouldn't it have had to come round to the front and down the drive?"

"No," Henry said. "There's a back entrance to the estate. You've no idea what time this was?"

"No, I haven't. I'm sorry. I never even thought about it until you started telling the sergeant about somebody going to the cliff path and tampering with evidence between your visit and Sir Robert's."

"Well," said Henry, "it doesn't really matter. It's just confirmation of what I was sure of all along. Somebody from the Manor—"

"Cartwright or Coe."

"Not necessarily. People can borrow other people's cars. Or it could have been one of the family."

"Henry, you're not suggesting—?"

"No, I'm not. Just thinking."

The tiny village of St. Lawrence lies on the clifftop, between Ventnor and The Needles. It is hardly large enough to be classed as a village, but it has a church, a pub, and a cluster of cottages. In the vicinity, a few retired people have built themselves comfortable homes in one of the few remaining quiet and unspoiled areas of the island.

It took only the briefest of inquiries at the pub to locate the Turnberry house. Down a rutted lane, with a left turn at the end, and there it was—an old renovated farmhouse, surrounded by a well-tended flower and vegetable garden of about half an acre. Henry pulled up outside the garden gate, and he and Emmy climbed out of the car.

The house was very quiet, but Henry was relieved to see that the curtains had not been drawn in an ostentatious show of mourning. All the same, he felt like an intruder as he rang the front doorbell. Weren't these people entitled to privacy in their grief? What good would it do to probe them with questions, to raise doubts about their tragic loss? Then he remembered that when you start unraveling a string of events, there is no knowing where it may lead, and he might—just might—be saving another family from bereavement. He also remembered that they were doomed to a visit from Sergeant Hemming anyway, so their afternoon was going to be shattered, one way or the other.

The door was answered almost immediately by a tall man with a square-jawed, sunburned face. He looked taken aback when he saw Henry and Emmy.

"Mr. Turnberry?" Henry said.

"I saw the car driving up," said Turnberry. "I thought it must be . . ." His voice had no soft West Country burr to it, but rather the brisk, self-assured accent of a middle-class London suburb. "I'm afraid I don't know you, sir, and obviously you don't know us, or what's happened to us, or you wouldn't be here. I don't want to be rude," he added with obvious sincerity, "but the fact is that I shall have to ask you and the lady to leave. You see, our son was killed yesterday, and my wife . . . well, I'm sure you understand."

"I understand and I know, Mr. Turnberry," Henry said. "That's why I'm here."

"Who are you, then?"

Henry pulled out his official identity card and handed it over to Turnberry, who studied it with an expression of growing disbelief.

At last he said, "Scotland Yard? Criminal Investigation Department? But there's been no crime here. It was an accident."

"Please let us come in," said Henry. "I must talk to you."

"And who's the lady?" Turnberry went on. "A policewoman, is it?"

"No, my wife."

"First time I've heard of a detective taking his wife along on an investigation." Turnberry's voice bristled with suspicion, and Henry could not blame him.

Emmy said, "Mr. Turnberry, this isn't an official investigation. My husband and I were spending the weekend at Carnworth when . . . when it happened. But my husband isn't sure that things are just what they seem to be. So—"

"If it's not an official investigation, then I don't see why I should talk to you. I'm expecting Sergeant Hemming, it's true, with Peter's things. But as for you—"

Mr. Turnberry's considerable bulk pretty well filled the doorway, but Henry was aware of somebody in the hall behind him. A woman's voice, gentle and sad, said, "Let them in, James."

Turnberry swung around. "Nora," he said, "you're supposed to be upstairs resting."

"I said let them in, James."

"Oh, very well." James Turnberry stood back to allow the Tibbetts to enter. He said, "Nora, this is Chief Superintendent . . . er . . ."

"Tibbett," said Henry. "Henry Tibbett. And this is my wife, Emmy. You are very kind to agree to see us, Mrs. Turnberry."

Nora Turnberry was plump but still pretty. Her gray hair was drawn back into an old-fashioned bun at the nape of her neck, and her smooth, scarcely wrinkled face bore only the merest suggestion of makeup. Unlike Pamela Oppenshaw, she had not been able to go straight to her wardrobe and select a black dress. Instead she wore a gray skirt and white blouse—the nearest thing to mourning that she could muster at short notice. She smiled at the Tibbetts—a sad smile, but sweet.

"Do please come in," she said. "I'm sorry James was not very welcoming. This has been a great shock to us, as you'll appreciate. James, take Mr. and Mrs. Tibbett into the lounge, and I'll make a cup of tea."

At half past two in the afternoon, this seemed less than suitable—but tea is the traditional English welcome and not to be refused. While Nora Turnberry was in the kitchen, her husband sat in the comfortable drawing room with his visitors, glowering at them in silence. Emmy was glad when Nora reappeared, bearing a tray with four cups, a teapot, a milk pitcher, and a sugar bowl. When the strong brew had been poured, Nora said, "I couldn't help overhearing what you were saying to James, Mrs. Tibbett."

"I know this must be very distressing for you—" Henry began.

Nora Turnberry cut him short. "I'm glad you came. I think there was something funny about Peter's death."

"You do?"

"Yes, and I'll tell you why. Peter knows that cliff path like the back of his hand, and heaven knows he's ridden Melly often enough not to make any silly mistakes."

"But the saddle girth broke, Mrs. Turnberry."

"I don't believe it." Nora Turnberry sounded almost serene in her certainty. "Peter was too good a rider to have mounted and set off on a long ride without checking over his gear. In any case, he always liked to saddle the horse himself, groom or no groom. It's only since he'd taken up with the Carnworth set—"

Henry said, "How long does the ride from Carnworth take, Mrs. Turnberry?"

"A good two hours or more, if you come by the usual cross-country route and take things moderate to easy. Quite a bit less if you take the cliff path and push your horse."

"I'm wondering," Henry said, "why Peter rode over to see you yesterday afternoon. He can't have spent long here."

"He didn't. Not more than a few minutes. I couldn't understand it. I saw him riding up, and I said to Father—didn't I, James?—I said, 'Why, there's Peter come for the afternoon, maybe to stay the night. I'll get him a cup of tea.' But all he says is, 'Hello, Mother, sorry I can't stay,' and he goes rushing up to

101

his room. 'Just fetching something,' he says, and he's downstairs and off again. Said he had an appointment at five, but where, I don't know. Melly had just got her head down into some of the nice grass in our meadow—"

Henry said, "He didn't tether the horse?"

"Bless you, no. Melly knows this place well. She wouldn't go off on her own. She likes it here."

Henry and Emmy exchanged a quick glance. Then Henry said, "You've no idea what it was that Peter came to fetch?"

Nora Turnberry shook her head. "None at all. Since it must have been something that would go in his pocket, I naturally thought of a letter or paper or such—but that's all I can tell you."

"Sergeant Hemming will be coming to see you this afternoon," Henry said.

"I told you that." This was James Turnberry's first contribution to the conversation.

"He told me," said Henry, "that he's bringing all of Peter's things—the contents of his pockets. There's nothing but keys, a wallet, a handkerchief. Nothing like papers or a letter."

Ponderously, James Turnberry said, "Look, Mr. Tibbett. We're just ordinary folk. Not like the Carnworth Manor set. I daresay Lady Oppenshaw told you."

"She said you owned a chain of stores," said Emmy.

Turnberry gave an unamused laugh. "She did, did she? I'll tell you what I am, Mrs. Tibbett—I'm a retail butcher, and a bloody good one, though I say it myself, and excuse the language. I had six shops in the Ealing area of London, which I sold a few years ago. Now I got two here on the island. I'm semiretired, and I leave the running to the managers—but I keep an eye on the quality of the meat, you can be sure. A chain of stores, indeed! No, we're simple people and we never thought Peter would turn out like he did—scholarships and Oxford and all that. Certainly never thought he'd end up engaged to Sir Robert's daughter, but that's the way life goes. One thing I'll say for him—he was never ashamed of us, was he, Mother?"

Mrs. Turnberry did not answer, but turned away, her eyes full of tears. James Turnberry went on, "Brilliant. That's what they all said about him at these posh places. And very soon he'd have been a proper lawyer. Well, I'm a God-fearing man, Mr. Tibbett, and I suppose the Almighty knew what he was doing, but I'm blowed if I can see why he should take a young life like that, just as it was starting, as you might say."

"Nor do I," said Henry, and he sounded grim. "Well, very many thanks for the tea, Mrs. Turnberry, and for your kindness. We'd better be going now." He stood up, hesitated a moment, then said, "I wonder if you'd do me a great favor, Mr. Turnberry?"

"If I can, Mr. Tibbett."

"When the date and time of the inquest are fixed, would you call and let me know? Here's my card."

In the hall, saying good-bye, Henry said, "By the way, Mr. Turnberry—just one more question."

"Yes?" Turnberry sounded suspicious again.

"When you opened the door to us, you said you'd seen the car driving up, and thought you knew who was coming to visit you."

"Well . . . I had an idea . . ."

"You recognized the car, did you?"

"No, no. I don't know what sort of car he has. I just thought that perhaps he'd come over and see us before he left the island, seeing that he and Peter were so close at one time."

"Who is 'he,' Mr. Turnberry?"

It was Nora Turnberry who answered. "Why, Professor Vandike, of course. He was staying at the Manor, so Peter told us."

"Yes," said Henry. "Yes, he was. You say he and Peter were very close?"

Nora Turnberry said, "It was he who—"

Her husband interrupted her. "He was Peter's tutor, up at Oxford. Thought the world of him. Used to take him for holidays during the vacations, rock climbing and suchlike, in Wales, wasn't it, Mother?"

"That's right, James," said Nora.

"So we thought," James Turnberry went on, "that it might be

only natural for him to come and see us. But—"

"I'm afraid he won't," Henry said. "He left for Oxford this morning."

"Ah, well, why should he, really? We only met him the once, didn't we, Mother?"

"Yes, James. When—"

"Well, you'll be wanting to be off, I daresay, Mr. Tibbett."

After leaving the Turnberrys, Henry drove back toward Ventnor. Shortly before Carnworth, however, he surprised Emmy by taking a left turn up a small lane.

"Where are we going?" she asked.

"Carnworth Manor."

"But I thought you said—"

"I know I did, but there's something I must know."

Another turn—to the right, this time—and Emmy saw that they were approaching the back entrance to Carnworth Manor, which led to the stableyard and parking area. Henry drove slowly past the gate, and noticed with approval that the police car was parked there. As he had hoped, Sir Robert was closeted with Sergeant Hemming. He stopped the car at the side of the road, out of sight of the gate.

"What do we do now?" Emmy asked.

"We wait," said Henry.

They did not have to wait long. A couple of minutes later, a jaunty boy on a bicycle came riding out of the back gate, whistling merrily. Henry was relieved to see that it was not the stable lad with whom he had talked. As the bicycle approached the car, Henry got out and called, "Hey!"

The bicycle stopped, the boy dragging his feet in the dusty lane as brakes. "Wot is it, then?"

"Want to earn fifty p.?" Henry asked.

The boy hesitated. "It's me afternoon off," he said. "What's it about, then?"

"Won't take you a moment." Emmy noticed that Henry, who was a good mimic, had lowered his accent a little in the social scale, and roughened it with a suggestion of vulgarity. He sounds like a cheap salesman, she thought.

"Orl right, then, let's hear it," said the boy.

Henry said, "You know Mr. Timmond?"

" 'Course I do."

"He's in the stables, is he?"

"Where else would 'e be?"

"Well, there's fifty p. for you if you go in and ask him to come out here and have a word. Tell him it's the feed salesman who called this morning."

"Why can't you drive in and see 'im yerself?" asked the boy.

Henry winked. "Ask no questions, lad, you'll be told no lies."

This indication of something a little fishy afoot intrigued the young man.

"Okeydoke," he replied. "Let's have the cash, then."

"Money-grubbing little brute," said Henry amiably, and handed over the coin. The lad wheeled his cycle around, mounted again with an athletic leg thrown into the air, and went back through the gate. A minute later he was out again and on his way, with a cheery thumbs-up sign. Quite soon he was followed by Timmond, wiping earthy hands on his ancient breeches. He came up to the car.

"Mr. Tibbett? This is a surprise, sir."

Henry said, "I couldn't come in. I don't want anybody at the Manor to know that I haven't left the island. You understand?"

"Of course, sir. Not that you need have worried. Sir Robert's with Sergeant Hemming now, so Sowerby tells me."

"Yes, but he won't be forever. What's more, Hemming is going to come and have a word with you afterwards."

"He is?"

"He is. I saw him this morning, and I told him . . . well, anyway, he's planning to see you." Henry paused. "When he asks you questions, Timmond, be sure to reply accurately, but . . . well, don't volunteer any more information than he asks for. Okay?"

"Okay, sir."

"Now lean on the car window as though you were talking to a nuisance of a salesman, and if anyone from the Manor comes, I'll drive off. I want you to tell me about car keys."

"Car keys?"

"Yes. If a guest arrives at the Manor by car, he is decanted at the front door, and the car is whisked off to the back here by a footman or somebody."

"By Higgins, the chauffeur, sir."

"Okay. Now what happens to the keys?"

"The keys are left in the car, sir. There's always somebody on duty around here to see that nobody unauthorized takes a car out. And it means that Higgins can shift the cars around if need be, and also bring them to the front door if ordered."

"That's what I thought," said Henry. "Now, yesterday afternoon, can you remember what cars were moved, and by whom?"

Timmond answered at once. "Sir Robert and Lady Oppenshaw ordered the Jaguar to be at the front door at three-fifteen, sir. And they brought her back at six, or thereabouts. The Bentley was in the garage all day, until the evening, when Sir Robert took her out to go to the lifeboat."

"And the other cars?"

"Well, there was just the two, sir. Dr. Cartwright's Lancia and Professor Coe's Ford—bit of a rattletrap, if you ask me," added Timmond.

"And did either of them go out?"

"Just the Lancia, sir. Dr. Cartwright drove her off at—oh, round about a quarter to four, it must have been. Yes, because I went in for a cuppa with Cook shortly after, and when I come out of the kitchen, the car was back."

"What time would that have been?"

Timmond reddened slightly. "Well, it being Saturday, sir, I think I may have lingered a little. It would be about five, I'd say."

"Did you hear the car coming in?"

"Can't say I did, sir. She's got a sweet-running engine, the doctor's Lancia, and there's always a bustle in the kitchen."

"Still, you're sure it was Dr. Cartwright who drove out of the stableyard shortly before four?"

Timmond scratched his head. "It was the Lancia, sir. I couldn't tell you for certain who was driving it, because I only

106

come out of the stables as it was turning off through the gate, and . . . I'm sorry, Mr. Smith, I told you this morning, we're very satisfied with the feed we're getting now."

Timmond nodded curtly and turned on his heel, as Henry let in the clutch and moved off down the road. In his rearview mirror, he could see that Barbara Oppenshaw had come riding out of the back gate on her chestnut mare. She stopped for a word with Timmond, who said something to her and went into the stableyard again. Barbara turned the mare in the other direction and was soon out of sight. She did not even glance at the little blue rental car.

10

Henry and Emmy drove back to Ryde, turned in the rental car, and took a taxi to the evening ferry. Henry was very silent on the journey. On the train back to London, he pulled a piece of paper out of his pocket and studied it intently. It was the practical-joke crossword puzzle. There were other people in the compartment, so Emmy made no remark, but continued to read the newspaper she had bought at the station. It was a London edition, and contained no reference to Peter Turnberry's death.

Back in their Chelsea flat, Emmy made supper while Henry continued to brood. As she was setting the table, Henry looked up and said, "It's all there, in that puzzle. It must be."

Emmy said, "It's interesting that Harold Vandike knew Peter at Oxford. Neither of them gave any sign of it."

"No reason why they should," said Henry. "Remember, all the other members of the party had been at Carnworth for nearly a week before we arrived. They weren't strangers to each other, as they were to us. I daresay Vandike and Turnberry did their reminiscing about the university during the first couple of days. Nevertheless, Vandike did compile that puzzle, and there's the clue about Peter holding the keys. I was meant to make something out of that, and I didn't. But somebody else did, and Peter Turnberry died."

"Surely," Emmy said, arranging knives and forks, "all the

Guess Who members must have seen the puzzle beforehand. It was a joke they all thought up together."

"The puzzle, yes. I'm not so sure about the clues. I don't think any of them are crossword fans—except Vandike, of course. However, we'll find out." Henry sat up straight, and seemed to give himself a little shake. "I'm sorry, darling. Let's forget it for the moment and have our supper."

The next day, James Turnberry telephoned Scotland Yard to say that the inquest had been arranged for the following Thursday at 10:00 A.M. The coroner's court would be sitting at the Ryde courthouse. There was no similar message from Sergeant Hemming.

Meanwhile, Henry was not entirely idle. During the afternoon, he put through a call to the London telephone number of Barbara Oppenshaw, which was listed in the directory. He had wondered if Barbara might decide to stay on at Carnworth, especially as she would certainly be needed at the inquest on Thursday. However, the telephone was promptly answered.

"Barbara Oppenshaw speaking."

"This is Henry Tibbett, Miss Oppenshaw."

There was a tiny pause. Then Barbara said, "If you want to know about the inquest, it's at the Ryde courthouse on Thursday morning at ten."

"I know that," said Henry. "I'll be there."

"Then why are you calling me?"

"Because I'd appreciate a talk with you, Miss Oppenshaw."

"Call me Barbara, for heaven's sake. Or aren't policemen allowed to use first names? Please tell me—it would be valuable information for my books."

Henry said, "It's unusual to use first names in the course of an investigation—Barbara."

"If you're not investigating anything, then why do you want to see me?"

Henry said, "I'm not investigating a case. I'm investigating a crossword puzzle."

"Oh." Barbara sounded a little taken aback.

"It'll have to be when I'm off duty, of course," said Henry. "How about this evening? Half past six at your apartment?"

Again there was a hesitation. Then Barbara said, "Oh, very well. If it will make you happy. Anything for a quiet life." She rang off.

So, when he left his office, Henry made his way not to Chelsea, but in the other direction, toward Islington, where he soon found the beautiful Carolean house—now restored and converted into apartments—where Barbara spent her time when in London. Hers was the ground-floor flat, and she opened the door to Henry with a marked lack of enthusiasm. Henry noticed, as she led the way into the sitting room, that she was wearing a sort of gypsy skirt in brilliant colors and a shapeless knitted blouse. Barbara Oppenshaw was certainly not in mourning.

She turned to Henry. "I expect you'd like a drink."

"I certainly wouldn't mind one. A scotch and soda, if possible."

"Of course." Barbara mixed two drinks and then sat down on the divan, motioning Henry to an elegant and very modern tubular chair, which turned out to be excruciatingly uncomfortable. She said, "Well?"

"First of all," said Henry, "I wanted to offer you all my sympathy, Miss Oppenshaw—I'm sorry—Barbara. Mine and Emmy's."

Coldly, Barbara said, "There's no need. Peter and I were no longer engaged when he was killed."

Henry let this sink in for a moment. Then he said, "You didn't appear after Peter's body was found, and I gathered from your parents that you were prostrate with grief."

"I didn't appear," said Barbara, "because I didn't want to be subjected to a whole lot of well-meant condolences about a man I didn't give a rap for."

"Then why did you get engaged to him in the first place—if that's not an impertinent question."

Barbara considered. "It is, of course, highly impertinent, but I'm prepared to answer it. I was introduced to Peter six months ago by Harry Vandike, who was staying at Carnworth. You probably know that Harry was Peter's tutor at Oxford, and had remained friendly with him ever since."

Henry said, "You and your family had never met the Turnberrys, even though you live quite close and on a small island?"

"The Turnberrys," said Barbara, "are not exactly the sort of people whom my family would know, in the ordinary course of events. However, Harry brought Peter over to Carnworth, and he appeared to be very much attracted to me. I was flattered, I suppose. Also, we had a hobby in common—horses. After that, he used to come over a lot when he was on the island, and we went riding together. Three months ago, he proposed to me and I accepted him."

"Were you in love with him then?"

"I was attracted to him," Barbara said. "And as I said, I was flattered. He knew that I was my parents' daughter, of course, but he had no idea that I was an established writer and an independent woman. Flattering again. However, I did have doubts, even then. I suggested that it would be best if we just lived together for as long as we both felt like it. But Peter was adamant. Marriage or nothing."

Henry smiled. "The roles of the sexes have certainly been reversed," he said. "It used to be the girl who insisted on marriage."

"The Turnberrys are very middle class," Barbara remarked. "To be honest, I suppose that was one of the things that began to get on my nerves."

Tentatively, Henry said, "Your parents seemed very happy about the engagement."

"Mother was," said Barbara promptly. "Probably because Harry Vandike gave him such a colossal buildup—how brilliant he was, how he was going to become a celebrated barrister, and so on. Also, Peter was good-looking, and Mother thought it was time I married. Father didn't think too much of the idea at first—but of course Mother can twist him round her little finger."

"So what happened?"

"It was quite gradual," said Barbara. "I think it started when I began to realize that Peter wasn't nearly as brilliant as Harry made out—rather stupid, really. Also, I could sense that he was becoming less . . . less attentive, if you'll forgive a quaint word. Then, just last week, shortly before the Guess Who house party, I heard that he'd been swanking around London, bragging that he was going to marry the Carnworth heiress. Not Barbara Oppenshaw. Not even Lydia Drake. The Carnworth heiress. The more I thought about it, the more I understood his insistence on marriage. He didn't give a damn about me as a person. He wanted my father's influence, my prestige, and eventually, through me, Carnworth and all that goes with it.

"The day before his death, I put it to him fair and square. Of course he denied it, but not convincingly enough. I told him again that I was prepared to live with him, but not to marry him. He was furious. We had a great row, and the evening ended with the air full of the fragments of a broken engagement. Thank God I found out in time. If he'd been a little cleverer, he'd have kept up the fiction until after the wedding."

Henry said, "But it was you who first got alarmed when he didn't come back after his ride."

Barbara gave him a sharp look. Then she said, "I was worried about Melisande." She stood up. "Let me get you another drink."

"Thank you," said Henry, surrendering his glass.

At the bar, with her back to him, Barbara said, "I suppose you think I was really madly in love with him, and that this is just a pose." She turned to face him, a glass in each hand. "Well, it's not. He was a jumped-up little fortune hunter, and I'm thoroughly glad to be rid of him. Of course," she added belatedly, "I'm sorry he's dead."

"Earlier," said Henry, "you talked about his 'being killed.' "

"It comes to the same thing."

"You don't think it's possible that anyone might have wanted to murder him?"

"Murder him?" Barbara laughed. "Whatever for? He was too unimportant."

Henry decided to change the subject. He said, "Tell me about the crossword puzzle."

"There's really nothing to tell. It was a silly, childish idea, and you stood it neatly on its head for us. We were talking at dinner about the difference between fictional and real-life detectives, and we wondered if you'd be able to solve some so-called classic fictional clues."

"Whose idea was it?"

Barbara wrinkled her brow. "I really can't remember. I think it was Bill Cartwright's. He and Fred had a friendly—well, more or less friendly—sort of wrangle about how each of them had inherited money from an old lady whom they might possibly have killed."

"More or less friendly?"

"Well." Barbara hesitated. "Bill seemed to suggest at one point that there really might have been some funny business over Fred's aunt's death, and Fred got very redfaced and cross. But it all blew over. Then Harry said that he needed a third theoretically possible murder for his crossword. Neither he nor Myrtle had anything to contribute, so he raked up the business of poor Jeannie's drowning. I reminded him that I was only six years old at the time, but he said never mind, it would do. It was only a joke, after all. So I said okay."

"The funny thing," said Henry, "is that far more of the clues in the puzzle relate to Jean Warfield's death than to either of the others."

"Oh, that was just coincidental," said Barbara. "Harry explained that. They were the little words, which happened to form themselves, as it were. The difficult thing was to get the long names, like Lady Fanshaw and William Cartwright, into the puzzle."

"Why was Peter's name mentioned?"

With some irritation, Barbara said, "Because it happened to fit in, that's all."

"The clue was strange, too."

"I didn't even look at the clues. I hate crosswords."

"I mentioned it at the meeting," Henry said. "The clue to Peter was 'He holds the keys to everything, of course.' "

"Oh, yes, I remember. And Harry explained that it referred to Saint Peter and the keys of heaven."

Henry said, "Can you think of anything else that Peter Turnberry might have held the keys to?"

"Oh, don't be childish, Henry. Of course not."

"In fact," Henry said, "what happened that day—when your sister drowned?"

"She wasn't my sister." The reply seemed like an automatic response to a frequently made error. "She was Mother's stepdaughter. To tell you the truth, I don't remember anything at all about it. I've been told over and over again what happened, and I suppose that has sort of jelled in my mind as the truth. But when I try to think back, I can only remember leaving the house with Jeannie to go swimming. Then everything goes blank. Shock, I suppose. I was very young."

Henry said, "You were fond of your"—he hesitated—"your stepsister?"

"I adored her," said Barbara simply. "I never knew my own mother, and Pamela seemed . . . well, remote and glittery and glamorous, but hardly a mother figure. Jeannie was quite different. From the moment we went to live at Carnworth . . ."

She stopped, and Henry was embarrassed to see that she was crying. He said, "I'm terribly sorry, Barbara. I didn't mean to upset you."

Barbara was in control of herself again. Raising her head, she looked straight at Henry. "I wonder," she said, "if that's quite true."

Henry said, "It's almost true."

"Like so many things," said Barbara.

"What do you mean?"

Barbara shrugged. "Just a generalization. How many things do you know that are absolutely and incontrovertibly true?"

Henry smiled. "A certain number," he said. "Relating to Peter's death, for example. I know that he rode over to his parents' house that afternoon to fetch some small object or piece of paper."

"You know that for sure?"

"Yes. I remembered a remark you made, and then his mother confirmed it."

Barbara raised her eyebrows. "You certainly are taking this seriously, aren't you? The inquest hasn't even been held yet."

"Trails go cold very quickly," said Henry. "Have you any idea what it was he went to St. Lawrence to get?"

"None. Cross my heart."

"Have you any idea what he wanted to see me about at five o'clock?"

"None."

"Is that true or almost true, Barbara?"

"I'm not prepared to answer that."

"It was something to do with the crossword, wasn't it?"

"I'm equally not prepared to get involved in guessing games, Henry."

Henry grinned at her. "Okay. You're perfectly within your rights. Tell me something else, if you will. The other members of the Guess Who club—have they all known your family for a long time?"

"Oh, yes, Oppenshaw and Trilby are the sort of publishers who stand by their authors. It makes sense for everybody. The publishers help the authors through sticky times, and the authors don't go flitting off to another publisher as soon as they get a best-seller."

"You're very much younger than the others," said Henry. "You must have known them since you were a child."

"Well, yes and no. I was brought up at Carnworth, and not all of our authors are actually on visiting terms with the family. In the old days, Bill Cartwright used to come down for weekends, and Fred Coe, too. Miss Twinkley was going strong even then. I didn't meet Myrtle or Harry until I started writing myself, and we formed the club. That was four years ago. Mother took to Harry at once, and he's been a frequent visitor ever since. I don't think she cares much for Myrtle. In fact"—Barbara frowned, trying to remember—"I *think* Bill was at Carnworth the day Jeannie drowned. Or perhaps not. It was so long ago, and I've probably got it muddled."

"That's very interesting," said Henry. "It clears up a point that was puzzling me—how any of the other club members would have known enough about what happened at Carnworth to suggest— But wait a minute. You just said that it was Harry Vandike who brought the subject up."

Barbara smiled. "Oh, there's no mystery about that. You may be sure that Mother has told him the whole story, probably many times over. It's one of her favorites," she added with an edge of bitterness. "A real tearjerker." There was a pause. Then Barbara looked at her watch. "I don't want to hurry you, but if you are through with me, I have a date."

Henry took the hint. On his way home, he wondered about Barbara's tears. Had they all been for Jeannie, or had the lady protested too much about her dislike of Peter Turnberry?

Later that evening, from his home, Henry telephoned Bishop Edwin Manciple in Fenshire. The Bishop was in fine fettle, as usual.

"My dear fellow, what a pleasure. Got another puzzle for me, eh?"

"Not really, Bishop," said Henry. "The puzzle has turned out to be one for me, this time."

"How do you mean?"

"There's been a death."

"A murder, you mean?"

"I'm not sure," said Henry. "Maybe. All I do know is that it is in some way connected with that crossword you solved for me. Now please tell me something technical."

"If I can. Certainly, if I can."

"You say Professor Vandike compiled that crossword?"

"I know it."

"Well, he would have built it around the long words—or rather names—wouldn't he?"

"Naturally."

"And the other words—the small words—would, as it were, form themselves?"

"Yes and no," said the Bishop. "Wait while I get my copy of the puzzle." A couple of minutes later he was back on the line. "Let's see now. If you look at the bottom line, 'whim' could as well have been 'trim' or 'brim' or even 'thin'—an en is a

116

printer's measure, just as an em is. So the compiler could use whichever word he found most appropriate."

"I see," said Henry. "Let's go a bit farther up. What about the word 'Peter'?"

"That's a name," said Edwin Manciple a little impatiently. "Surely that's one of the names necessary to this tarradiddle."

"That's what I'm not sure of," said Henry. "Could the compiler have used a different word there?"

There was a silence, while the Bishop considered. Then he said, "Of course, a row of two-letter words like that is downright unethical, but Vandike had to fit in all those names. Let me think. He could have used 'loser,' with 'let' as the down word. 'BO'—body odor—is quite legitimate. And of course, 'as' is just as good a word as 'at.' But wait a minute. You said something about writers. Maybe Vandike wanted to bring in the word 'pen.' Well, what's the alternative? Go on, Henry, use your mind."

It took Henry about ten seconds. Then he said, "Of course. 'Poser.' A puzzle. The perfect word, I should have thought."

"Certainly. But I told you that I thought Vandike had a reason for every word he used. He must have wanted to introduce the name 'Peter.' It's obvious from the clue. Peter holds the keys to something. To what?"

"I wish I knew," said Henry.

"Well, ask him."

"I can't. You see, he's dead."

"The death you mentioned?"

"Yes."

"Well," said Edwin Manciple, "you're the detective, but if I were you, I'd have a word with Professor Harold Vandike, and right speedily. He deliberately put that name into the puzzle, and he wrote that clue. Vandike knows what this mysterious key is all about, you mark my words."

"Right as usual," said Henry. "Thank you very much, Edwin. Good night."

"Good night, Henry. Keep in touch, won't you? This is really becoming rather exciting for an old fogey like me. A very good night to you."

Harry Vandike, however, proved elusive. When Henry finally contacted his Oxford college the next day, he was told that Professor Vandike was away. Yes, certainly, he lived in rooms at the college, but it was the summer vacation, and the professor had left for a mountain-climbing holiday in Wales. He would not be back for at least ten days, maybe longer. No, he had left no address. He called the college every few days for messages. Henry added his name to the list of those who had been anxious to contact Vandike.

He put down the telephone thoughtfully. A mountain-climbing holiday in Wales, doubtless in the company of one or more of his undergraduates, just as he had taken Peter Turnberry on similar holidays some years earlier. He remembered the little sailing boat disobeying Sir Robert's orders and leaving the shelter of the bay, in the direction of Smuggler's Cove, and the cliffs. An accomplished mountain climber could have scaled that cliff—or another, equally expert, could have climbed down it. Master and pupil might well have met that afternoon.

Oh, well. Back to the Limehouse stabbing, which was no mystery, but meant a lot of work, all the same. The next day and Wednesday, office as usual, and then the train to Portsmouth Harbor in the evening, for the inquest on Thursday morning. Henry had booked himself and Emmy a double room at a good but unpretentious hotel in Ryde. He had no intention of taking up Sir Robert's invitation to stay at Carnworth. He did, however, do a certain amount of wondering why he had not heard officially from Sergeant Hemming, or been subpoenaed to give evidence.

11

The inquest was a sleepy and extraordinarily dull affair. The courtroom was stuffy and conducive to drowsiness, and while the coroner himself was an alert and obviously intelligent man, the jury sat stodgily in their box, regarding the witnesses with cowlike gazes.

In the body of the courtroom, Henry noticed Sir Robert and Lady Oppenshaw, with Barbara; Dr. Cartwright, Dr. Spenceley, Sergeant Robinson, and Detective Sergeant Hemming, as well as the captain of the lifeboat, were also present. The Turnberrys were there too, holding hands and showing the only outward signs of distress. A bored-looking young man with a stenographer's pad in his hand was presumably a cub reporter from a local newspaper. There was no sign of Timmond.

The evidence was given in due form, each witness testifying to what he or she had actually seen and done. Any signs of straying into hearsay were promptly rapped into silence by the coroner. All the salient and undisputed facts were laid before the jury.

When Sir Robert was describing how he and Barbara had spotted the body from the clifftop, maps were produced and handed to the jurors—quite unnecessarily, because they were all local people and knew the terrain like the backs of their hands.

Nevertheless, Sergeant Hemming was obviously determined that everything should be done properly. Sir Robert went on to describe his ride home and his summons to the lifeboat. He added that when he was unable to contact the local doctor, he had suggested that Dr. William Cartwright, one of his houseguests, go along in the lifeboat. Mr. Tibbett had accompanied him.

"Mr. Tibbett? Who is he?" The coroner's eyebrows went up a fraction, in a way Henry did not like.

"Chief Superintendent Tibbett of the C.I.D.," Sir Robert amended. "He was another of my houseguests."

"And why did he go with Dr. Cartwright?"

"It was at his own request, sir," replied Oppenshaw. "I saw no harm in it."

The coroner grunted, asked Sir Robert to stand by, and continued to hear the witnesses.

And so, in due course, the whole story unfolded. The saddle was produced as evidence—the spot where it was found being marked with an X on the maps. The coroner himself then asked Sir Robert's opinion as to why the mare had taken so long to get home. Sir Robert said that he could only make a guess, but that the animal was in such distress that she had probably galloped off in panic and lost her bearings.

The coroner then turned to the jury and asked if they felt they had heard enough evidence. It seemed to be a case of a straightforward and tragic accident. Did the detective sergeant wish to call any further witnesses? Hemming rose to reply that he did not. He was in complete agreement with His Worship. As he sat down, he gave Henry a smug smile from his suet-face. Without leaving the box, the jury returned a verdict of accidental death.

Outside in the sunny street, Emmy turned to Henry in fury.

"How dared they?" she demanded. "They didn't even call you!"

To her surprise, Henry smiled. "If they had been going to," he said, "I'd have received a subpoena. I think it was foolish of them." He paused reflectively. "I wonder who 'they' are? Just the police, or—ah, good morning, Sir Robert . . . Lady Oppenshaw . . ."

"Well, that's that," said Sir Robert flatly. "I'm afraid you had a wasted journey from London, Mr. Tibbett."

"I wouldn't say that," said Henry, with a smile. "It was all very interesting. I thought Sergeant Hemming handled the whole matter most efficiently, didn't you?"

"We are proud of our local police force," said Sir Robert, a little stiffly. Then, "Well, mustn't keep you. I daresay you'll be wanting to get back to town. Lots to do, and so forth."

"Yes," said Henry gravely. "I expect to be pretty busy."

The Oppenshaws were just leaving in the chauffeur-driven Bentley when Dr. Cartwright came up to the Tibbetts.

"Well, that all went off very smoothly," he remarked, rubbing his small white hands together. "These things are nearly always prosaic in real life, don't you find? I'm glad Miss Twinkley wasn't there to make a mystery of it," he added with a sort of giggle.

"Perhaps she was," said Henry. "I noticed an old lady in the back row with flowers on her hat, who might easily have been your—"

"Now, now," said Dr. Cartwright, embarrassed. "Don't forget our pact. Not a word outside the club."

"Not a word," Henry agreed.

"What I really wanted to say," Cartwright went on, "was that I shall be driving back to London, and I wondered if I could persuade you and your wife to accept a ride with me this time."

"I think we'd be delighted," said Henry. "Wouldn't we, Emmy?"

"We certainly would," said Emmy.

"Saw as much of the island as you needed to last time, eh?" said Cartwright.

"Quite as much," said Emmy.

"Well, there's a ferry leaving soon, so if you're all set . . ."

In the car, conversation naturally turned to the inquest, and to Peter Turnberry. Henry said, "By the way, Timmond tells me that you took your car out that afternoon?"

Cartwright did not appear to react, except with faint surprise.

"Timmond told you? What an extraordinary thing. Why should he?"

"Probably because I asked him," said Henry.

Cartwright sniffed, indicating his opinion of Henry as an officious busybody. He said, "Yes, you're perfectly right, I did. Much earlier in the afternoon. I'd been for a walk, and remembered that I was out of cigarettes."

"Cigarettes?" said Henry, remembering the constantly refilled boxes all over the Manor.

"Tobacco, I should say. I like a certain brand of pipe tobacco, which the village store fortunately stocks. So I took the car and nipped down to get a couple of ounces."

"Oh, well, that's simple enough," said Henry. He could not remember ever seeing Dr. Cartwright smoking a pipe.

"I didn't see Timmond," added the doctor, sounding piqued. "What was he doing—spying, or something?"

"No, no." Henry was reassuring. "He was going to have a cup of tea in the kitchen when he heard the car starting up. He got to the stable door just in time to see you driving out of the gate."

"Timmond should stick to his horses," said Cartwright snappishly. "The cars are the chauffeur's concern."

"Of course," said Henry, and changed the subject.

A little later he remarked, "I believe we go through Myrtle Waterford's home town."

Cartwright looked surprised. "Yes, we do. Great Middleford. About half an hour's drive from here."

"It's extraordinary," said Henry, "that someone like her should write those tough, violent books. I wonder where she gets her ideas."

"From other authors," said Cartwright, a little grimly. "You don't imagine Myrtle's ever been nearer to violence than an argument at the Women's Institute, do you? She simply reads all the hard-hitting American authors, transposes the scene to Britain, and changes the hero's name to Tex Lawrie. Talk about plagiarism! But it's very difficult to prove—or so Harry Vandike says. Nevertheless, between you and me"—Cartwright broke off to hoot his horn angrily at another motorist—"see that? Cutting

122

in when it was clearly my road . . . what was I saying? Oh, yes. Between you and me, I've been told that Sir Robert is getting worried. There used to be a certain originality about Myrtle's work, but lately it's been so obviously derivative—to use a kind word—that I understand he's seriously considering the possibility that there might be lawsuits. Not the sort of thing that Oppenshaw and Trilby needs at the moment, when publishing in general is in the doldrums. Yes, Myrtle had better watch her step." Dr. Cartwright spoke with gloomy relish. Henry had heard of professional jealousy, and presumed that this was just another manifestation of it.

He said, "How well did you know Peter Turnberry, Dr. Cartwright?"

"Know him? I didn't know him at all. Never met him until the Carnworth week. Vandike knew him at university, I believe, and of course Barbara was engaged to marry him, but as far as I know, neither Myrtle nor Fred had met him before, either."

"So you have no idea what he wanted to see me about the day he died?"

There was a little pause as Cartwright accelerated to pass a dawdling car ahead. Then he said, "No. No idea. But it seemed to me that he was worked up over that ridiculous crossword puzzle, for some extraordinary reason. Can't imagine why. It had nothing to do with him."

"You noticed that too?" Henry was interested. "His name appeared in it, you remember, and there was that clue about Peter holding the keys."

"I really can't remember the puzzle," said Cartwright, "but it struck me that the word 'Peter' was just a filler-up, as you might say. The important names for Vandike to work in were the ones connected with possible mysteries."

"Yes," said Henry. "Yes, I know."

It was a few minutes later that a sign informed drivers that they were entering the town of Great Middleford, and the car made its way into a broad street, lined with attractive Georgian and early Victorian houses, most of which had been converted into shops. The centerpiece, as it were, was a beautiful Elizabethan timbered structure, the Tabard Inn, which did not seem to have changed either its name or appearance for over four hundred years.

Henry said, "I wonder if you'd mind dropping us off here, Doctor?"

Cartwright grinned. "Have you got some rooted objection to my driving you into London, Tibbett—or are you thinking of paying Myrtle a visit?"

Blandly, Henry said, "I've often heard about the Tabard at Great Middleford. I thought we might have lunch."

"Wish I could join you," replied the doctor, equally bland. "Unfortunately, I have to get back to my surgery. Good-bye, Tibbett . . . Mrs. Tibbett. I don't imagine that we shall meet again—unless you need my services professionally, of course."

"Good-bye, Dr. Cartwright," said Henry. "You've been very kind. It would be a pleasure to meet you again—but in a non-professional capacity. On both sides," he added with a smile.

The Lancia moved off toward London, and Henry and Emmy, with their one small suitcase, walked into the oak-beamed bar, festooned with horse brasses and warming pans, of the Tabard Inn.

The Tabard lived up to its reputation. Even though it was nearly two o'clock, the Tibbetts were welcomed warmly, told that they were certainly not too late for lunch, and invited to take a drink at the bar while they studied the menu. This was in the best tradition of old-fashioned English cooking, featuring grilled Dover sole, prime ribs of beef, local roast lamb, and steak-and-kidney pudding. With some difficulty, because everything was so tempting, Henry and Emmy placed their orders and started on two glasses of dry sherry.

Henry said to the pretty, dark-haired barmaid, "Do you have a telephone I could use?"

"Of course. Just through that door over there."

"And a local directory?"

"There's one in the phone booth, unless somebody's pinched it again," said the barmaid. "People are awful, aren't they? Take anything that isn't nailed down."

Her pessimism was unjustified, however. The directory was there, and only one Waterford was listed—Gerald, The Chimneys, Rabbit Lane. Just right, Henry thought, and dialed the number.

Myrtle answered the phone almost immediately, as if she had been waiting for a call. "Mrs. Waterford speaking."

Henry said, "Oh, sorry. I was hoping for Jack Harvey."

There was a sharp intake of breath, but before Myrtle could slam down the receiver, Henry added, "Just a joke, Mrs. Waterford. This is Henry Tibbett. You remember me from Carnworth?"

The breath was exhaled—a long sigh. Then, unruffled and impeccably upper class, Myrtle said, "Why, of course, Mr. Tibbett. How nice to hear from you. But you really were naughty to play that trick on me."

"Is your writing identity really such a dark secret?" Henry spoke lightly, amused.

"It's not . . . well, no, not exactly that, although I wouldn't like the local people to know—"

"Mrs. Waterford," said Henry, "I've just come from the inquest on Peter Turnberry."

"Oh?" Myrtle's voice expressed no more than polite concern. "What was the verdict?"

"Accidental death," Henry said.

"Of course. What else could it have been?"

"My wife and I," Henry went on, "are in Great Middleford at the moment, on our way back to London. In fact, we're about to have lunch at the Tabard."

"An excellent choice, Mr. Tibbett."

"And afterwards," Henry went on, "I wondered if we might drop in and see you."

There was a distinct pause. Then Myrtle said warmly, "But of course. How very nice. What time can I expect you?"

"About half past three?"

"Splendid. Gerald won't be—that's to say, I'm afraid my husband will still be at work then, but I'd be delighted to see you both."

"You're very kind," said Henry. "See you later."

The lunch was delicious. It was not a meal to be hurried, and the dessert, *bananes flambées,* was well worth waiting for. Con-

125

sequently, it was after a quarter past three when Henry returned to the bar, closed now, but doubling as a reception desk. He asked, first, whether he might leave the suitcase until later in the afternoon and, second, if a taxi could be ordered.

The Chimneys turned out to be a small but exquisite Elizabethan farmhouse on the outskirts of the little town. It had been restored with expert and loving care, and the garden was immaculately tended. As the taxi drove in through the open wrought-iron gates, Henry was doing a little mental calculation. A small-town bank manager, while a respected and by no means indigent citizen, could hardly afford to live in a place like this, unless he had some source of income beyond his salary. It could be a private fortune, but if so, why soldier on as a bank manager? The source must surely be Myrtle, or rather Jack Harvey.

The front door was opened by a maid, who ushered the Tibbetts into a comfortable drawing room with a huge fireplace, unlit but piled with logs.

"Madam will be down in a moment," said the maid, and withdrew.

Emmy looked at Henry, eyebrows just slightly raised. He grinned back, guessing correctly that they had both had the same thought. Jack Harvey was doing well.

Then the door opened and Myrtle came in—the Lady of the Manor, country-wholesome in a striped cotton dress and cashmere cardigan. Neat gray hair, strong hands, sensible shoes. As unlike the world of Jack Harvey and Tex Lawrie as could be imagined.

She said, "Mr. and Mrs. Tibbett! This is a delightful surprise. May I offer you a cup of coffee?"

Emmy said, "Not for me, thanks. We've just had a magnificent meal."

"Yes. The Tabard has a very fine cook, I am told. Of course, Gerald and I hardly ever eat there. Rather like living in London and never visiting St. Paul's."

Henry and Emmy smiled politely, and then Henry said, "The inquest this morning was interesting, I thought."

"Really?" Myrtle sounded bored, a shade too bored, perhaps. "I should have thought it would be a mere formality."

"That's what was interesting," said Henry.

"I'm afraid I don't quite understand . . ."

Henry said, "There were people with important evidence to give who were not called."

"Such as?"

"Myself, for one," Henry said.

There was an awkward pause, and then Myrtle said, "Would you care to see the garden? The roses are at their best just now."

"I'm afraid we haven't the time, Mrs. Waterford," said Henry. "I have to get back to London. I only called to ask you a couple of questions."

"Me?" Myrtle's manner became glacial. "Questions? What about?"

"About how well you knew Peter Turnberry."

Again, a pause. Then, "You're not trying to tell me that you are here in your official capacity, I hope, Chief Superintendent?"

Henry smiled. "Of course not. I'm just . . . curious, that's all. Force of habit, I suppose. I'd be very grateful if you'd help me fill in a few blanks."

"In what?"

"Oh, just an idea I have. Had you met Peter Turnberry before the Carnworth week?"

"No, I had not." No hesitation whatever.

"But during the week, before Emmy and I arrived, you got to know him quite well?"

"I really don't see where this is leading, Mr. Tibbett. Of course, people at a small house party like that are bound to get to know each other."

"You knew he had an appointment with me at five o'clock on the day he died?"

"Everybody knew it. We were all there when it was arranged."

"Have you any idea, Mrs. Waterford, what he wanted to say to me?"

"None. How could I have?"

Henry felt that he was losing ground. He had no right to ask these questions, and Myrtle had no reason to answer them. Without being downright rude, she was letting him understand that she was well aware of the fact, and would not put up with much more. He decided that an outright attack was the only hope. After all, he could only fail.

He said, "I understand that Oppenshaw and Trilby may not be publishing any more of your books."

Myrtle went pale. Anger? Fear? It was difficult to tell. Then she said, a little shakily, "I can't imagine where you heard such a silly story, Mr. Tibbett. Oppenshaw and Trilby are not the kind of firm to drop an author with whom they have dealt for years, just because—"

"Just because what, Mrs. Waterford?"

"Nothing. In any case, Jack Harvey is very well known. I could easily find another publisher."

"So you have considered the possibility?"

"How dare you put words into my mouth!" There was no doubt about the anger now. Emmy was forgotten. So was the Lady of the Manor and the roses at their best. This was a fight, and Henry's heart lifted. People do not become aggressive unless they have something to defend.

He said, "I suppose what you really need is a good, original plot for your next book. Something that nobody could possibly call . . . derivative."

"Are you accusing me of—"

"I'm accusing you of nothing at all, Mrs. Waterford. The rumor that I heard about you and Sir Robert was probably just jealous professional gossip. However, all authors must be in search of inventive ideas for books, and I don't suppose that any one of them would be so philanthropic as to suggest one to another writer. On the other hand, Peter Turnberry was not an author. I just wondered if he might have come to you with an idea for a new Tex Lawrie story."

For a moment, Myrtle seemed to be wrestling between throwing Henry out and passing the whole thing off gracefully. He had given her the opportunity to do either. Lacking any brawny

128

aid, she would have to do the job herself, and do it verbally. This might give the impression of some sort of guilty conscience. Myrtle quickly made up her mind. She actually smiled.

"Well, Mr. Tibbett, I can see that Scotland Yard trains its officers well. No wonder you solved our little crossword with no difficulty. Yes, Mr. Tibbett—or should I say Mr. Holmes?—you are quite right. Peter Turnberry did come to me with an idea for a book. If you were a writer, you would know that this happens all the time. Everybody in the world has a wonderful idea for a book, if only somebody would write it down for him. I expect Peter hawked this idea around our whole group. I can tell you that it was quite hopeless. Sir Robert would certainly never have published it. So you see . . ." Myrtle shrugged her shoulders.

Henry said, "Having hawked it around the group, as you say, don't you think he might have intended to come to me with this idea?"

"To you?" Myrtle laughed, but it was not entirely convincing. "Since when, Mr. Tibbett, have you been a writer of mysteries?"

"Of course I'm not an author, Mrs. Waterford," said Henry, "but my impression from what you said just now, and from what I gathered at Carnworth from the others, is that when a layman comes to an author with a perfectly marvelous idea for a book, it is generally based on a real-life incident—something in which that person has been involved. In America, there is an expression which I'm sure you've heard—'Boy, I could write a book!'—meaning, of course, that some experience of the speaker's would provide material for—"

"Peter Turnberry's idea," said Myrtle, in a voice of ice, "could not possibly have come from his own experience."

Henry was unruffled. "Then perhaps from somebody else's—somebody he knew well." Myrtle said nothing. "After all, Mrs. Waterford, I may not write mysteries, but my profession is trying to solve them." Another pause. "Would you tell me what this idea of Peter's was?"

"Certainly not."

"If it was so bad, and not based on any real incident—"

Myrtle, quite in control of herself now, smiled. "I said no, Mr. Tibbett. I meant no. Now, would you like to see the garden, or must you be on your way?"

"I think we should be going, Mrs. Waterford. I have a lot to do."

Myrtle turned to Emmy. "It has been most delightful to see you again, Mrs. Tibbett," she said. She stressed the word "you" very slightly.

"You have a most lovely house and garden here, Mrs. Waterford," said Emmy with perfect sincerity, intending only to soothe ruffled feathers. "I'm sorry we haven't had time to see it properly, but . . . well, good-bye."

She held out her hand. To her surprise, Myrtle was looking at her with a sudden hostility, as marked as she had shown in her exchanges with Henry. She shook hands silently, walked out of the drawing room to the front door, and held it open without a word. The Tibbetts left.

Outside the gates on the country road, Emmy said, "That was pretty odd, wasn't it? What did I say to upset her so much, for heaven's sake? And how do we get back to Great Middleford from here? Walk?"

Henry grinned. "To answer your questions one at a time—yes, but no odder than I'd expected. You mentioned the house, which is obviously affordable thanks to Jack Harvey, and would be in jeopardy should that author cease to write, for any reason. And—what was the last one?"

"How do we get back to the Tabard, pick up our suitcase, and get to the railway station? We're miles from anywhere. I thought at least she'd call a cab for us."

"There's a bus-stop sign," said Henry. "We'll wait."

They were comparatively lucky. Half an hour later a bus arrived and took them back to Great Middleford, the Tabard, and the railway, whence there were twice-hourly trains to London. By half past six, they were home.

12

The London School of Economics informed Henry that Professor Coe lectured every Monday and Thursday morning. Henry had called the school as a last resort, for Fred and Alice Coe were not listed in the London telephone directory, and—apart from a complete lack of justification—Henry did not wish to use his status as a senior officer of the C.I.D. to force the post office to divulge the number. Out of interest, however, he got Inspector Reynolds to turn up an old London telephone book, the one for the year preceding the death of Miss Felicity Orwell. In it, Frederick Coe was listed, with an address in a modest northeastern suburb, a respectable but by no means expensive area. A call to that number had produced a surprised and faintly Cockney response from the lady of the house.

"Professor Coe? Oh, you mean the people what lived here some time ago. No, can't help you, I'm afraid. I did gather from Mrs. Donovan next door—now dead and gone, poor creature—that they'd come into a lot of money and left the district. No, I couldn't say where they went. Perhaps the police might be able to help you."

"I doubt it very much," said Henry gravely. "Thank you all the same."

And so he put through his call to the London School of Economics. It was a Friday, so there was nothing more to be done that day, but the following Monday, Henry called again, and

131

was told that Professor Coe was indeed in the building, but could not be interrupted in the middle of his lecture.

Henry said that he had no intention of interrupting a class, but requested that the professor might be given a message that Chief Superintendent Henry Tibbett of Scotland Yard wished to talk to him on a private matter, and would he be kind enough to call the Chief Superintendent's extension at Scotland Yard as soon as he was free to do so.

Coe could, of course, have ignored the message entirely, and then Henry would have had to resort to other tactics. However, he had a feeling that the call would be returned, and sure enough, at half past twelve, the switchboard operator informed him that Professor Coe was on the line.

Henry was all quiet affability. "Fred, how very kind of you to call back. Hope it didn't sound too official, but I knew I'd be in my office. I've been trying to trace you, but either you live out of London or your phone's unlisted."

"Yes, it is unlisted. I don't want to be bothered by frivolous callers. I'll give you the number."

Henry scribbled it on a notepad. Then he said, "But that must be quite near us, out along the King's Road. I can see that you live on the fashionable side of Berkeley Square . . ."

"I live nowhere near Berkeley Square," said Fred Coe, with some irritation.

"Forget it . . . just a literary allusion. I hope it doesn't sound impertinent, but I wondered if I might drop in and see you. Perhaps this evening."

"Of course. Alice and I would be delighted." There was no hesitation, in fact Coe sounded positively pleased. "And you'll bring Emmy, won't you? I've been telling Alice about you both, and she's most anxious to meet you. I had no idea that we were such close neighbors."

"You're very kind," Henry said. "You must think it odd, my inviting myself like this."

"Odd? Not in the least. Very flattered that you should."

Henry said, "I must warn you, Fred. I want to talk about Peter Turnberry."

132

"Ah, yes. Poor fellow. Were you at the inquest?"

"Yes, I was."

"Barbara called and told me. Accidental death. Such a pity. A nice young man, even if not very bright."

"Not very bright? I understood from Sir Robert that he'd done exceptionally well at Oxford, and was completing his studies in—"

"Shall we say six o'clock, or is that too early for you?" Coe broke into Henry's sentence with what sounded like a little spurt of irritation. Henry was intrigued.

"Six o'clock will be fine," he said. "Just tell me exactly how to find your house . . ."

The Coe residence turned out to be a small but charming Regency town house on a quiet street off King's Road, Chelsea. It had a little front garden, with roses blooming behind the iron railings and gate. The house was painted white, with a pale blue front door. There was a gleaming brass knocker in the form of a human hand, and a more practical electric bell at the side of the door. Henry rang the bell, and the door was opened almost at once by a trim, well-dressed, gray-haired woman, as neat as a pin and a complete contrast to the untidy, shambling professor.

The woman smiled warmly. "Mr. and Mrs. Tibbett. How delightful. And how refreshing to meet somebody who takes the trouble to be punctual. Do please come in. I am Alice Coe."

The small hallway was paneled in pine, and smelled deliciously of furniture polish. Through a door to the left, Henry glimpsed an elegant little dining room with a circular table and antique chairs with needlepoint covers. The door at the end of the hall presumably led to the kitchen. The staircase leading down from the upper floor had been stripped down to the pale pinewood and meticulously polished. Mrs. Coe led the way up the stairs.

"Let's go up to the drawing room. These narrow little houses keep us in good shape, don't they? Always climbing up and down stairs."

The staircase led directly to a beautiful drawing room, which stretched the length and (such as it was) the breadth of the house. At the far end, French windows opened on a small balcony, from which a flight of stone steps led down into a little back garden. Like the front, this was impeccably tended—a central paved courtyard surrounded by beds of roses, delphiniums, geraniums, and larkspur. An English country garden in miniature. Inside the paling fence, beyond which lay other similar town gardens, privacy was ensured by trees—a couple of graceful lilacs, a flowering cherry, and even an apple tree. Henry knew that houses like these, so close to the center of town, commanded astronomical prices. A contrast, indeed, to the northeastern suburb. Was Miss Twinkley responsible for all this luxury—or was it that other little old lady, Miss Felicity Orwell?

"I think it's just a little too cold for drinks in the garden," Alice Coe was saying. "Now sit down and tell me what you would like."

Henry and Emmy sat down on the comfortable sofa (curly Victorian cherrywood, upholstered in thick cotton scattered with a pattern of tiny blue and white flowers), and asked for Scotch and soda.

A Regency armoire turned out to be the façade for a well-stocked bar. As Alice poured the drinks, she said, "I'm afraid Fred isn't home yet. Typical of him. I just hope he's remembered that you're coming. I've given up trying to apologize for him. I suppose you just have to accept the fact that he's the original absentminded professor."

"And also an author," said Henry. "It must keep him very busy."

For a moment Alice looked surprised, even alarmed. Then she relaxed and said, "Of course, Fred met you at Carnworth, didn't he? So you know he's a writer."

"Or perhaps one should say, half a writer," said Henry. "The Freda, one presumes, in Freda Wright. I've often wondered how collaborators work on a book, I mean, the actual methods. Does Dr. Cartwright think up the plots and Professor Coe do the writing? Or do they share both jobs?"

Alice turned, with the full glasses in her hands. She did not look pleased. "I see that you know a great deal, Mr. Tibbett. I hope that you will keep it to yourself. It would damage Fred greatly if it was generally known."

"Naturally," said Henry. He thanked Mrs. Coe as she handed him his drink. "Being at Carnworth made us sort of honorary members of the club, and bound by its rules of secrecy."

"I understood," said Alice Coe, "that you were the visiting celebrity. I thought that the actual identities of the writers weren't disclosed to—"

Emmy said, "Henry's a policeman, Mrs. Coe. He couldn't resist a challenge like that—especially after the crossword puzzle."

"The what?" Alice had poured herself a small gin and tonic. Now she sat down abruptly in one of the wing chairs that matched the sofa, put her drink on a table beside her, and looked really surprised. "I'm afraid I don't understand."

"Didn't Fred tell you?" Henry asked.

Alice shook her head.

"Well," said Henry with a smile, "it was just a little joke that the members of Guess Who thought they'd play on me, to see if I could function like a classic whodunnit detective. They sent me a blank crossword puzzle and a series of clues. You can guess who compiled the puzzle."

"Vandike," said Alice, with deep distaste. "Just the sort of idea he would have."

"I'm not actually sure whether it was his idea or somebody else's," said Henry. "Anyhow, I managed to solve it—by cheating, of course."

"What do you mean, cheating?"

"I happen to know one of Britain's most dedicated crossword fans. I passed the whole thing along to him, and he solved it for me."

Alice said, "I fail to see what a crossword could have to do with a whodunnit."

"Most of the clues," said Henry, "when correctly solved, turned out to produce names. Yours, among them."

"Mine?"

"Yes, and your husband's. In connection with Miss Felicity Orwell."

"In that case," said Alice Coe in a voice of pure ice, "I am not in the least surprised that Fred told me nothing about the crossword. And what, Mr. Tibbett, were you supposed to do?"

Henry said, "The main clues came in batches—three of them. Each contained names which were in some way connected to each other. In your batch were Fred Coe, Alice, and Felicity Orwell. I presumed, correctly, that I was to find the connection between the names."

"And you say that you succeeded?"

"Yes, Mrs. Coe. I found out that Miss Orwell was an aunt of yours, whom you brought to live in your house and nursed devotedly until her death. I fancy it was not in this house."

Alice managed a frigid smile. "You also know, without any doubt, that Aunt Felicity left us quite a lot of money. It enabled us—with the help of Fred's work in both his fields—to leave the . . . the place where we were living and move here. You seem to have solved the puzzle, and I sincerely hope that you made Harold Vandike look very silly."

"There was a little more to it than that, Mrs. Coe. You see, the three sets of clues, each of which related to a member of the club, hinted that a crime might have been committed."

"A crime, Mr. Tibbett?"

"Murder for money," said Henry. "In two cases, at least."

"Including ours?"

"Well, obviously. Now please believe me, I didn't take any of the cases at all seriously, once I had solved the crossword and seen its implications. I realized that it was a bunch of sharp-witted people having a little harmless fun at my expense." Henry paused and sipped his drink. "But then an odd thing happened. Peter Turnberry was accidentally killed by a fall from his horse."

"Peter who?"

"You didn't know him?"

"I've never even heard of him."

"So you didn't know that he was—"

At this point the front door opened, slammed shut again, and Professor Frederick Coe came lumbering up the stairs, shouting good-naturedly as he came.

"Late again! Late as usual! Apologies, my good people!"

Fred Coe's bearded face appeared as he hurried up the stairs, still in the process of divesting himself of an old raincoat. "Sorry, Alice. Just stopped at a pub with a few of my students to thrash out a couple of points . . . didn't realize how the time was going by . . . Hello, Henry. How are you, Emmy? This is my wife, Alice . . ."

"I have already had ample time to introduce myself," said Alice coldly. "You'd better go upstairs and comb your hair. What will you have to drink—or have you had enough already?"

Fred Coe gave a great roar of laughter. "Hell hath no fury like a woman whose husband turns up late. Pour me a stiff whisky, Alice dear. Be down in a moment."

With that, he went at a shambling run up the flight of stairs leading to the bedroom floor. Alice prepared his drink in a silence alive with hostility. A minute or so later, Professor Coe reappeared minus raincoat and rubbing his hands. If he had combed his hair, the fact was not apparent. Alice handed him his drink.

"Thank you, my dear. Henry and Emmy—your good health." He sat down. "Now, what's all this about Peter Turnberry? Nothing mysterious, surely?"

Before Henry could answer, Alice Coe said, "The Chief Superintendent seems to think that between us we murdered Aunt Felicity for her money."

"Mrs. Coe," Henry protested, "I said no such—"

"Ah, you're thinking of the crossword puzzle," boomed Fred cheerfully. "I don't think I told you about that, Alice."

"You certainly didn't, and I'm not surprised. To think that a group of grown and intelligent people—"

"It was only a joke," said Coe, shuffling his feet a little.

"Not a very funny one," remarked Mrs. Coe. "In any case, the Chief Superintendent seems to have solved it very competently, and now we are all suspects."

Henry said again, "Please, Mrs. Coe, I said no such thing. But

137

I do want to talk to your husband about Peter Turnberry."

"Of course." Alice became gracious again, with an obvious effort. "Would you care to see our little garden, Mrs. Tibbett?"

"I should love to," said Emmy.

So the two women went down the stone steps to the small backyard, and the men were left alone in the elegant drawing room that Miss Felicity had so kindly financed.

Henry said, "First of all, had you met Peter Turnberry before the Carnworth get-together?"

"I . . . er . . . no. Goodness me, no."

"Then why did you say on the telephone that he wasn't very bright?"

"I'm a teacher, you know," said Fred. "A week is quite long enough to spot a bright young fellow—or one who isn't."

"And yet both Sir Robert and Vandike seemed to rate him very highly, intellectually."

"Oh, that." Coe lit a pipe and puffed at it, fanning away the smoke with a contemptuous gesture that seemed to encompass Peter Turnberry's mental ability. "He was one of Harry's protégés, you know. Any young man who will go mountain climbing with Harry automatically becomes a genius, whatever the evidence to the contrary. If he ends up with a bad second or even a third, Harry will find an excuse for him. I have no idea what kind of degree Peter Turnberry got, but you can be sure it wasn't a first, dear fellow."

"Mr. Vandike isn't married, is he?" said Henry.

Coe roared with laughter again. "You don't have to pussyfoot around it, old man. Harry's as queer as a three-dollar bill—but don't quote me. He keeps his nose clean, and I wouldn't want to be sued for slander. Or would it be slander nowadays," he added, puffing reflectively, "now that it's no longer a crime? Interesting point. You'd know more about that."

Henry smiled. "Slander would come under civil law," he said. "I'm not a lawyer, only a policeman, and my field is crime. And talking of crime, did Peter Turnberry come to you during the Carnworth week with a suggestion for a plot—I mean, a plot for a Miss Twinkley book?"

138

Fred Coe looked surprised. "Funny you should say that," he remarked. "Yes, as a matter of fact, he did."

"I thought he might have," said Henry. "When was this?"

Coe thought for a moment. "It was a couple of days before you arrived. He cornered me and—"

"You and Dr. Cartwright, I suppose?"

"No, just me. Actually, Bill thinks up the plots and I do the writing, but Peter didn't know that." Fred Coe chuckled. "I must say I'm glad I'm not generally known to be a mystery writer. I'm told that if you are, the world and his wife come pestering you with ideas for plots, most of which are completely useless."

"And was Peter Turnberry's useless?"

Coe hesitated. "I thought there just might be something in it," he admitted, "although it was ridiculously complicated. However, I did go so far as to mention it to Bill, but he turned it down right away. Said he wouldn't touch it."

"What was the plot?" asked Henry bluntly.

"Oh, I can't remember the details. The usual thing—wills and inheritances and something about an illegitimate child . . . the usual rigmarole . . ."

"And what was to be the method of murder?"

"Very unoriginal," said Coe. "Drowning. Made to appear accidental. Very difficult to prove without actual witnesses. That's why it's popular with writers—and maybe in real life, for all I know."

Henry said, "The third set of crossword clues concerned the accidental drowning of Barbara Oppenshaw's stepsister."

"That's obviously where he got the idea," said Coe. "He must have known the story, and I suppose he thought one could make some sort of a mystery novel out of it. I've never heard the whole story myself—only the snippets that came out at the Guess Who dinner, when we got the idea for the crossword."

Thoughtfully, Henry said, "If you thought the plot had possibilities, why do you imagine that Cartwright was so much against it?"

"Several reasons. First, because it wasn't very good. Second, because it didn't seem to be a Miss Twinkley story at all. But mainly, I think, because of something I had no idea of until then."

"What was that?"

"Simply that Bill, quite by chance, had been visiting Carnworth and was there when the elder girl drowned. If Sir Robert were to get a Freda Wright manuscript with a drowning in it, he might assume that Bill was in some way drawing on his own experience of the girl's death. Being a doctor, and on the spot, he was naturally involved. Well, Oppenshaw and Trilby are very good publishers, my dear Henry, and we certainly didn't want to risk upsetting Sir Robert. So that was that."

"You told Turnberry you couldn't use the story?"

"Yes, I did."

"What was his reaction?"

Fred Coe rubbed his chin. "I'd quite forgotten until now," he said. "He made an odd remark."

"What was that?"

"He said, 'Then I'll just have to wait for Tibbett.' Struck me as peculiar at the time, but then I forgot all about it. Oh, well, poor young fellow, nobody'll write his story for him now."

"No," said Henry. "Nobody will. Unless he told it to Harry Vandike. He might make a Gothic of it."

"No, no, no. He obviously took it first to Harry, since they're such friends. Or were. Harry must have handed him the pink slip before anybody else." Coe paused. "Did he try it on anyone else, do you know?"

Henry said, "This is in confidence. He tried to sell a plot idea to Myrtle Waterford. She turned it down, and refused to tell me what it was about. Maybe the same one. Maybe not. Well, thank you very much, Fred. You've been a lot of help."

"Help? Help in what? The whole thing's closed now, surely?"

"I hope so," said Henry.

Fred was puffing noisily at his pipe. "Damn thing always goes out," he complained.

"By the way," said Henry, "I knew there was something I meant to ask you. Does Bill Cartwright smoke a pipe?"

"If he does, I've never seen it," said Coe. "The occasional cigarette, that's all."

Just then, Alice and Emmy came back from the garden. Alice seemed in a much better mood.

"If you two men have had your mysterious discussion," she said, "I suggest we all have another drink and talk about pleasant things."

And so they did.

13

For the next few days, Henry concentrated on routine work and office matters. He had a feeling that the Turnberry affair would somehow seek him out, rather than the other way around. He had slipped enough ferrets down holes to start a scamper of rabbits, and the thing to do now was to wait. Besides, Harold Vandike was still somewhere up a mountain in Wales.

Bearing this in mind, it was no great surprise when his office telephone rang on Friday, and he was told that Professor Vandike was on the line and wished to speak to him. He grinned to himself.

"Tibbett? This is Harry Vandike."

"Nice to hear from you. I thought you were in Wales."

"I am."

"What did you want to talk to me about?"

Vandike chuckled. "The other way round, dear fellow," he said. "I check with the college by telephone every few days for messages, and I've just heard that you've been trying to contact me. Naturally, I'm curious to know why."

"Oh, that." Henry sounded offhand. "That was before the Turnberry inquest."

"What's that got to do with it?"

"Oh, just a notion I had—but the jury had no difficulty in coming to a verdict of accidental death, so the matter is closed."

There was a short silence. Then Vandike said, "As a matter of fact, I have to make a quick trip to London next week, Tuesday, to be precise, just for the day. Then I'll come back here and finish my holiday. I thought perhaps we might lunch together, if you're free."

"What a delightful idea," said Henry blandly. "I won't suggest the canteen at Scotland Yard, unless you're interested in a tour of—"

"Certainly not." Vandike sounded almost alarmed. "My club. The Explorers, in Pall Mall. I daresay you know it."

"From the outside only," Henry said. "My explorations are of a rather different nature from those of your members."

Vandike ignored this remark. He merely said, "Will twelve o'clock be too early for you? I have an afternoon appointment."

"Twelve will be fine."

"Splendid. Just ask the porter for me."

"I look forward to it," said Henry.

When Vandike had hung up, Henry took up a notebook and began making some jottings, doing quite a bit of serious thinking at the same time. Then he sent for Inspector Reynolds.

"Sit down, Derek. Got a moment?"

"Yes, sir. You heard about the Limehouse fellow? Open-and-shut case, if the prosecution doesn't bungle it. So, for the time being . . ."

"Derek, you remember that crossword lark, and the weekend that Emmy and I spent at Carnworth, on the Isle of Wight?"

"Yes, sir. And some poor young man was thrown from his horse and killed. Bit of bad luck, that."

"Extremely bad luck," said Henry. "Look, I'd like to tell you all the facts, as I know them, and get your reactions."

"You're not happy about the inquest verdict, then?"

"I didn't say that. I just want you to listen."

"Of course, sir."

Henry spoke for about half an hour. Derek Reynolds was a good listener. Only occasionally did he interrupt to ask for a point to be clarified. When Henry had finished, there was a long silence.

Henry said, "Well?"

With no hesitation, Reynolds said, "There's a cover-up going on, sir."

"Cover-up? Of what?"

"Young Turnberry was never thrown from his horse because the girth broke, sir. Why he went over the cliff, nobody knows—or rather, somebody knows and isn't saying. If you ask me, Mr. Turnberry knew something that was inconvenient to someone . . . no, I'll be more definite. To someone important. So it was fortunate that he had a fatal accident just when he did. And that local man, Hemming—he's in on it."

"In on it?"

"Well, any decent copper would have subpoenaed you, sir, and Timmond the groom too, and at least let the jury hear the evidence. So the 'someone' is someone local. Or someone local covering up for yet another person."

"This begins to get awfully complicated, Derek," Henry remarked.

"Obviously it's complicated, or it wouldn't have happened," said Reynolds enigmatically. "Now, who's the most important local person involved?"

"Sir Robert Oppenshaw—or his wife."

"Exactly, sir."

"But they both have perfect alibis, Derek."

"They do, do they? If I were you, sir, I'd get down there and see if you can't break them."

"They were taking tea with the Dowager Lady Whitstable, who lives near Ventnor. Drove themselves over in the Jaguar." Reynolds made a note. Henry went on, "I can't take that idea seriously, Derek. But it is possible that Sir Robert might be trying to protect one of his authors. Don't forget that these people are his bread and butter."

"Are they, sir?"

"He's the publisher, and they're all best-sellers."

"Yes," said Reynolds, "but he has money of his own, as I understand."

"Why did Peter ride to his parents' house?" Henry asked.

"That's to say, we know he had to ride, because his driving license was temporarily revoked. What I mean is, why was he so anxious to go there?"

"Simple, sir. He picked something up—papers, probably—to bring back and show you at five. And he never got to see you, and there were no papers on his body when it was found. Somebody removed them."

"The same person who moved the saddle, and tethered the mare so that she wouldn't get home until much later?" Henry asked.

"That I couldn't say, sir," admitted Reynolds. "But it looks like it, doesn't it?"

Henry beamed. "I'm delighted," he said.

"Delighted, sir?"

"That you've reached the same conclusions I have. The question is, what do we do now?"

Reynolds sighed. "You tell me to go and do some bloody dull work that you know I don't enjoy, sir." They grinned at each other.

Henry said, "Okay, Inspector Reynolds. Off you go and do it. And if it's humanly possible, get me the results by Tuesday morning."

Searching through old records is a time-consuming business, even with police authority and a charming staff doing their best to help. Derek Reynolds, however, went at it like a beaver, and by Monday evening he had photocopies of the documents he needed. As he followed the trail he had set for himself, he began to experience a rising excitement. It was leading somewhere. Just where, he wasn't sure, but at least he would have something to show the Chief Superintendent that might make him think.

Consequently, it was with some satisfaction that he knocked on Henry's door on Tuesday morning and entered with a file in his hand. Henry looked up from the papers he was studying.

"Hello, Derek. Anything to report?"

"Yes, sir. Some positive, some negative."

"Well, sit down and tell me."

Reynolds pulled up a chair and said, "I'll give you a bit of negative for a start, sir. The Oppenshaws' alibi seems watertight."

"So you checked on it, did you? How?"

"I got on to that Robinson bloke at Ventnor, and he's a pal of Lady Whitstable's gardener. He made a few discreet inquiries, and it seems that the gardener is deputed to look after the guests' cars during these parties of Her Ladyship's, which are pretty big affairs. It so happens that he—the gardener—is especially interested in Jaguars, and he swears to Robinson that the Oppenshaw car was there from half past three until a quarter past five. What's more, sir, the gardener remembers that at about half past four, Sir Robert came out to the car to get some cigarettes for his wife, and they started chatting about the Jag. Then Sir Robert looked at his watch and said he must get back inside or there'd be trouble."

"I told you so," said Henry. "All right. What about the positive?"

Reynolds opened his file. "It's hard to know where to start, sir. I think the best place is with Lady Oppenshaw."

"Pamela Oppenshaw?"

"Yes, sir. You see, I got the impression from what you said that Sir Robert owned Carnworth Manor."

"So he does," said Henry. And then, thoughtfully, "And yet—come to think of it, he never said so in so many words. I remember him saying something that gave me the idea the place was his . . . what was it? Oh, yes. That after he married Lady Oppenshaw, he naturally had her stepdaughter, Jean, come and live with them at Carnworth—" Henry suddenly slapped his hand to his forehead. "I am a blithering idiot, Derek."

"Sir?"

"Lady Oppenshaw owns Carnworth, doesn't she? Barbara Oppenshaw told me so herself, but I didn't take it in at the time."

"How was that, sir?"

"We were talking about her relationship with Jeannie, and she got upset and started to cry. Among her tears, she said, 'From the moment we went to live at Carnworth . . .' If Sir

Robert had owned the place, Barbara would have been living there all along, and she'd have said, 'from the moment *she* came to live at Carnworth.' I apologize, Derek. I've given you a lot of work to find out what I should have known all along."

"You'd still need the proof, wouldn't you, sir?" said Reynolds soothingly.

"You're very tactful, Derek. Okay, tell me about it."

"Well, sir, Lady Oppenshaw inherited Carnworth from her late husband, a Mr. Francis Warfield, who was a very rich man. Made a fortune in copper or zinc or something shortly after the war. I haven't had time to find out too many details, but there's no doubt that he bought Carnworth Manor in the 1950s. Then, ten years later, he died of a heart attack."

"Leaving his fortune and Carnworth to his widow."

"Well . . . not exactly, sir."

"How do you mean?"

Derek Reynolds did not exactly smirk, but he evidently felt quite pleased with himself. He said, "I've got a copy of his will, sir. It's an interesting document." He burrowed in the file. "It's in here somewhere . . ."

"Don't bother," said Henry. "Just summarize it for me. On the back of a postcard."

"Sir?"

"Sorry. Just a reference to what Winston Churchill is supposed to have said to his aides. Long before you were born."

Reynolds cleared his throat. He said, "Well, the gist of it is this, sir. Warfield left the house and the interest on the capital to Lady Oppenshaw—that's to say, Mrs. Warfield—for her lifetime. After that, everything was to go to his daughter by his first marriage, his only child Eugenia. There was a board of trustees looking after the investment of the money and so on. However"—Reynolds paused to let the full import sink in—"however, if Eugenia should predecease her stepmother . . ."

"Pamela copped the lot," said Henry.

"Yes, sir. But there's another proviso—a rather strange one."

"Go on."

"The will specifically states that should Eugenia have a

child—issue of her own body, or some such legal term—then he or she should inherit."

"After the stepmother's death?"

"Yes, sir. That is, unless Mrs. Warfield married again."

"Which she has done," Henry remarked.

"Precisely, sir. In the case of the girl Eugenia, she would have inherited lock, stock, and barrel at the age of twenty-one, should Mrs. Warfield remarry."

Henry said, "So it was obviously greatly to the advantage of the Oppenshaws that Eugenia should not live to be twenty-one."

"Yes, sir."

"And that she shouldn't have a child. Well, that's just about out of the question. She was only eighteen when she died, and not married."

Reynolds said, "There's nothing in the will about marriage, sir."

There was a long pause. Then Henry said, "What happened to this board of trustees?"

"It was disbanded, sir, once Eugenia was dead, leaving no issue."

"Irrespective of whether Mrs. Pamela Warfield remarried or not?"

"That's right, sir."

Another long pause. Then Henry said, "I wonder if Sir Robert . . . was he Sir Robert then?"

"No, sir. Oppenshaw and Trilby didn't exist. It was just the old firm of Trilby & Son, and it was on the rocks, so I hear. Oppenshaw bought it for very little, and proceeded to build it up into what it is today. He was knighted ten years ago, sir, for services to literature."

"Well," said Henry, "there seems no doubt that Jeannie's death was an accident. There was nobody with her except six-year-old Barbara, and I can't imagine even a wicked stepmother coaching Baba on how to drown an eighteen-year-old girl. As I was saying, I wonder if Oppenshaw knew about the provisions of the will."

"I couldn't say, sir. But somebody did. Certainly the present

148

Lady Oppenshaw and the people who were on the board of trustees."

"You have their names?"

"No, sir. There seems no way I can find out, except from Lady Oppenshaw herself."

Slowly, Henry said, "If there had been a child . . ."

"That seems very unlikely, sir. The girl Eugenia was very well brought up, and young people in those days didn't—"

"Young people always have and always will," said Henry with a grin. "Still, I do agree it's unlikely. What's much more probable is that somebody knew about the will, and was using it to try to exert some sort of hold over Sir Robert. It also strikes me that this story—or a fanciful version of it—was the one that Peter Turnberry was trying to hawk around the writers at Carnworth."

"Hawk around? I hadn't heard."

"No, Derek, you hadn't." Henry smiled. "You've done extraordinarily well. Thank you. Can you leave the file with me? I'll take it from here."

The Explorers Club, in fact, had very few actual explorers among its members, although it had been founded in the early nineteenth century as a meeting place for those intrepid English gentlemen who put on pith helmets and strode their way with trains of native bearers over the map of Africa, marking off an Empire with their solid boots. However, it did attract a younger and more energetic type of member than did, for example, the Mausoleum. It had a reputation for fine food, and Henry had not been lying when he told Vandike that he was looking forward to his lunch.

The porter had Professor Vandike paged, and Harry soon appeared, dapper in a dark gray suit.

"Ah, Tibbett, delighted to see you. You don't mind if we go straight to the dining room? As I told you, I have an appointment—and in any case the wine list here is quite exceptional. Personally, I don't believe in spoiling my palate with spirits beforehand. So . . ."

By this time he had guided Henry upstairs and into the spacious and virtually deserted dining room. The headwaiter appeared, and Vandike asked for his usual table, which turned out to be a secluded one in a remote corner. Then began an animated discussion on food and wine, in which Henry took no part except for an occasional nod if his opinion, for the sake of form, was consulted. When the first bottle—a deliciously light and dry Meursault—had been opened and approved by Vandike, the headwaiter withdrew.

Vandike then sat forward, nursing his glass in his hand. His week in Wales had left him handsomely tanned and fit.

"Now, Tibbett," he said, "I'm interested in this notion of yours, as you called it."

"I explained on the telephone—"

"Coroners' juries," said Vandike, "are notoriously stupid. Either they bring in a verdict of 'murder by person or persons unknown,' which leaves the police in a damned awkward position when they know perfectly well that the death was an accident, or else they ignore the most blatant evidence and say 'accidental death' in an obvious case of murder."

"I've had quite a bit of experience with them," said Henry gently. "I've always found them pretty reliable. Common sense generally follows the right instinct, you know."

"You were at the Turnberry inquest?"

"Yes, I was."

"Subpoenaed?"

"No. Just out of interest. The proceedings were very short. The police presented an admirable and lucid case, borne out by medical evidence."

"And they didn't call you?"

"I told you they didn't, Professor."

"You said on the telephone that you had no further interest in the affair. At least you implied it."

"Yes, I did, didn't I?"

"Well I happen to know that's not true. You've been talking to Myrtle and Fred and even to Barbara. And you've been trying to get hold of me." Harold Vandike sat back and smiled. "Forgive me, but it's an uncomfortable feeling to know that a senior police official is taking an interest in . . . in something one is involved in."

"Involved? In what way?"

"Oh, I don't mean Peter's death, naturally. But you must have heard that I was his tutor, and that we were . . . friends. Apart from Barbara, I was the only person at Carnworth who knew him well."

"Barbara and her parents," amended Henry.

"And her parents, of course," agreed Vandike, a little hastily.

Henry said, "Apparently he was trying to sell a mystery plot to the Guess Who members before Emmy and I arrived. I presume he came to you first, since he knew you best."

"A plot?" Vandike sounded genuinely surprised. "First I've heard of it. What sort of a plot?"

"From what I've been able to gather, something complicated about wills and illegitimate babies," said Henry, deliberately vague. "I've no idea of the details."

"The young idiot," said Vandike. "God preserve us from amateurs. Anyhow, he certainly didn't suggest any plot to me."

Henry said, "Well, you write Gothic mysteries, don't you? And this was a modern whodunnit. Fred Coe thought it might have possibilities, but Cartwright turned it down flat. So did Myrtle."

"And Barbara?" For the first time, Harry Vandike sounded a little on edge.

"I don't know if he approached Barbara with it," Henry said. "Since he was engaged to her, one would think she would be the obvious person, but he may have been afraid of upsetting her."

"Upsetting her?"

"Yes. You see, the murder method was drowning, and there was a young girl involved. In view of her experience with her stepsister—"

"Oh, that's ancient history."

"Nevertheless, it must have made a great impression on her as a child." Henry paused. "She didn't object to your using it in your crossword?"

"Not in the least."

"It did occur to me to wonder," Henry said thoughtfully, "why you concentrated so much on that mystery, rather than on the others, when you compiled the crossword."

"Concentrated? I don't understand you."

"The final solution," said Henry, "contains far more references to what we may call the Oppenshaw case than to either of the others." He pulled a paper out of his pocket. "I brought it along, just for fun. You'll notice that as well as the names, we have 'beach,' 'Baba'—which I'm told was Barbara's nickname as a child—and even 'Peter.' Why drag him in? And in the clues to the two words making up 'alibi,' it's clearly implied that you hope Barbara has one. You see what I mean? Even the clue to 'whim' connects with Peter. Can you explain?"

Vandike smiled, a tightly knowledgeable and superior smile, such as he might well have bestowed on a stupid but enthusiastic pupil.

"If you knew anything about crossword compilation, Tibbett," he remarked, "you would realize that my task was extremely difficult. I had to incorporate a number of names into a small puzzle. Naturally, I had intended to make the pattern symmetrical, but even I had to abandon that idea. As for the small, intersecting words—I simply had to use whatever would fit and seemed to have some connection with one or another of the mysteries. It just so happened that more of them concerned the Warfield girl."

Henry remembered what Bishop Manciple had said, but did not put it forward as a theory. He said, "You told me before that the clue about Peter holding the keys was a reference to Saint Peter and the Pearly Gates of heaven."

"And so it was."

"Well," said Henry easily, "now that he's dead, we'll never know whether or not he held the key to anything else. You've no idea why he wanted to see me that evening, or why he rode over to his parents' house in the afternoon?"

"To answer your questions in the reverse order," said Vandike dryly, "he rode over to St. Lawrence because he wanted to see

152

his father and mother. What other reason could there have been? He rode, as you may have found out, because some oaf of a magistrate had suspended his driving license. As to why he wanted to see you—perhaps he wanted to expound this famous plot to you. That, of course, is no more than a guess, arising out of what you have just told me."

Henry smiled. "An amusing idea," he said. "You may well be right. Well, I'm only sorry that such a pleasant week should have been spoiled by a tragic death. I was much impressed by Carnworth."

"Yes," agreed Vandike. "A beautiful place."

"You're a climber," said Henry. "Have you ever climbed the cliff by the old smugglers' route?"

"Of course I have," said Vandike. "The first time I ever visited Carnworth. It was put to me as a sort of challenge. In fact, it's laughably easy, if you know what you're doing. The only people who get hurt are the amateurs. I always think it is the greatest mistake for amateurs to attempt to vie with professionals—don't you?"

The smile was the same as ever, but Henry suddenly felt a sense of menace and strong hostility. No, not exactly hostility. More like warning. Yet when it came to the detection of crime, he, Henry, was the professional. Interesting.

Vandike added, "A professional knows what he is doing. If he decides to abandon an enterprise, for any reason, it is foolhardy for an amateur to persist."

The conversation had, of course, been punctuated by the periodic arrival of the headwaiter, who seemed to be serving the professor himself as a mark of special favor. He produced various delicious dishes and a bottle of Volnay to accompany the roast ribs of beef and the ensuing cheese. Each time the waiter approached, Vandike was careful to break off the conversation, and did not resume it until he had withdrawn.

Henry declined coffee. He could get a cup from the canteen, and Vandike had been consulting his watch in a marked manner for several minutes. So the two men rose to leave. It was ten minutes past one.

153

"Sorry to hurry you like this," said Vandike, "but I have so little time. Can I offer you a ride back to the Yard? I have my car in the club's basement garage."

"That's very kind of you," Henry said, "but I don't want to delay you, and I have plenty of time. Thanks for a delicious lunch."

And that seemed to be that.

14

That evening, back in the shabby but comfortable Chelsea flat that was their home, Henry said to Emmy, "Oh, by the way, I've applied for a few days' leave."

Emmy, who was making a salad in the kitchen, put her head around the door. "What do you mean, 'leave'?"

"You know what 'leave' is, darling. A few days off."

"But Henry, I thought we were saving up your leave as well as money to go to Burgundy in the autumn."

"I know we were, love," Henry said, "but I'm afraid I must do this." He paused, then added, "When it's all over, you may find that it isn't counted against my leave allowance after all."

"I knew it," said Emmy resignedly. "I knew the Turnberry thing wasn't over. We're going back to the Isle of Wight, aren't we?"

"Right the first time."

"To see the Oppenshaws?"

"I don't know," said Henry. "They're certainly not the first on the list."

"Then who is?"

"The Turnberrys. Peter's parents."

"How can they help?"

"You'll see, I hope," said Henry.

This time, making an early start, Henry drove his own elderly but well-preserved car down to Portsmouth. The weather was still beautiful, the crossing calm, and the Solent speckled with white sails. Soon the Tibbetts were ashore, had lunched, and were bowling along the coast road, bypassing Ventnor, on the southern tip of the island, and regaining the coast on the clifftops near St. Lawrence. They reached the Turnberrys' house at three.

Henry had given no prior warning of their arrival, and could only hope that James and Nora would be home. In fact, Nora Turnberry was weeding the garden when they arrived. She straightened up, looked puzzled for a moment, then broke into a smile.

"Why, it's Mr. and Mrs. Tibbett. How nice. What are you doing in these parts? Wait while I take off my apron. You must come in and have a nice cup of tea."

After polite greetings, Henry and Emmy were ushered indoors and invited to sit down while Nora put the kettle on. From the kitchen, which was connected to the living room by a serving hatch, Nora called, "James will be disappointed to miss you. He's out seeing to the shops. Always goes around to both of them midweek. James is most particular that the quality and service is always the best it can be. We're not a big business, Mr. Tibbett, but we do try to keep high standards. There, the kettle'll be on the boil in a minute. Milk and sugar? And you'll take a slice of my walnut cake, won't you?"

A minute or so later she came in with a laden tray, which she put down on a low table. As she poured tea, Nora Turnberry chatted on. "Having a bit of a holiday, are you? I've often said to James, there's something about the island. People don't come down here just once. Back and back they come. Well, look at us, always lived in Ealing and came here on holiday—and here we are. Can't explain it, but there it is."

Henry smiled. "You're quite right, Mrs. Turnberry—but this is a bit more than a holiday."

"More than a holiday? What's that mean?"

"We came to talk to you and your husband," said Henry.

"About Peter," Emmy added.

For the first time a trace of reserve crept into Mrs. Turnberry's voice. "That's over and done with, isn't it, Mr. Tibbett? Wasn't it bad enough when it happened? James and I—well, we've decided that you can't put the clock back and go on moping all your life—but it's not what I call very nice to come down here raking everything up again."

Henry said, "I know just how you feel, Mrs. Turnberry, and I'm terribly sorry. But I have to ask you."

"Ask me what?"

Quite deliberately, stirring his tea, Henry said, "Did Peter know that he was adopted?"

Without thinking, Mrs. Turnberry began, "No, we never—" and then broke off and turned angrily to Henry. "You trapped me into that. Unfair, I call it. What James would say—"

"I'm sorry, Mrs. Turnberry," Henry said. "I had a strong hunch that it was true. But I had to hear it from you."

"Well, there's only one person who could have told you, and I'm ashamed of him. I supposed lawyers had to keep people's secrets—like priests, almost. But then I always did think he was a shifty one, whatever Peter said."

"You mean Professor Vandike?"

"Who else? He was the one who arranged it all, and under what he called the seal of secrecy. Some seal, I must say." Mrs. Turnberry did not offer either Henry or Emmy a slice of her delicious-looking walnut cake—a sure sign of real fury.

"Well," said Henry pacifically, "it doesn't make any difference now, does it?" Nora Turnberry stirred her tea, glaring at him. He went on, "You knew the identity of the actual parents, I suppose?"

"No, we did not." The words were almost spat out. "If Mr. Vandike told you so much, why didn't he tell you that too, I wonder? He's the only person who knows."

"I gather this was a private adoption, arranged through Vandike."

"Of course it was. When James and I found out we couldn't have kids of our own, we started thinking about adoption."

"Did other people know this?"

"Know what?"

"That you were looking for a child to adopt?"

"Certainly not. It's not the sort of thing one goes around discussing with all and sundry, is it? We did what we thought was the proper thing. We asked our doctor."

"Your doctor in Ealing?"

"Well . . . no, as a matter of fact. Gossip gets about so fast in the suburbs. But it happened that James had been having some trouble with his hearing, and the doctor recommended him to a specialist."

"William Cartwright!" cried Emmy.

Nora looked at her, surprised. "How did you know that?" she asked. "Why, I'd almost forgotten the name myself until you mentioned it. Yes, he did wonders for James. Hears as well as anybody now." The bitterness seemed to have left Mrs. Turnberry, and there was almost relief in the way she spoke. "Well, Dr. Cartwright said it wasn't really his province, and suggested we go to an adoption society. But we didn't fancy that. We knew we wouldn't be told the name of the parents, but we did want a sort of personal guarantee about the baby, if you know what I mean. So he told James that he'd keep it in mind, and make some inquiries. That's how we got in touch with Professor Vandike. Or rather, he with us."

"He with you?"

"Yes. He called on us in Ealing one day—drove up in a very flashy motorcar, for those days, and said he'd heard from Dr. Cartwright that we were looking for a baby to adopt, and that he knew just the one, and could arrange it."

"And you believed him, just like that?" Henry asked.

"Oh, no. James did a very thorough check, you can be sure. First he contacted Dr. Cartwright, who said that this was a lawyer friend of his from Oxford. Then James checked with Oxford and found that Professor Vandike was really what he said he was. That's to say, he wasn't a professor back then, but he was teaching law, and he was a lawyer, all right. So we thought that was good enough."

"What did he tell you about the baby?"

"Not very much," said Nora Turnberry. "Just that he was two weeks old, a boy, white of course, and that both parents were healthy and of good family. I always remember him saying that—of good family. They say breeding will out, and look how handsome and clever Peter grew up. I mean, it just goes to show."

"And you never told Peter?"

"No, Mr. Tibbett. I don't know if we were wrong—"

Emmy broke in, "You were quite right, Mrs. Turnberry. At least in my opinion. I can't imagine anything more unsettling for a child when he's looked on you as his parents all his life—"

Nora Turnberry smiled gratefully at Emmy. "It's nice to think you understand, Mrs. Tibbett. Have some walnut cake."

In the car, Emmy said, "Jeannie's child?"

"It's much too early to say that yet," said Henry, his eyes on the road. "What's for sure is that at least two of the Carnworth party—Cartwright and Vandike—knew that Peter Turnberry was adopted."

"And the Oppenshaws?"

"Very hard to say. I doubt that Sir Robert knew. If Peter was Jeannie's child, he'd have been born before Oppenshaw married Pamela Warfield. I suppose she must have known about the baby, but Jeannie could have gone off and found a doctor somewhere—"

"Cartwright?"

"He's an ear specialist. Still, he could have been a contact, I suppose. The question is, did Jeannie herself know what was in her father's will?"

"That's something we'll never be able to answer," said Emmy. "Well, what's the next step? Go and confront the Oppenshaws?"

"No, not yet," said Henry. "There are other things to do first. Back to London, I think. Got some calls to make tomorrow. And notice that I'll be back in the office, saving the rest of my leave for Burgundy."

The following morning, Henry called the Explorers Club and

asked for Professor Vandike. He was told that the professor had not been there for some time, that he was on holiday in Wales. The secretary was extremely friendly.

Next, Henry telephoned Vandike's Oxford college, to be told that the professor was not expected back until the following week.

Henry was just contemplating how he could discover the name of the hotel in Wales, when his phone rang again. This time the operator told him that Mrs. Tibbett was on the line.

"Henry, have you seen this morning's paper?"

"Haven't opened it yet, as a matter of fact."

"Well, you should. And if you remember, neither of us saw a paper yesterday, but it was in last evening's *Star*."

"What was?"

"I'll read it to you," said Emmy. There was a slight rustling of paper. " 'Fears for safety of mountaineering professor,' is the headline. And it goes on, 'Mr. Roger Talbot, twenty-one, raised the alarm in the small Welsh village of Aberpriddy when his friend Professor Harold Vandike, fifty-eight, of Oxford, failed to return from a lone ascent on Tuesday. It is understood that a search party has already set out."

"Tuesday?" Henry repeated. "You're sure it says Tuesday?"

"Quite certain. And in this morning's paper—"

"Okay. I've got my own copy here. Thanks for calling, darling. You've got sharp eyes."

Emmy said, "I thought you had lunch with him on Tuesday in London."

"I did," said Henry. "This requires a little investigation."

The morning paper carried quite a few more details. Professor Vandike had been identified by the press as the compiler of crosswords, the pontificator on television panels, the literary critic—in fact, a personality. Consequently the story had moved up several notches in the estimation of the sub-editor, and reached page two.

Henry read that Vandike had apparently set out early on Tuesday morning to make a lone ascent of a difficult climb known as the Devil's Chimney. He had forbidden young Mr. Talbot to

160

come with him, saying that he was not sufficiently experienced. As a result, Roger Talbot had joined another group of young people for a long but fairly easy climb, returning to the hotel at 5:00 P.M. He did not begin to worry until after seven, when it began to grow dark. He knew that the Devil's Chimney, although difficult, was not a particularly long climb.

As a result, a search party had set out at once, but by darkness had found nothing. The following day, the Wednesday that Henry and Emmy had spent on the Isle of Wight, searchers had been out again, and had again found nothing. It was pointed out by local guides that the climb involved circumnavigating some deep ravines where a body might lie undiscovered. Indeed, a cross surmounting a cairn of stones indicated where one such unfortunate was presumed to have fallen some years before. His body was never found.

Some local men had remarked that it was a foolhardy thing, and uncharacteristic of Professor Vandike, to go off on a dangerous climb like that by himself. No blame, of course, could attach to his young companion, one of his law students from Oxford, to whom he was teaching the rudiments of mountain climbing. The search continued, but hopes for the professor's safety were fading.

Henry picked up the telephone and called the Explorers Club again. The porter was quite definite. No, they had not seen Professor Vandike for some time. Everybody at the club was very distressed at the news of his probable accident.

"Were you on duty at noon on Tuesday last?" Henry demanded.

"Yes, sir. I was."

"Then you must remember that I lunched with Professor Vandike. Chief Superintendent Tibbett of Scotland Yard. Well, I gave my name as Mr. Tibbett. You had the professor paged—"

"That's right, sir. I remember it well. And he wasn't in the club, so you went away again, saying there must have been a mistake."

Angrily, Henry went to the Explorers Club in person. The porter greeted him with obvious recognition, but stuck to his story. Producing his police identity card, Henry demanded to see the headwaiter. He was met by the same polite, blank stare. The headwaiter did not recollect ever having seen him before. Professor Vandike had not reserved a table on Tuesday—in fact, he had not lunched in the club for some weeks. Tragic, isn't it, sir, that he should be lost like that? Still, never give up hope. They have found people after quite a long time . . .

Full of frustration, Henry telephoned Barbara Oppenshaw.

Her first words were, "Oh, Mr. Tibbett. You've heard about Harry?"

"That he's missing from a climb?"

"Yes. The papers keep talking about possibilities, but I don't see how he can be alive . . ."

Henry said, "Now look here, young lady. I've had enough of these practical jokes. First the crossword, now this."

"What on earth do you mean?" Barbara sounded genuinely bewildered.

"Harry Vandike was a great practical joker, wasn't he?" Silence. "Well, wasn't he?"

"I . . . yes, I suppose he was."

"The crossword puzzle was his idea, wasn't it?"

"I told you before, I can't remember."

"Never mind. What I'm telling you is that I think this is another example of his warped sense of humor."

"I don't understand you."

Grimly, Henry said, "Harry Vandike wasn't climbing any mountain last Tuesday. He was lunching with me here in London at his club."

Barbara gave a little gasp. "Well, in that case, the club staff can surely—"

"No, they can't. That is, they won't. I don't know how much he paid them, but it's only a question of the hall porter and the headwaiter. They both swear that he wasn't there, and certainly didn't lunch with me."

Sweetly, Barbara said, "Your work must be a terrible strain, Mr. Tibbett."

"I beg your pardon?"

"Don't you think you may have been . . . imagining things?"

"Of course I don't."

"Two people's word against yours is quite convincing, you know," said Barbara. "Not to mention the young man in Wales, and the hotel staff there and—"

"I'm going to find Harry Vandike if it kills me." Henry was losing his well-known professional calm.

"Are you an experienced climber, Mr. Tibbett?"

"No, I've never so much as climbed a wall. But—"

"Then it may well kill you, Mr. Tibbett," said Barbara, and hung up.

The local police in Wales were most helpful, although depressed. It didn't do the neighborhood any good to lose a climber, especially a popular, celebrated, and expert one. So the search parties went on searching doggedly, even with little or no hope left.

"I wish you'd call them off, Superintendent," said Henry.

"So long as there's a chance he might be alive, sir—"

Henry said, "You've only my word for this, but you're risking valuable lives on a wild-goose chase. Professor Vandike wasn't even in Wales on Tuesday. He was in London."

"But . . . that's not possible, sir."

"He was not only in London," said Henry. "He lunched with me."

"Well, in that case, sir, there must be people who remember—"

Trying to be patient, Henry said, "The professor is a well-known practical joker, Superintendent. We lunched at his club, but he has persuaded or bribed the few members of the staff who saw us to deny the fact."

"You mean they say they never saw either of you, sir?"

"The hall porter says I turned up asking for Vandike," Henry admitted, "but went away again when told that he wasn't there."

There was a pause. Then the superintendent said, "It's an odd story, sir."

"I'm well aware of that," said Henry. "Now, will you do something for me?"

"Of course, sir." The superintendent sounded wooden.

"Go to the hotel where he was staying—the Mountainside, I believe it's called—"

"That's right, sir."

"Go there and get every detail you can—when he arrived, what luggage he had, what he was wearing when he arrived, what time he left the place on Tuesday morning, what he was wearing then, whether he came by car, and if so, where is the car now? Did he take an early train to London on Tuesday, or did he hire a self-drive car locally? You know what I mean."

"Yes, sir." The superintendent sounded bedazzled. This sort of high-speed, high-power inquiry was a novelty in his quiet Welsh valley. "I'll call you back, sir."

Henry had only just hung up, and was contemplating the best way of bullying the staff of the Explorers Club to come clean, when the switchboard operator called to say that a boy named Richard Perkins was downstairs and wished to see him.

"What about?" Henry demanded.

"He won't say, sir. He's only a bit of a lad, about eighteen."

"Then get one of the sergeants to see him."

"Yes, sir."

A moment later the phone rang again. "Switchboard here again, sir. Perkins says to tell you it's about the Explorers Club."

"Send him up at once," said Henry.

Richard Perkins was a fresh-faced, red-haired boy, and Henry recognized him at once. "Come in and sit down, Richard. You're the page boy at the Explorers, aren't you?"

"I was." The cherubic face was sulky.

"You were last Tuesday."

"Yes, I was, sir. And that Mr. Grafton—the hall porter—he got me fired. That's why I come to you."

"How did you know where to find me?" Henry asked.

"Well, it come about like this, sir. You come to the club this morning, didn't you? Talked to Mr. Grafton."

"Yes, I did. I didn't see you."

"No, you wouldn't, sir. I got a sort of cubby'ole where I sits and waits till there's someone to be paged, or baggage carried.

Well, when I 'eard you was a chief superintendent at the Yard, I thought to meself, That's too much."

"What was too much?" said Henry.

"I know for a fact," Perkins added bitterly, "that Mr. Grafton got a hundred pound out of it. And not a penny did 'e give me, you can be sure. So after you'd gone, I come out and I sez to 'im—"

"Just a moment," said Henry. "It was you who paged Professor Vandike last Tuesday, wasn't it?"

"Yes, sir, it was. You was at the front desk, and the professor come down and took you up to the dining room."

"Thank you, Richard," said Henry, with a grin. "You've set my mind at rest."

"I 'ave, sir?"

"I really thought I might be going mad. All right, what happened then?"

"Well, sir, Mr. Grafton sez it's just a joke of the professor's, like 'e's always playing on people, and that if anyone asks me, I must say like 'e did, that I paged 'im but 'e wasn't there, so you went off again. And I sez, 'Okay, Mr. Grafton, but what's in it for me?' "

"And what did he say?

" 'E sez there's nothing in it for anyone, it's just to oblige the professor. ' 'E's a very generous tipper, as well you know, young Perkins,' sez Mr. Grafton—and that's true, sir, so 'e is. Then after lunch—Tuesday, that is—I seen you go out, and a few minutes later down come the professor and 'ad a talk with Mr. Grafton, confidential-like, leanin' over the desk. And after the professor went, I saw Mr. Grafton countin' ten-pound notes, and there was ten if there was one, sir. And not so much as fifty p. did come my way. D'you call that fair, sir?"

"No, I don't," said Henry reasonably. "So what did you do?"

"I didn't do nothing till you come this morning, sir. That's when I 'eard you tell Mr. Grafton you was a copper from the Yard. So after you'd gone, I come out and I sez, 'Mr. Grafton,' I sez, 'you was tellin' lies to the police,' 'You shut your impudent mouth, Perkins,' 'e sez. I sez, 'It's the duty of every citizen to 'elp the police and tell 'em the truth, and if 'e comes and asks me personal, I won't tell 'im a lie for a penny under ten quid.' That made 'im proper mad. 'You're fired, Perkins,' 'e sez. 'Wot for?' I sez. 'Unsubordingnation,' 'e sez, or some such long word. 'Very well,' I sez, 'I'm off and you can carry the members' bleeding baggage yerself.' Just then a party of members arrives, and I'm off to the staff cloakroom, change out of me uniform, and out the back way before you could say knife. And I come straight 'ere."

"You did very well, Richard," said Henry, who had been keeping a straight face with some difficulty. "Ten quid was the very least you could have expected. I suppose Professor Vandike gave money to the headwaiter too."

"You bet, sir."

"And you say this wasn't the first time?"

"Oh, no, sir. Up to all sorts of larks is the professor. I remember once 'e invited a big group of guests to what 'e called a special gourmet lunch, and then 'e ordered the chef to serve nothing but bread—no butter, mind—apple jelly and water. Cor, I wish I'd seen their faces. All the dining room staff was laughing fit to bust. Seems the professor went on about the special sort of apple for the jelly and the flour for the bread, and wot 'e called the vintage of the water. I *did* see the blokes' faces when they come out, and they was a proper study. After, I asked the professor—'im and me bein' on good terms—'Wot did you do it for, Mr. Vandike?' And 'e sez, 'To take 'em down a peg, that's what, Dicky. Serve 'em right for talkin' big about food and wine.' Well, you couldn't 'elp but laugh, could you, sir?"

"It sounds rather a cruel joke to me," said Henry.

"Well, jokes is cruel, ain't they?" replied Perkins matter-of-factly.

"Yes," said Henry. "Yes, I suppose they are. Now, young gentleman, I can't give you a tenner for telling the truth, nor can I give you a gourmet lunch, but if you'd like to come to the canteen with me and have a bite to eat, be my guest."

"Your guest, sir?" The boy's eyes grew round with wonder and delight.

"Yes. And afterwards I'll have somebody show you around the Yard, if you'd like that."

"Oh, yes, please, sir. Thank you, sir."

Several eyebrows were raised at the sight of Detective Chief Superintendent Tibbett treating a shabbily dressed youth to lunch at Scotland Yard, but any amused questioners were simply told that the boy was a key witness.

Meanwhile, in his office, Henry had no little satisfaction in sending a constable to bring Mr. Grafton and the headwaiter of the Explorers Club to the Yard for questioning. It took very little to get the truth out of them, once they heard of Perkins's treachery. Each admitted to having received a "small honorarium" from Professor Vandike for what seemed no more than a harmless prank. Henry berated them soundly, frightened them badly, and finally let them go with their tails between their legs. It made him feel better, but got him no further in real terms. The question remained—where was Harold Vandike?

Later, the superintendent from Wales called. Vandike and his young friend had arrived ten days previously at the Mountainside Hotel. They had come by train, and had been driven to the hotel in the local taxi. The young man, Talbot, was wearing tweeds, and the professor a dark gray suit. Each had had a large suitcase and a knapsack. Since then, they had been out climbing every day, dressed in regulation climbing gear—they seemed well equipped—and had changed into informal clothes for dinner. Nobody had seen Vandike leave the hotel on Tuesday morning, as he was up and off early. His luggage was still at the hotel, but there was no sign of the gray suit. His climbing gear and clothes were missing, as might be expected. Also his knapsack.

The hotel, a favorite resort for climbers, stood at the foot of the mountain, and no transport was necessary to reach the most popular climbs. However, the hotel maintained a fleet of bicycles for the convenience of guests. Nobody at the railway station remembered the professor boarding the early train for London, but the small station was deserted at that hour, apart from the ticket clerk in his little cubicle, and if Vandike had had a return ticket, he might well not have been seen. The search parties were continuing.

"Last time I told you to call them off," said Henry, "I wasn't one hundred percent certain that I was right. Now I am." He outlined his recent interviews with the employees of the Explorers Club. "So for heaven's sake don't risk any more lives or injuries. Got it?"

"Yes, sir." The superintendent paused and then said, "Must be a proper joker, this professor chap, to go to all that trouble just for a leg-pull."

"I don't think," said Henry, "that this was just a leg-pull."

15

Henry was in a state of indecision. He had work to do at Scotland Yard, and he did not want to waste any more days of his precious leave allowance. A chief superintendent of the C.I.D. had no business shoving his nose into the disappearance of a mountaineering professor, a disappearance that was in any case being handled by the local force. It was much later in the afternoon when he had an idea. There was no danger in it, after all. Just some discreet inquiries that might help. He telephoned Emmy.

"Will you do something for me, darling?"

"Of course. Anything that I can." Emmy sounded surprised.

"Then telephone the Mountainside Hotel at Aberpriddy and book a room for a couple of nights, starting tomorrow. Pack a suitcase with a few essentials and look up the trains—no, better still, ask the hotel. They're bound to know the best way to get there from London. You're off on a short holiday."

"Alone?"

"I'm afraid so. I'll explain this evening what I want you to do."

Henry then telephoned his friend the superintendent at Aberwithy—the small town whose police area included Aberpriddy—and explained the somewhat unusual situation: that Mrs. Tibbett was coming to the Mountainside purely as a visitor, but with instructions to keep her eyes and ears open. She might,

Henry remarked soothingly, be able to pick up information that a local policeman could not. On the other hand, she might possibly need some assistance, and if she did . . .

"She'll call me, of course, sir," said the superintendent promptly. "I much look forward to meeting your lady. Just tell her to ask for Superintendent Evans."

The next morning, Emmy set out by train at the indecently early hour of half past six, and having passed through Reading, Bristol, and the Severn Tunnel, and changed twice at small junctions with long names that seemed to consist entirely of *L*'s and *W*'s, she arrived at Aberpriddy Halt at midday, just as Harry Vandike and Roger Talbot had done two weeks earlier. Like them, she took the only taxi from the station to the Mountainside Hotel.

For a Welshman, the driver was garrulous. "Was you ever hearing such a terrible thing as the poor professor? Rode in this very cab, sitting where you are now, very smart in his London suit," he began with some relish.

"You know him quite well, do you?" Emmy ventured.

"Knew him. Ah, knew him. He's no more, and we'll not see his like again."

"You think there's no hope, then?"

"Not from Devil's Chimney. They say the devil claims one man's life in each ten years. It was due." The driver hardly seemed in a merry mood.

Emmy pressed on. "What I mean is, Professor Vandike used to come here often?"

"Every year. Every year since I left the pits and took to my taxi, which is ten if it's a day."

"And he was an expert climber?"

"He—" the driver was suddenly silent. Then he said, "You one of these journalists, then?"

"No, no," Emmy assured him.

"That's good. We don't want any of them in the valley." But all the same, the driver unaccountably clammed up, and no more was said until the wheezing vehicle drew up outside the forbidding gray stone building that was the Mountainside Hotel.

Emmy obtained a room with no difficulty. Professor Vandike's accident had evidently put a damper on business, since the clientele consisted entirely of climbers. That Emmy should have arrived on her own, without climbing gear, was enough to set the village talking, and the taxi driver's suspicion that she might be a newspaperwoman in disguise was widely held. However, by sitting quietly in a corner of the bar before lunch, and at an inconspicuous table in the dining room during it, she was able to sample a slice of local gossip.

Two things emerged. One was that Professor Vandike had been well known and admired, but not greatly liked. His constantly changing retinue of young men was looked at askance. The second fact was that his death was taken absolutely for granted. More than once she heard the story of the devil exacting his due of a human life each decade, and people were already talking about the second cross to be erected near the ravine.

She also learned that Roger Talbot, Vandike's young friend, had left the previous day to complete his vacation elsewhere. He had been very upset and, not surprisingly, had lost his enthusiasm for mountain climbing. He had also, apparently, lost his driving license, which had annoyed him greatly, even though he was leaving Aberpriddy by train.

"Going on as if *we* had something to do with it," remarked the proprietress to Emmy tartly. "My belief is he left it at home, and home's where he'll find it. I didn't want to bother you before you'd had your dinner, Mrs. Tibbett, but I'd be grateful if you'd look into the office and sign the register when you have time."

This was a moment that Emmy had been waiting for. After lunch the office was quiet and there was no sign of Mrs. Jenkins, the proprietress, whose sharp little black eyes missed nothing. A bored teenaged girl pushed the guest register over the desk to Emmy, and returned to her magazine.

Quickly, Emmy flipped back the pages. There were the two

signatures. Harry Vandike had penned his name in an illegible but characteristic scrawl, but immediately underneath it, Roger Talbot had signed in a fine italic hand. Obviously he was a student of calligraphy.

The girl looked up from her love story, and Emmy quickly turned to the current page of the register and wrote her own entry. Then she said, "I thought I might hire a car while I'm here. Can you tell me how to set about it?"

The girl looked at her as if she thought Emmy were mad. "People don't hire cars here," she said. "They go climbing. Or bicycle. The hotel has bicycles."

"I see. Thank you."

Not wishing to telephone from the hotel, Emmy walked down to the village. It was a depressing little place, gray and dark and dwarfed by the majestic but menacing mountains around it. A place to eat and sleep in, and then to get away from, up to the summits and the sun.

Little shops sold souvenirs but didn't seem to have their hearts in it. There was the usual grocery and butcher's shop. The only prosperous-looking establishments were the ones that sold and rented climbing gear and equipment, and the pharmacy, which provided first aid to wounded mountaineers. However, there was a post office, and outside it a public call box. Emmy went in and dialed the number of Superintendent Evans in Aberwithy.

Evans was all affability, and told Emmy at once that a world-famous car-rental firm had an office in the town. He suggested that she should take the bus ("Stops right outside the post office") for the ten-minute drive. "You could take the train," he added, "just one stop, but there's none till this evening." He paused and cleared his throat. "Will you be wanting help from the force, madam?"

"I don't know," said Emmy. "I'll try to manage on my own. But I'd very much like to come and meet you, if I may."

"Of course, madam. Of course. I'll be in my office. Anybody will direct you."

Emmy was lucky. A bus arrived within a few minutes, and the car-rental office was empty except for a girl in a bright green uniform. They had plenty of cars. The summer season was ending, and trade was very slow. The girl gave Emmy the details and prices.

Thumbing through the catalogue, Emmy remarked, "Tragic business about Professor Vandike, wasn't it?"

"Vandike? Oh, the chap who fell off the mountain. Well, they will do it. Bring it on themselves, if you ask me . . ." Aberwithy was evidently not taking the affair to heart in the same way as Aberpriddy.

"I believe he hired a car from you while he was here," said Emmy.

The green-uniformed girl looked surprised. "Vandike? Oh, I don't think so. We don't get people from Aberpriddy. Climbing's all they think of."

"Yes, I suppose it is. Well, I'd like a Fiat Panda for twenty-four hours—now until tomorrow afternoon. What do I have to do?"

"Just fill in this form and show me your driving license. Got a credit card? Good, you won't have to pay a deposit." The girl pushed a complicated-looking form toward Emmy, who, in turn, fished her driving license out of her handbag.

British driving licenses must be among the last in the world that do not require a photograph of the holder. However, they have to be signed, and for this reason, car-rental firms scrutinize the signature on the form carefully to make sure it matches the one on the license.

When the formalities had been completed and Emmy had the keys of the car in her hand, she said, "I was recommended to you by a friend of mine—Mr. Roger Talbot. I think he hired a car last week."

"Not that I know of. But then, I was on my holiday."

"Oh, I see . . . thank you."

Emmy drove the Panda to the parking lot in the middle of the small town, and then made her way on foot to the police station.

The superintendent seemed genuinely delighted to see her. He immediately agreed to her request to speak to Henry at the Yard.

"Henry? I'm in Superintendent Evans's office. I've hired a

173

car—there's only one firm. The girl knew nothing about Vandike, but she was on holiday last week, so that doesn't help. I also mentioned Roger Talbot, but that didn't ring a bell either."

"Why did you mention him?" Henry asked, surprised.

Emmy said, "I saw their signatures in the hotel register. Vandike's is the usual scribble, but Roger Talbot's is in that italic script—"

"The same as the crossword clues!"

"Exactly. *And* he left the hotel yesterday complaining that he had lost his driving license!"

"How very interesting," said Henry. "Anything else?"

"Not much. Everybody assumes that Vandike is dead, and that his body will never be found. There's a superstition that the Devil's Chimney claims a life every ten years, and one was due. Oh—and the hotel has bicycles, which they lend to their visitors. Just a moment, the superintendent wants to say something . . ."

"Then put him on the line, will you, darling? And then get back to me yourself."

"Okay. Superintendent?" Emmy handed over the phone.

Quickly, and with some excitement, Evans said, "Mrs. Tibbett mentioned the hotel bicycles, sir. Well, they reported one missing, maybe stolen, on Wednesday last. We found it that same day in the parking lot here in town. It never crossed my mind until—"

"Why should it have?" said Henry. "But it's interesting all the same, don't you think? Now, my wife has done her best with these car-rental people, but we'll need your help. I don't want to get them alarmed. You'd better send a uniformed constable around to the office with a story about hired-car thefts. The main thing is to be able to take a look at the records for last week. I want to know if a car was hired out to a Mr. Roger Talbot, and if so, get his license number and a good look at his signature, and make a report. I know you can't describe a signature, but I think this one may be distinctive. Do you know what's called the italic hand?"

Evans looked blank. "Something they write in Italy, would it be, sir?"

"No. It's a sort of formal and very flowery handwriting, like a . . . like you get on a diploma or a citation or something. I think Roger Talbot's signature may be something like that. Now—what's become of Professor Vandike's belongings?"

"As far as I know, the hotel has them, sir. Officially, you see, we haven't given up hope . . . and anyway, we don't know the next of kin."

"Find a pretext and go through them," said Henry.

"Looking for something special, sir?"

"Yes. His driving license."

"That's all, sir?"

"That's all," said Henry, "unless, of course, you come across anything else interesting. An inventory would be useful. My wife will come and see you tomorrow before she leaves, and she can bring it."

"Right, sir. I'll put you on to Mrs. Tibbett again."

Emmy said, "I'm afraid I haven't been able to do much, darling."

"You've done a great deal."

"Nothing that Superintendent Evans couldn't have—"

"Ah, but you did it privately, anonymously. Now take a drive, enjoy the scenery, and spend the night at the hotel. Tomorrow afternoon, hand back the car, get whatever data the superintendent has been able to muster, and come home. It'll probably mean a night journey. Did the hotel give you a rail timetable?"

"Yes, they did. Wait a moment, I think it's in my bag. Yes, here it is. Aberpriddy Halt, 6:15 P.M. Aberwithy, 6:22. Change at those unpronounceable places. Leave Bristol 8:30, arrive London, Paddington, 1:20 A.M. That seems to be it."

"I'll meet you at the train," Henry said, "unless I hear from you."

"Oh, Henry, that's not necessary. I'll just take a cab—"

"I'll meet you," said Henry firmly. "I hope we've been able to do this unobtrusively, but you can never be sure."

"It all sounds to me," Emmy said, "like another of Harry Vandike's little practical jokes."

"I hope it is," said Henry. "But I'm afraid this time the joke may be on him. See you tomorrow night. Take care."

Emmy spent an enjoyable couple of hours driving up to a beautiful spot recommended by Evans and admiring the glory of a mountain sunset. Then she went back to the hotel.

The bar was deserted, having only just opened. Mrs. Jenkins herself was presiding behind it in obvious boredom. "That Mary's late again. I don't know what young people are coming to." She seemed glad of a chat with Emmy, agreeing to join her in a half-pint of bitter.

"Thank you very much, my dear. I hope you had a pleasant day."

"Very," said Emmy. "I hired a car and drove up to St. David's Rock."

"Beautiful view from there," remarked Mrs. Jenkins. Then, after a pause, "I thought you might have been to look at Devil's Chimney. Not to climb it, I mean—oh, goodness me, no. But to get a story for your newspaper."

"Newspaper?"

Mrs. Jenkins leaned confidentially across the bar. "Now, dear, you can't fool me. People don't come to this hotel except to climb, and you're not one of those. Well, you'll not find out a lot about poor Professor Vandike, but you can always send them what's called an atmosphere piece, can't you? But there's no sense in thinking he'll come back, because he won't. Not from the Chimney, not after all this time."

It suddenly occurred to Emmy that it might be useful not to deny that she was a journalist. She gave a rueful smile and said, "Well, Mrs. Jenkins, you seem to have found me out. Now that we're alone for a moment, is there anything you can tell me about the professor that might be useful to me?"

"I'll tell you one thing, useful or not," said Mrs. Jenkins, snappily. "His bill's not been paid, and all his things are still in the room. The young gentleman, Mr. Talbot, he took his own stuff, of course, but what am I to do with Professor Vandike's things, that's what I'd like to know. Suppose I want to let the room again? Well, I know we're not full, but it's the best room in the hotel, and some of our regulars are very particular about having it." She paused for breath and a drink of beer. "I've a good mind to ask the police to come and take them away. After all, they'd keep them safe, wouldn't they, in case he did come back—which he won't."

"I think that's an excellent idea, Mrs. Jenkins," said Emmy. "I'd do that first thing tomorrow."

"Well, I'm glad you agree, dear. It's taken quite a weight off my mind. The police around here are very good, you know. They found a bicycle of ours left in Aberwithy only the other day. Some guest must have cycled over there, decided to take the bus back, and just left the bicycle in the parking lot. Talk about being inconsiderate with other people's property. I'll never find out who did it, though I've my suspicions and nobody can stop me."

"You don't think it could have been Professor Vandike or Mr. Talbot?" asked Emmy tentatively.

Mrs. Jenkins looked at her scornfully. "How could it have been, considering that the professor was off to Devil's Chimney, and young Talbot joined a party with a professional guide? Oh, no. But there's some . . . well, I'll say no more. But Professor Vandike was a real gentleman, even if he did bring along a different young man each year, which I thought peculiar to say the least." Mrs. Jenkins sniffed. "Still, none of my business, so long as the bill's paid."

"Did Mr. Talbot pay before he left?" Emmy asked.

"He paid his bar bill, as you'd expect," said Mrs. Jenkins. "As for the room, the professor always paid for both of them. I didn't feel I could ask Mr. Talbot for it. Oh, I'm not worrying. The police will find the next of kin. It'll be paid."

"Do you remember," said Emmy, "a young man called Peter Turnberry, who came here one year with Professor Vandike?"

"Turnberry? Turnberry? It wasn't last year, that was Mr. Hepplewhite . . . nor the year before, that was the Jones boy, I shan't forget *him* in a hurry . . . let's see now. Yes, it must have been three years ago. A nice young fellow, just finished at Oxford and going in for the law. That the one you mean?"

"That's him," said Emmy.

"He and the professor were *very* close," confided Mrs. Jenkins. "Always sitting talking in corners and shutting up like clams when anybody came near. And yet, it's a funny thing . . ."

"What is?"

"Well, not to speak ill of the dead, but, as I said, I always thought there was something . . . well . . . not quite *normal* about the professor and his young men, if you follow me. And yet, with Mr. Turnberry, I remember thinking—he's not one of *those*. You get my meaning? They were close, all right, but it seemed more like they were discussing a business deal or some such thing."

Sharp little black eyes, missing nothing, Emmy thought. "Well, I can see you've got customers arriving," she said. "I'm just going to make a phone call before dinner."

She left Mrs. Jenkins muttering, "That Mary! I'll teach her to be late," and made her way to the hotel's phone booth. The superintendent was no longer on duty, and the telephone book had pages of Evanses in it—but a sympathetic sergeant divulged his superior's home number. It was answered by a soft Welsh female voice, which said that Ivor was watching telly, but she'd get him.

Emmy told Evans that he would not have to resort to any subterfuge to get access to Vandike's belongings. Mrs. Jenkins would be calling to ask him to remove them. "So it's only the car-rental firm you have to worry about," she added. "I'll see you in your office tomorrow evening, around five." Then she had dinner, and went to bed early.

The next day was a long and tedious one for Emmy, even though she enjoyed driving up to a well-known mountain restaurant for lunch. She wished heartily that she could have taken an earlier train back to London, but she had to give the local police time to do their work—and in any case, the car was hers until three. However, it was with relief that she handed it back to the girl in green.

The girl seemed less bored and quite eager to talk. "You'll never guess," she said as she checked the mileage. "We had the police in this morning!"

"The police?" said Emmy, with all the innocence she could muster. "Whatever for?"

"Said there'd been a lot of hired cars stolen recently," said the girl. "I said there'd been none stolen from us, thank you very much, but he looked at our files all the same. Said he might be able to pick out a name. I thought it was all a bit fishy."

"I expect the police knew what they were doing," said Emmy.

"Yes, that's just it. I expect they did, and it wasn't to do with car thefts."

"Oh? What was it, then?"

"Checking up on us, to see if we keep our records right and report our income for tax," said the girl. "Well, of course we do, but there's some as doesn't, and the income tax are in with the police, whatever anybody may say. It gave me a nasty feeling, like being in Russia or somewhere."

Emmy was soothing. "I wouldn't worry," she said. "Especially as you've nothing to hide."

"Well, I've always said it's a free country. Here you are. Just sign here, please. And here, for the credit card. Thanks a lot."

Emmy filled the next half hour exploring the amenities of Aberwithy, which were minimal. She ended up reading a newspaper in the public gardens, and was heartily glad when her watch told her it was a quarter to five, and she might decently make her way to the police station.

Evans greeted her with jubilation. "I think the Chief Superintendent's going to be well pleased," he said. "For a start, Constable Jones found out about the car."

"The girl told me the police had been around," Emmy said.

"Yes, and with a beautiful story about car thefts that nobody could have disbelieved. He's a good lad, is Jones."

"Yes," said Emmy, suppressing a smile. "Well, what did he find out?"

"Last Monday," said the superintendent impressively, "just before the office closed, that is, about a quarter to six, Mr. Roger Talbot came in and hired a car. And he signed for it in that italic way that the Chief Superintendent was describing."

"And has the car been returned?"

"Not to here. It wasn't meant to be. You know this firm has offices all over the country, so you can hire a car in one place and turn it in somewhere else. Well, this car was hired for

179

twenty-four hours, and was returned and paid for as agreed. A big expensive car it was, with a good turn of speed."

"And where was it handed in?"

"In London. The branch office near Waterloo Station."

"And the license number?"

"Written down here, Mrs. Tibbett. Jones thought of everything."

"Could I have some paper to copy all this down for Henry? Did Constable Jones manage to find out what Roger Talbot looked like?"

"Well, no, madam. You see, the girl was on holiday last week, as you pointed out, and the constable didn't want to go making a fuss. But he did note the car's number, as you'll see, and he did get to nosing around the park where the cars are kept—oh, I tell you, there's not much Jones misses. He confirms the car's not there."

This seemed something of an anticlimax to Emmy, but Evans went on enthusiastically. "So it looks as though the car will be in the Waterloo establishment, unless it's been hired out again in the meantime. I've no doubt the Chief Superintendent will check."

"I'm sure he will," said Emmy, with little hope. The car was sure to have been cleaned and re-hired by now.

"Now, to proceed," said the superintendent, proceeding. "I must congratulate you, madam. How you persuaded Mrs. Jenkins of Mountainside to call me—"

"I didn't have to—" Emmy began.

"You're a lady of great cleverness and persuasion, as I can see," Evans went on gallantly. "She rang me this morning and asked if I'd take charge of the professor's things. They're here, in an empty office next door. You'd like to be seeing them?"

"I certainly would," said Emmy. "Was there a driving license?"

"Yes, there was. And . . . well, come and see."

Professor Vandike's belongings were neatly laid out on the desk of the unoccupied office. They were much that one would expect to find in the luggage of somebody on a three-week holiday. The usual assortment of underwear, socks, shirts, slacks, and sweaters, including the heavy variety used by climbers, but with a selection of lighter-weight items suitable for evenings at the hotel. There was no climbing gear—no crampon-spiked boots, no rucksacks, no knitted woolen hat, no belaying rope or pitons or other climbing necessities. These were presumably at the bottom of the ravine with Harold Vandike. There were also no wallet, checkbook, credit cards, or cash.

There was, however, a driving license made out in the name of Harold Vandike, giving his Oxford college as his address, and signed with the scrawl that Emmy recognized from the hotel register. There were also a bunch of keys, a sponge bag with the usual toiletries, two pairs of pajamas, a dressing gown, slippers, and a dozen white handkerchiefs of fine linen. And that was that.

Emmy made a list, meticulous to the last detail (one tube of toothpaste, half-used). She also noted the number of the driver's license.

Emmy said good-bye to the superintendent, remarking truthfully that it had been a great pleasure to meet him, and made her way to the railway station. The journey was tedious but uneventful. As she alighted from the train under the great glass arches of Paddington Station, she saw no sinister characters. In fact there were very few travelers, but nevertheless it was with relief that she spotted Henry on the platform. Half an hour later they were home again.

16

Half past two in the morning. Emmy was brewing another cup of strong coffee while Henry pored over her inventory of Vandike's possessions and made notes. He looked up with a tired smile as she came in from the kitchen.

"Well," he said, "it all seems pretty obvious, except for the missing names."

"How do you mean?"

"To begin at the beginning," Henry said, "Harry Vandike and his young friend are on holiday. Vandike called his Oxford college, and heard that I wanted to get in touch with him. He may have heard something else from somebody else, but we'll leave that aside for the moment. He decided to come up to London on the quiet to see me and find out what I was up to. He didn't want anybody to know, not even Roger Talbot, so he invented the story about climbing the Devil's Chimney. He left the hotel early, cycled to Aberwithy, left the bicycle in the parking lot, and transferred to the car that he had hired the previous day and left there."

"He must have been in climbing clothes, with his equipment," said Emmy, stirring her coffee.

"Exactly. Now, notice what's missing from your list. The dark gray suit in which he arrived at Mountainside, and his wallet with cash and credit cards. Nobody in their senses would take those things on a climb. He must have put the suit in his ruck-sack, together with town shoes, a shirt, and a tie. He hired the car in Roger Talbot's name, showing Talbot's driving license."

"I had figured that out for myself," said Emmy, "as soon as I saw the italic hand in the register."

"Just so. I daresay Vandike was teaching Talbot. And, as our experts pointed out when the crossword clues arrived, it's deliberately designed to remove personal characteristics from handwriting. So Vandike's signature on the car rental form looked—to a layman, anyhow—just like Talbot's."

"But he left his license behind," said Emmy. "Surely that must mean that he intended to go back to the hotel."

"I'm sure he did," said Henry. "Something evidently happened to prevent it."

"He must have changed his clothes somewhere," said Emmy. "The girl said the car had been turned in at the office near Waterloo Station. He could have gone to the men's room there, and—"

"No," said Henry. "Wait a minute. He told me he still had the car when we lunched together. So he changed somewhere en route."

"I suppose he had to drive through a lot of deserted countryside," said Emmy. "Easy enough to nip behind a bush and . . . but what happened to his climbing gear, then? He must have planned to arrive back wearing it, but he wasn't driving back. He—"

"He changed somewhere, at some house, where he stopped on the way from Wales to London," said Henry, slowly. "He must have left his climbing gear there. He told me he had an appointment, which was why we lunched so early. He then drove off and turned in the car near Waterloo Station. That meant that he wasn't thinking of taking a train back to Wales. As we know, they leave from Paddington, which is on the other side of London. No, he was going to take a train from Waterloo, back to the place where he had left his gear. That's where his appointment was." He paused. "Have you got an atlas anywhere of England and Wales?"

"I think I've got my old school one somewhere," said Emmy. "Wait a minute. I'll go and look."

When Emmy returned with the atlas, Henry opened it at the page showing Wales and southeastern England. "I thought so," he said. "Come and look."

"It's an old atlas," said Emmy. "It won't show the new highways or—"

"Never mind. This is just in general terms. See this?" Henry put his finger on the black dot marked GREAT MIDDLEFORD. "Draw a line from there to London. Now draw a line from London to South Wales."

"Why," said Emmy, "they almost cross. I mean, it would only be a few miles' detour, coming from Aberwithy by car, to go to—"

"Myrtle's house. And the train to take him back again would leave from Waterloo."

"But," said Emmy, "why didn't he just keep the car, call in at Myrtle's on the way back to change, and drive on? And why go to the elaborate lengths of pretending not to have lunched with you?"

"I'm guessing," Henry admitted, "but this is what I think. Somebody contacted Vandike and a meeting was arranged at Myrtle's house. He was supposed to get there by train, having no car of his own in Wales—a long and tedious journey, I should imagine—"

"And how was he to get back to the Mountainside Hotel, for heaven's sake?"

"I think," said Henry, "that somebody volunteered to drive him. He might arrive somewhat late, but he was always capable of inventing a good story to cover that. The search parties wouldn't have been out at that stage. The meeting was to be early in the afternoon, hence his hurry to get away from the Explorers Club. The practical joke was just his way, as he thought, of ensuring that it would be denied that he had been in London or seen me that day."

"But—" Emmy shivered slightly. "What went wrong? He never got back to Aberpriddy."

"No, he didn't." Henry sounded unusually grim. "The person who volunteered to drive him knew that he would never arrive. It was a nice little set-up for a murder. If Harold Vandike hadn't wrecked it by hiring a car and driving to London first and lunching with me, there'd have been a subscription taken for a second cross on the Devil's Chimney, and a nice memorial service."

"But surely Myrtle would have told—?" Emmy began.

"One would have thought so. But she hasn't, has she?"

"You're sure he's dead?"

"He's either dead or a magician," said Henry. "I can't produce his body. But you can be sure it's not in a ravine at Aberpriddy."

"Then where is it?"

"That," said Henry, "is what I propose to find out."

"Starting with Myrtle?"

"She seems the obvious place to begin. So we'd better get some sleep."

"How about the Yard?" Emmy asked.

Henry yawned. "I've had a talk with the Assistant Commissioner and told him roughly what I'm doing, or think I'm doing. He's agreed to let me take what leave I want, unless something really important turns up. Meanwhile, Reynolds can cope with what's going on."

"Our holiday in Burgundy," said Emmy, "seems to be retreating farther and farther into the distance."

"Maybe next year, darling."

"Maybe."

The Waterfords' house outside Great Middleford was as tranquil and beautiful as ever when Henry and Emmy drove up to it around eleven o'clock the following morning. Henry had given no notice of his arrival, and just hoped that Myrtle would be at home.

He was unlucky. The same maid who had admitted the Tibbetts on their previous visit informed them cordially that madam was in Great Middleford doing her shopping. Of course,

Henry and Emmy might wait. They had, as it were, established their credentials by their first visit. She showed them into the living room, with its big windows overlooking the garden, and was about to leave them when Henry said, "By the way . . . what's your name?"

"Doris, sir."

"Well, Doris, you may be able to help us. We've come to collect the things that Professor Vandike left here with Mrs. Waterford last Tuesday."

"The chap with the beard and all those funny boots and rope and stuff?" asked Doris, intrigued.

"That's right. He drove here in the morning, didn't he, and changed into a town suit."

"That's right. I pressed it for him. Proper crumpled it was, out of that knapsack thing."

"Well, he asked us to drop in and pick up—"

"But he didn't leave nothing here, not that I know of, sir."

"You mean he came back and collected his things?"

"Yes, sir. In the afternoon. I was off duty, strictly speaking, but I did hear voices, and I recognized his. Then a car drove off, and when I come to get tea, he'd gone. And taken his stuff with him."

"Oh, well," said Henry, "if he did leave anything, Mrs. Waterford will know. We'll wait until she gets home."

Myrtle was back within half an hour. Henry and Emmy heard her car drive up to the house, and obviously Doris did too, for she was at the front door in no time. Henry heard her saying, "I'll take those packages to the kitchen for you, madam. Just you put them on the hall table, and I'll get the rest from the car."

"Thank you, Doris."

"And, madam—"

"Yes? Any messages for me?"

"Not so much a message, madam. There's Mr. and Mrs. Tibbett, who was here the other day. That's their car in the drive. They're waiting for you in the drawing room, madam."

"Oh, are they?" Myrtle sounded far from pleased. "I hoped the car belonged to the man who's supposed to come look at the

186

drains. Well, I suppose I shall have to see them."

A moment later the door opened and Myrtle came into the drawing room. "Well, fancy," she said. "*What* a surprise." Her tone of voice made it clear that the surprise was not a pleasant one, and that the drain expert would have been a much more welcome visitor. "Just passing through Great Middleford again, Mr. Tibbett?"

"Not exactly," said Henry. "I'm trying to trace the movements of Professor Harold Vandike last Tuesday—the day he died."

It was difficult for a woman as stolidly constructed as Myrtle to look disconcerted, but for a moment she managed it. Then she said tartly, "Well, I can't imagine why you came here. I understand the poor man had a climbing accident and that they're still looking for him. Somewhere in Wales, I believe."

"I think you know that's not true, Mrs. Waterford," said Henry. "Let me tell you what I know so far. Harold Vandike left the Mountainside Hotel in Aberpriddy early last Tuesday, in full climbing gear, having announced that he intended to do a dangerous climb alone. Actually he turned his back on the mountain and cycled to the nearest town, where he jettisoned his bicycle and picked up a self-drive car, which he had hired the previous day under an assumed name. He drove the car directly here, to this house, arriving about half past ten or eleven, I imagine. He changed his clothes—he had brought a city suit with him in his rucksack—and drove on in his hired car to London, where he lunched with me."

"That's ridiculous," said Myrtle, but she did not sound quite sure of herself.

"It may be ridiculous," said Henry, "but it's what happened. In fact, your maid Doris confirmed it just now, before you came home. She told us she even pressed his suit for him."

"The little fool," said Myrtle, with real anger. "All right, Harry Vandike did come here. I expect you know he loves playing jokes—not always very kind ones. Apparently he intended to let his friends at the hotel think he had met with a climbing accident, and then turn up as right as rain. His idea of an amusing prank. He also mentioned that it would enable him to keep an important engagement in London without anybody knowing."

"Why didn't you tell somebody this right away, Mrs. Waterford? Why didn't you inform the Aberwithy police? After all, his disappearance was reported in the papers, and you must have known—"

Myrtle had the grace to look uncomfortable. "I promised Harry," she said. And, gaining a little confidence, she went on, "I have no idea where he is now, or whether he's dead or alive."

"One of the men in the search parties might have been killed!" Emmy spoke angrily and spontaneously.

"That's really none of my affair," remarked Myrtle, "and in any case, nobody was hurt."

Henry said, "He told you that he would return here by three o'clock, resume wearing his climbing clothes and drive back to Wales?"

"Yes," said Myrtle. "And that's exactly what he did."

"Where do you think he is now?"

"Well, I won't disguise from you that I'm very worried, Mr. Tibbett. I thought he would turn up at his hotel that same evening. But I cannot be held responsible—"

Henry checked her. He said, "So he drove back here in the same car, changed, collected his things, and drove off again?"

There was a tiny hesitation. Then Myrtle said, "I presume it was the same car. I was busy at my typewriter—I like to work in the afternoons—and I didn't even see him. Just heard the car drive in and then out again about ten minutes later."

Henry said, "He didn't come back here by car, Mrs. Waterford. He turned the car back to the London office of the rental firm and came on by train."

"Well, then, I suppose he must have come by taxi from the station and left the same way. We are three miles from the railway, Mr. Tibbett. You would scarcely have expected him to walk."

"You think, then," said Henry, "that he took a cab from the station, asked it to wait while he changed, and then took it back to the station?"

Carefully, Myrtle said, "That is my guess, Mr. Tibbett. I told you, I didn't even see him."

"So you don't know for certain that he did come back?"

"No, I suppose I don't. But somebody came, and his things had gone when I came down to tea, so I naturally—"

"Doris says," Henry persisted, "that she heard voices."

"Like Joan of Arc, I presume?" Myrtle's nervousness showed through her sarcasm.

"You know what I mean," said Henry patiently.

"Well, if she did, I suppose it was Vandike and the cab driver."

Henry said, "I'm sorry, Mrs. Waterford. I think you have the last part of the day's events all wrong, and I think you know it. Vandike may have taken a cab from the station back here, but from here, somebody volunteered to drive him back to Aberwithy. It would have been an impossible railway journey from here. Have you looked at the timetables?"

"Why on earth should I have looked at the timetables?"

"Well, I have, and he couldn't have made it before the next day, after a nightmare journey. In fact, his best plan would have been to go back to London from here, cross London to Paddington, and start for Wales from there the following day."

"Well, perhaps that's exactly what he did." Myrtle stood up. "I think you are taking this prank too seriously, Mr. Tibbett. Harry will reappear in a few days, laughing his head off. He has a curious sense of humor, but there you are."

"And where do you think he is now?"

"I haven't the remotest idea," said Myrtle stiffly. "I told you."

"Well . . . let's hope you're right to be so optimistic." Henry stood up and held out his hand. "I'm sorry to have taken up your time, Mrs. Waterford. Good-bye."

Myrtle shook Henry's hand reluctantly, as if it were a dead rat. She said good-bye a little more cordially to Emmy, saw them to the door, and watched the little black car drive away.

Henry was silent during the drive back to London. He found a parking space for the car, and he and Emmy walked back to their apartment, where Emmy prepared a salad lunch while Henry drank a cold beer. When Emmy announced that the meal was ready, he seemed to come out of deep meditation.

"Sorry, darling," he said. "I'm not very good company, I'm afraid."

"You've been thinking," said Emmy.

"Yes," said Henry. "This spinach salad is delicious."

"It's the mushroom and garlic that make it—"

"I shall go to the Assistant Commissioner this afternoon," Henry went on, as if he had not heard her. "I must. He'll have to fix it somehow with the local force. I can't go on like this, alone and with no official resources. One murder was bad enough. Two is too much."

Emmy said tentatively, "Remember what Myrtle said. You don't want Harry Vandike popping up alive and well, shouting 'April fool!' do you?"

"He won't pop up, I very much fear," said Henry. "Then I think I should see young Roger Talbot. And I have to find some way of getting her there."

Emmy was too used to this sort of remark to make the elementary mistake of asking, "Getting who where?"

Instead, she simply said, "There's some cheddar and some quite decent Brie, if you'd like it."

"What? Oh, yes. Thanks, love."

"And some fresh bread," Emmy added with a touch of pride. She had only recently taken to home baking, having been driven to the edge of despair by mass-produced, pre-sliced loaves.

When lunch was over, Henry departed for Scotland Yard. Emmy, still tired after her late-night journey from Wales, went somewhat listlessly about the cleaning of the apartment, for which she had had no time in the morning. As she did so, she considered the characters in this case that was not a case.

The Oppenshaw family, for a start. Sir Robert: bluff, good-natured, apparently easygoing but very shrewd, standing to lose a great deal if an illegitimate child of Jeannie Warfield's did turn up. And yet—Sir Robert was now a very successful publisher. It was impossible to think of him as a murderer. Lady

Oppenshaw would have the same motive as her husband, but all the objections were the same. A courageous woman. Emmy remembered how she had driven over to break the news of Peter's death to Mrs. Turnberry. That took the sort of guts that never makes the headlines, but is nonetheless worthy. In any case, Emmy remembered that Sir Robert and Pamela had been at a highly respectable tea party when Peter Turnberry was galloping Melisande back along the clifftop.

Barbara . . . Emmy paused in her washing up, rinsing her sudsy hands. Barbara was a curious girl. Was it possible that at the age of six, precocious child that she was, she might have contrived her stepsister's death? Harry Vandike had certainly hinted at it strongly in the crossword puzzle. Barbara had become engaged to Peter Turnberry with, as it seemed to Emmy, little or no affection for him, although Henry seemed to think differently. Anyhow, the evening before his death, she had broken the engagement. Curious.

What about the others? Dr. Cartwright had been there when Jeannie drowned, and also when Peter was killed. Funny, that. And he had taken his car out during the afternoon, ostensibly to buy pipe tobacco when he didn't smoke a pipe. Fred Coe . . . no, nobody would be suspicious of Fred Coe. Brilliant, but in an academic way. Not a plotter, not a schemer.

Myrtle, on the other hand, was a different matter altogether. Emmy could not see her as a murderer—but then, human nature can take odd twists and turns. Myrtle was frightened, for all her bluffing. Not only physically frightened, but frightened for the loss of her solid country-house life. Myrtle knew too much about something, and knew that she did. That was why she hadn't told the police about Harry Vandike's visit.

And Vandike himself? He was too clever by half, if you asked Emmy. Like a slyly malevolent puppeteer, pulling the strings that manipulated the others. Now, if Henry was right, the tables had been turned on him.

Phrases came floating back into her mind, from the weekend at Carnworth, from the Ventnor police, from the day of the inquest—even from that morning . . . Emmy suddenly realized that she had washed the same plate three times, and decided that she must be more tired than she thought. Stupid, filling her head with things that didn't concern her. She dried the last plate briskly, and was just getting out the vacuum cleaner when the front doorbell rang.

Surprised and not pleased, she went to answer it. Probably somebody collecting for charity, or trying to sell hairbrushes or religion. She wiped her hands on her apron and opened the door, to find herself face to face with Barbara Oppenshaw.

Without preamble, Barbara said, "I want to see Henry."

"I'm sorry," said Emmy, with a conscious effort at politeness, "you can't. He's at Scotland Yard."

"That's a lie, for a start," said Barbara.

"I beg your pardon?"

"I said 'That's a lie,' in case you didn't hear me. I called the Yard just before lunch, and they told me he'd taken the day off. I'll come in, if I may."

"Come in by all means," said Emmy, standing back from the doorway. Barbara's easy, expensive elegance made Emmy actually aware of her own slightly grubby apron, the untidy apartment, and the confusion visible through the open broom-cupboard door.

Barbara looked around the lived-in un-chic room and out to the small, straggling garden. "I can't think why people who can't afford it persist in living in Chelsea," she said. "It used to be such a pleasant place."

Ignoring this blatant insult, Emmy said, "I'll tell you what happened, Miss Oppenshaw, if you'll just listen. It's perfectly true that Henry took the day off, and we drove down to the country this morning. But we were home for a late lunch, and he then decided to go back to the Yard. If you really want him, you'll find him there, but he may well be busy."

Barbara hesitated a moment, then said, "You can give him a message for me, I suppose."

As if I were a servant, thought Emmy, but she choked down her resentment. "Very well. What is it?"

"My parents and I," said Barbara, "are extremely annoyed at

the way your husband is interfering in our affairs."

Emmy raised her eyebrows. "Interfering?"

"Yes, interfering. And when I say 'our affairs,' I also mean those of Oppenshaw and Trilby's authors. He has thoroughly upset a number of people by his prying and his insinuations, and it has got to stop. Do you understand?"

"I understand what you are saying," said Emmy.

Barbara went on. "The inquest on Peter was perfectly straightforward and the matter is closed. There was no need for Henry Tibbett to come down to Ryde for it. He wasn't subpoenaed. Since then, he has badgered me, Peter's parents, Fred Coe, Bill Cartwright, and even poor old Myrtle."

"And Harry Vandike?" Emmy suggested.

"It's tragic that Harry should have been killed," said Barbara, not sounding as if she gave a damn one way or the other, "but mountain climbing is an extremely dangerous sport, and Harry knew it."

Emmy said, "You mentioned that your parents were upset. Why? Henry hasn't seen or spoken to them since we were at Carnworth, except for a word or so at the inquest. And in fact, Sir Robert—"

"My parents are upset at the effect your husband is having on valuable authors," Barbara snapped. "And I'm worried about them—especially Mother."

"I didn't think Lady Oppenshaw had anything to do with the publishing business," said Emmy.

"She doesn't, but she's very unhappy at what Father is going through. In fact, she—that is, both of them—asked me to tell Henry that if he has anything to say concerning Oppenshaw and Trilby, or any of its authors, he should come to Carnworth in person and say it."

"Is that an invitation?" asked Emmy. Despite herself, she could not suppress a grin. "If it is, it's hardly the warmest I've ever received."

"It is an invitation," said Barbara. "I shall be going to Carnworth next weekend, and we hope to see you both there, and get things settled once and for all."

"What things?" Emmy asked innocently.

"If we knew that, they'd be settled already," retorted Barbara. "Please tell Henry what I've said, and ask him to telephone my father as soon as possible."

"I'll tell him," said Emmy.

17

Henry was intrigued to hear about the invitation to Carnworth when he got home that evening.

"Certainly we'll go," he said. "In fact, if I can work fast enough, we might even turn this into a classic whodunnit."

"What do you mean?"

"I mean, reassemble all the people who were at the literary weekend—"

"And unmask the murderer? Oh, Henry, you can't mean that."

"I mean exactly that," said Henry. "But I haven't much time. I hope Reynolds has located the fellow."

"What fellow?"

"Roger Talbot."

In fact, Inspector Reynolds was, at that very moment, speaking to Roger Talbot on the telephone. It had not been very difficult to find him. He had obtained Talbot's home address from the Mountainside Hotel, and had been informed by Mrs. Talbot that her son had cut short his climbing holiday after Professor Vandike's accident and was staying with a group of undergraduate friends in London, where one of them had a flat. She gave him the telephone number and address without a murmur.

Roger Talbot was very surprised to be telephoned by a detective inspector from Scotland Yard, and was inclined to be suspicious. Reynolds invited him to allay his doubts by hanging up and calling back to the Yard, where he would discover that Inspector Reynolds was not a fraud. Roger, mollified, agreed. He also agreed to come to the Yard first thing in the morning for a talk with Chief Superintendent Tibbett.

He turned out to be a personable young man with lank, fair hair. He sat opposite Henry, looking pale and upset, and demanded to know what this was all about.

"Please don't be alarmed, Mr. Talbot," said Henry. "I'm just making a few routine inquiries about Professor Vandike's death."

"You are? But there's no mystery—"

"We have to be sure," said Henry smoothly. "Get the loose ends tied up, as it were. You were a close friend of the professor's, weren't you?"

"I suppose you could say that, yes." Roger Talbot flushed a little. His skin was smooth and fair, like a girl's. "He was such a wonderful person," he added with a burst of genuine enthusiasm. "I mean, he was so much more than a teacher of law."

"I believe he taught you italic calligraphy."

"Yes. I use it all the time now."

"You need a special pen, I believe?"

"Not really," said Roger. "They make a fountain pen with a broad flat nib, which works very well. Look." He took a conventional-looking fountain pen out of his pocket, and wrote his name on a sheet of paper.

"Very elegant," said Henry.

"Of course, if you're a purist, like Harry, you keep a special stock of quill pens and inks. He liked to use sepia."

"I know."

"You know? How on earth—?"

"Never mind. Go on and tell me more about Professor Vandike."

"Well, he was a tremendous athlete, you know. Climbing, sailing, swimming—not the sort of things you'd associate with an academic type. And then there was his writing, you know, as well as the crosswords he compiled. Talk about an all-rounder."

Not believing that Talbot could be referring to Elaine Summerfield, Henry said, "When you say 'writing,' you mean literary criticism?"

"Oh, yes, that of course. But he was also working on a book, you know."

"Was he?" said Henry thoughtfully. "No, I didn't know that. Something pretty erudite, I imagine."

"Oh, I wouldn't say that," said Talbot. "It was a history of Oppenshaw and Trilby, the publishers. Old Oppenshaw more or less commissioned it, I gather, and of course they're—that is, they *were* going to publish it. Most of it is eighteenth-century stuff about Richard Trilby and the early days—but Harry was bringing it right up to date. The firm nearly failed after the Second World War, you know, and Oppenshaw stepped in and saved it. He was quite a junior member of the business at that time, but he had this great vision that if only he could buy the firm before it went bankrupt, he could make a great house of Trilby's again." Talbot's voice had taken on the fervor of someone expounding on his favorite subject. "It was touch-and-go, you know. If Oppenshaw hadn't been able to find the money just when he did, Trilby's would have gone bankrupt and simply disappeared."

"You seem to know a lot about the subject," said Henry.

"Well, I was doing research for Harry on it, actually." Talbot paused, and blushed again. "Actually, the money came from Oppenshaw's wife, although Harry's rather soft-pedaling that. I mean he *was*. You see, it was just after Oppenshaw got married that he was able to buy the firm. Another few weeks, and it would have been too late. But in Harry's manuscript, he just says that Robert Oppenshaw managed to raise the money at the last moment."

"What other research have you been doing for Vandike?" Henry asked.

"Oh, old documents and things. I was looking up facts about Carnworth—that's his estate on the Isle of Wight, you know. Harry used to go and stay there."

So this is the link I've been looking for, Henry thought. How easy, once you know. Quite casually, he said, "I expect you looked up for him how Sir Robert came by the property—just like the money, through his wife. Francis Warfield's will and all that."

"Yes, I got him a copy of the will. Didn't read it myself. As I told you, Harry was going gently on the fact that the money and the property came through Oppenshaw's wife. After all, it was Oppenshaw himself who pulled the firm together and made it what it is today. Who cares where the finance came from?" Talbot paused and cleared his throat. He said, "I think I know just how Harry was going to handle it. I even thought I might try to finish the book myself, now that Harry's . . . gone."

Henry said, "Well, I wish you luck. Now about the actual accident. You'd been at the Mountainside with Vandike for about a week?"

"Six days, actually."

"Did he get a lot of mail?"

Roger looked surprised. "Letters, you mean? No, nothing that I remember. Of course, he called the college and his London club several times to get messages."

"And were there messages?"

"I don't know. If there were, he never told me. He did make several phone calls, but I don't know to whom."

"I see," said Henry. "Now, about climbing gear."

"I hired mine from a shop in Aberwithy, but of course Harry had his own. First-rate stuff."

"But he didn't travel down to Wales in climbing kit?"

"Good Lord, no. He was wearing a dark suit, like a city gent. He had all his gear in a big suitcase."

Henry pretended to make a note. "It was on the Monday evening, was it, that he told you he was going to do the Devil's Chimney?"

"Yes. He'd cycled into Aberwithy to do some shopping after we came back from the mountain. He got back at dinnertime, and that was when he told me. I wanted to go with him, but he said it was much too difficult for a beginner like me. I don't suppose I could have saved him, but I'll never forgive myself for not going, all the same." The young man sounded near tears. "At least I'd have been able to raise the alarm sooner. As it was, I didn't do anything until nearly dinnertime, when it was far too late."

"He left the hotel early, didn't he?"

"I don't know when he left. I was asleep. He was certainly gone when I woke up at eight."

"Would you have expected the climb to take so long?" Henry asked.

"Not the Chimney itself, no. But there's quite a climb—well, more of a walk, really—to get there. Some people even do it by car, which Harry always said was cheating. And he said he was taking a picnic to eat at the top, and would take his time coming down. He said he might even stop off in the village for a beer. So I wasn't worried."

"Well, I think that's all, Mr. Talbot," said Henry. "Thank you. You've been very helpful."

Talbot smiled shyly. "I don't feel I've helped at all," he said, "but I must say I've enjoyed talking to you, sir, which is more than I expected." He flushed again. "I'm terribly sorry, I didn't mean . . . that is, I never thought I'd enjoy an interview at Scotland Yard."

"Most people don't," Henry assured him with a grin. "At least not the guilty ones."

When Talbot had gone, Henry telephoned the offices of Oppenshaw and Trilby. He seemed to remember that this was one of the two days in the week when Sir Robert was driven to London in the Bentley and actually did some work in his office. He was right, but Henry had to fight through a battery of secretaries and personal aides before he was finally connected with Oppenshaw himself.

Sir Robert was friendliness itself. "My dear Tibbett, how kind of you to call. What can I do for you?"

Remembering Emmy's account of her talk with Barbara, Henry was surprised at this geniality. He said, "Spare me a little of your valuable time, if you can, Sir Robert. I know you don't have very long in London, so I suppose that to suggest lunch would be—"

"Not possible, I'm much afraid, dear fellow. I am lunching with"—he mentioned a world-famous, best-selling American author—"who is here for a few days, and thinking of changing his publisher. This is in confidence, of course. He feels that his present people do not project a sufficiently—how shall I put it?—a sufficiently high-class image. I have ventured to suggest to him that Oppenshaw and Trilby might be just what he is looking for. So . . ."

Henry stemmed the flow. "That's why I was going to suggest a quick drink before your appointment. The bar of the Orangery, perhaps, if that would suit you."

There was a hesitation. Henry knew that Sir Robert must be curious to know what he had to say. He also knew that the choice of rendezvous, one of the most expensive and elegant restaurants in London, would intrigue him. It did. Sir Robert made up his mind. "Very well," he said. "I could make it at twelve, for half an hour or so. You did"—he hesitated—"you did mean the Orangery? The place just off Park Lane—never can remember the name of the street—"

"That's right," said Henry. "Thank you very much, Sir Robert. Twelve o'clock in the bar." He hoped very much that he would be able to charge the bill to petty cash.

Henry then put through a telephone call to the Isle of Wight, and had a pleasant conversation with Mrs. Turnberry. He intended to suggest to Oppenshaw that the Turnberrys should be invited to the weekend gathering, and he felt that they should be warned in advance that they might receive such an invitation. He imagined that since Peter's death there had been little communication between the two families.

Then, at twenty to twelve, he went out into Victoria Street to find a cab to take him to the Orangery.

Henry and Emmy were by no means part of the gilded aristocracy—nor of anything else gilded, for that matter—and he did not go to places like the Orangery every day. However, it had figured in a few other cases where he had dealt with wealthy people, and it was a place where he felt at home. The doorman greeted him like an old friend, and soon he was sitting at the empty bar (expense-account lunches started later than midday), waiting for his guest.

Sir Robert arrived at ten past twelve (the one-up position of the slightly late). The two men ordered drinks and took them to a corner table. Sir Robert glanced fleetingly at his slim gold watch.

Henry said, "This is really kind of you, Sir Robert. I know your time is precious, but I felt I must see you personally. You know that Barbara visited my wife yesterday afternoon?"

"She did mention it."

"With a very kind invitation for Emmy and me to spend next weekend at Carnworth. Naturally, we'll be delighted."

Sir Robert muttered something patently untrue about the pleasure being his.

Henry went on, "She said something else, however—something that has worried me very much."

"Indeed? What was that?"

"She said that you and Lady Oppenshaw, not to mention Barbara herself, were all very upset about some of my activities."

There was a ponderous silence while Sir Robert sipped his drink. Then he said, "Barbara always exaggerates a little—the artistic temperament. However, Tibbett, I don't mind telling you that I am a little disquieted. Not on my own account," he added hastily. "As you know, I've neither seen nor spoken to you since the inquest. No, my concern is for my authors."

"What have they been telling you?" Henry asked.

"Nothing directly. But they keep in touch—the members of the Guess Who club in particular—and I get news of them through Barbara. It seems that you have visited or spoken to them all, making insinuations that Peter Turnberry's death might not have been an accident. This has distressed them, very understandably. It provoked some sort of row between Bill and Fred, with the result that the new Freda Wright is badly behind its deadline. Myrtle got hold of some ridiculous idea that I am displeased with her work, and had a telephone conversation with my junior partner, which was highly unpleasant, not to say abusive. She is talking about taking her new book to another publisher. I think I shall be able to bring her around, but she's very temperamental, you know, despite her placid exterior."

"And poor Harry Vandike—" Henry began.

"A tragedy. A great tragedy." Sir Robert sighed heavily. "I

feel it deeply and personally, for he was an old friend. As far as Oppenshaw and Trilby is concerned, however, I hope you won't think me callous if I say that he is not such a loss as some of the others would be. The Elaine Summerfield books have a certain following, but Gothics are not in the tradition of the firm."

"I understand," said Henry, "that he was writing a book for you, under his own name. A history of Oppenshaw and Trilby."

"That's quite true," agreed Oppenshaw. "Fortunately it was almost complete when he died. I can easily find a competent authority to finish it off from Harry's notes."

"The young man who was doing the research for Harry is very keen to—" Henry saw no harm in putting in a word for Roger Talbot.

However, Sir Robert cut him short. "I said an *author*, Tibbett. I have received a letter from the boy. He is a mere undergraduate, with no expertise, no technique. Out of the question." He paused and cleared his throat, indicating a change of subject. "Now, to revert. Of all my authors, my greatest anxiety is for Barbara. I am speaking now as a publisher, not as a father. The Lydia Drake books are enjoying a considerable vogue at the moment, and she has told me in so many words that she finds it impossible to write under these conditions."

"What conditions?"

"To be blunt, Tibbett, the fact that Scotland Yard seems to think that a member of the Guess Who club may be a murderer. I have told her not to be silly, that no official steps have been taken or even hinted at, that the verdict of the coroner's jury was final, and so on. But it's no good. The doubt remains. She has not written one word since the Carnworth week."

"I'm awfully sorry about all this," said Henry meekly. "I do realize that my pesky curiosity may have upset people. I'm afraid I didn't stop to think of it like that. However, I can assure you that the whole thing is now cleared up in my mind." He paused. "Since I have offended these people, I really wanted to see you in order to ask a favor of you."

"A favor?"

"You have kindly invited Emmy and me for the weekend, and I understand that Barbara will also be at Carnworth. Would it be asking too much if you were to reconstitute the Carnworth literary weekend—as far as that's possible?"

"I'm afraid I don't understand, Tibbett."

"I feel I owe you and your authors an explanation," Henry said. "If I could meet them again, all together, I could set their minds at rest. If you would indulge me, and invite—"

"I can't reconstitute that weekend," said Sir Robert, "as you know very well. Peter Turnberry and Harry Vandike are both dead."

"That's unfortunately true," said Henry, "but you could invite Fred Coe and William Cartwright and Myrtle. And—I hope I'm not presuming—I think it would be a gracious gesture to let Peter's parents in on this. Then everybody concerned can go about their business with no worries. Everything will be over."

"Everything will be over," Sir Robert repeated. There was a long silence. Then he said, "There's something in it, I suppose." Another hesitation, then he made up his mind. "Very well, Tibbett. I'll do it. Of course, I can't guarantee that they'll all be free to come."

"I think they'll accept," said Henry.

Ignoring this, Sir Robert said, "And now I really must be off, or I shall be late for my luncheon guest. Thanks for the drink, Tibbett. I'll get my secretary to arrange the other matter. Oh—and just let her know what time you'll be arriving on Saturday, and whether you want to be met. She'll fix it all. Good-bye till then, Mr. Tibbett."

18

Henry and Emmy did not need to be met. They drove down on Saturday morning, taking the now familiar car ferry from Portsmouth to Fishbourne and the beautiful coast road.

Carnworth Manor looked as serene as ever in the pale sunlight of early September. As before, the Tibbetts were met at the front door, but this time by Sowerby, the butler. There was no sign of the Oppenshaws. As before, their suitcases were whisked away, and their car was driven around to the parking area near the stables.

They had been given the same blue bedroom, and it was with a shock of déjà vu that Henry, looking out of the window, saw two figures on horseback riding through the dappled greenery of the park. Indeed, one was Barbara—but beside her, instead of Peter Turnberry, was Sir Robert himself, mounted on the big bay.

Combing her curly brown hair in front of the dressing-table mirror, Emmy said, "I'm still completely in the dark, darling. What are you going to do?"

Hernry grinned. "I told you. Stage a classic detective story ending."

"I don't see how—"

"You don't have to see how." Henry kissed the back of her neck. "It would spoil it all. Just leave it to me."

"I know," said Emmy gloomily. "You think if you told me, I'd go and put my foot in it and give everything away."

"I never said that."

"You meant it, though." Emmy turned to him, smiling. "All right, darling, play it your own way. I'm just here for the ride."

"Oh, no," said Henry seriously. "You have an important part to play."

"I do? Then you might tell me about it."

"You'll find out soon enough," he assured her. "Now let's go down and see if we can get a drink before lunch."

Fellow guests from the mainland had evidently made an early start, or perhaps come down on Friday evening, for Fred Coe, Bill Cartwright, and Myrtle Waterford were already in the drawing room, chatting over drinks with Lady Oppenshaw.

"Ah, there you are! The guests of honor. Come on in, Henry and Emmy. No need for introductions. Let me get you a drink." Pamela sounded lighthearted enough, but it struck Emmy that there was a brittle edge to her voice. "That means that when Robert and Barbara come in from their ride, we can have lunch. Now, what's it to be?"

Pouring two glasses of pale sherry for the Tibbetts, she went on, speaking almost in an aside to Henry, "The Turnberrys aren't coming until after lunch. And they're not staying here, naturally."

"Naturally," Henry agreed. He accepted his drink and turned back to the rest of the party.

"So, no more sleuthing, eh?" remarked Coe genially.

"No, that's all finished," Henry said.

"Quite a relief, although we might have got a book out of it. Ah, well, Bill will be coming up with a good plot for Miss Twinkley once all this is over. Isn't that so?" he added to his co-author; any bad blood between the two men seemed to have vanished.

"I will do my best." Dr. Cartwright was as prim and precise as ever.

Myrtle said, rather too loudly, "Such a shame that Harry can't be with us."

"Yes, indeed," said Fred. "He'd have enjoyed hearing the Chief Superintendent's exposition no end. Fitted it all together like a crossword puzzle, have you, Tibbett?"

"Something like that," Henry agreed.

Lady Oppenshaw was saying to Emmy, "I can't tell you what a relief it will be to have all this wretched suspicion out of the way. Don't think I'm blaming your husband—he has his job to do—but I've been really worried about Robert and Barbara. And the others, of course."

Soon afterward, Sir Robert and Barbara came in, still in their riding clothes. They had a quick drink and went up to change. A few minutes later the whole party sat down to a cold lunch. Although the subject of Peter Turnberry was not mentioned, there was a general air of expectancy throughout the meal. Only Myrtle seemed nervous. She ate little, and when she spoke, it was too loudly. Lady Oppenshaw, however, kept up a flow of easy conversation, while Barbara looked both angry and sulky. The others all appeared to be in good form.

After the meal, they went back into the drawing room. It was arranged as it had been for the Guess Who meeting, with chairs in a semicircle facing the same little Georgian table. This time, however, there was also a chair at the table. The lecture was expected to be less formal than that of the previous occasion.

Henry sat down at the table, as the others bustled in a hap-hazard pattern, seating themselves. Emmy sat as far back as possible, and wondered what her role was to be. When everybody was settled, Henry smiled at his audience.

"Just like old times," he said. "Sorry to keep you waiting, but Mr. and Mrs. Turnberry have not yet arrived."

"Is that important?" asked Sir Robert "Surely they can't be—"

"It's very important, I'm afraid, Sir Robert," Henry said. "You see, as I go through this story, I'm going to ask some or all of you to corroborate both my facts and my theories with your testimony. And that of the Turnberrys is vital. I shall also need Mr. Timmond to come in for a short time."

"So you told me," said Sir Robert. "He's waiting in the kitchen, and he'll come as soon as I ring."

Almost at once came the peal of the front doorbell, and a moment later Sowerby was ushering Mr. and Mrs. Turnberry into the drawing room. They looked stiff, formal, and ill at ease, dressed in their Sunday best.

Pamela Oppenshaw rose immediately to greet them. "Nora, my dear . . . and James . . . come along in . . . Now let me see, Robert and Barbara you know, of course, and I believe you've met the Tibbetts. Now this is Mrs. Waterford . . ."

Introductions were made, and the Turnberrys took their places in the semicircle.

"Right," said Henry. "Now we can begin. The difficulty is to know exactly where. I think it's best to go right back to the death of Mr. Francis Warfield, first husband of Lady Oppenshaw, and the owner of a considerable fortune, including this property of Carnworth."

If any of the group were surprised, they did not show it. The Turnberrys looked uncomprehending, and Sir Robert put his hand over his wife's in a protective gesture. Otherwise there was no reaction.

Henry went on. "Mr. Warfield had a daughter by a previous marriage—Eugenia, known as Jeannie. She was fifteen when he died. Now we come to the crux of the matter—Mr. Warfield's will. It left an outright but not large sum to his widow. The rest—including Carnworth Manor—was also willed to the widowed Mrs. Warfield for her lifetime, provided that she did not remarry. Should she do so, everything would revert to Jeannie on her twenty-first birthday."

Sir Robert had turned purple. "Really, Mr. Tibbett, is it necessary to go into all this?"

"Yes, I'm afraid it is," said Henry. "I'm sure that everybody here will treat it in confidence. As I was saying, if Mrs. Warfield did not remarry, then Jeannie would have to wait until her stepmother's death to inherit. That is quite a usual arrangement. However, there was another strange clause. It stated should Eugenia die before the age of twenty-one, all bequests relating to her should apply to any child she might leave, legitimate or not. In other words, the child would inherit immediately if Mrs. Warfield remarried, otherwise on her death."

"It sounds very peculiar to me," remarked Myrtle.

"It was a strange provision to make on behalf of a fifteen-year-old girl," Henry agreed. "Mr. Warfield may have had a reason—but we shall never know it. What we do know is that within two years of Mr. Warfield's death, his widow did remarry, and became Mrs.—now Lady—Oppenshaw. Her second husband and his little girl, Barbara, moved into this house, and the new ménage was set up.

"Now, on the face of it, this meant that Jeannie's death before her twenty-first birthday would be of great benefit to Sir Robert and Lady Oppenshaw. There was, of course, no question of her leaving a child."

In a choked voice, Pamela Oppenshaw said, "If you think that we'd have murdered Jeannie . . . especially when we knew she had so little time . . ."

"So little time?" Dr. Cartwright spoke sharply, puzzled.

Henry appealed to Pamela Oppenshaw, who was now sitting with her handkerchief pressed to her eyes. "Lady Oppenshaw, your husband told me the truth in great confidence. Now that you have mentioned it, do you agree that I should tell these people? After all, it was a long time ago."

Without removing the handkerchief from her eyes, Pamela Oppenshaw nodded.

Henry went on, "Well, the sad truth is that Jeannie, although outwardly healthy, was suffering from a fatal disease—multiple sclerosis. She might well never have survived to her twenty-first birthday. The Oppenshaws' one idea was to make her last years as happy and carefree as possible—and they were succeeding. Jeannie obviously got on well with her stepfather and adored her new little sister. The family was very close—the more so, perhaps, because of the impending tragedy that only the parents knew about.

"Meanwhile, under Mr. Oppenshaw's guidance, the old firm of Trilby & Son, now Oppenshaw and Trilby, was beginning to flourish. Not many years later, Mr. Oppenshaw became Sir Robert, recognized by a grateful country for his services to literature. Nevertheless, when Jeannie drowned just as the purchase deal for the firm was going through, it was more than a personal tragedy for the Oppenshaws. It put them in what might be an awkward position vis-à-vis anybody who knew about Mr. Warfield's will.

"Consequently—I am now guessing, and need confirmation—I think it was decided not to mention the fact that the house and estate had not been Sir Robert's all along. A simple and harmless deception, to protect the family and its integrity." Henry turned to Sir Robert. "Am I right, sir?"

Oppenshaw, still holding his wife's hand, had listened in silence, his face darkening with anger and embarrassment. He said, "Since you ask me, and I am an honest man, I must admit that you are right. After Jeannie's death, Pamela and I decided to refer to Carnworth as my house. We saw no harm in it."

"None whatsoever," Henry assured him. "Right. Now, for a complete change of scene, we go to the University of Oxford, and the late Professor Harold Vandike."

A little ripple of a sigh went through the room. Whether it was relief at a change of subject or mourning for Vandike, it was hard to tell.

Henry went on. "You all knew Harry Vandike. And when I say 'all,' I include Mr. and Mrs. Turnberry. Correct?"

Nora and James Turnberry nodded in unison, like mechanical dolls.

"That being so," said Henry, "you also knew that he was brilliant and entertaining, but had a streak of near-sadism in him. He delighted in practical jokes, some of them very cruel.

"As a young lawyer, he arranged a number of private adoptions for people who did not care to go through adoption agencies. Among his clients were Mr. and Mrs. Turnberry."

Again the two heads nodded in unison.

"They were recommended to him by a doctor who was treating Mr. Turnberry for an ear complaint. Dr. William Cartwright, in fact."

"Nothing wrong about that, is there?" demanded Cartwright. "What did I know about adoptions? I told them to consult a lawyer, and Vandike came to mind. I had known him at the university."

"Good so far," said Henry. "Vandike produced a little boy for the Turnberrys—Peter. Incidentally, the Turnberrys lived in Ealing in those days and had no connection whatsoever with the Isle of Wight. As is usual in these cases, only the lawyer knows the identity of both the true and adoptive parents, and it is a grave breach of legal ethics to divulge this knowledge. So I have no idea who Peter Turnberry's real parents were. Nor did he, nor do Mr. and Mrs. Turnberry. And his real parents, wherever they may be, have no idea that it was their son who was killed—even if they happened to read of Peter's death in the paper. The break is made clean and complete, as it should be. The only evidence of identity lies safely locked up in a lawyer's office.

"So matters stood, and life went on quietly. Barbara grew up, and turned out to be a talented writer. Dr. Cartwright, an old family friend, started to collaborate with Professor Coe on the Freda Wright books—just as a joke at first, I suspect. Naturally, Dr. Cartwright submitted them to Sir Robert, who saw possibilities in Miss Twinkley. The indefatigable Harry Vandike, another old friend of the Oppenshaws, was pursuing his career at Oxford, compiling crosswords and writing literary criticism, excelling as an athlete, and also producing the Elaine Summerfield Gothic novels. Sir Robert hinted to me the other day that Oppenshaw and Trilby published them more out of friendship than admiration, although I know they have a big public among what I believe are known as class-C readers."

There was a small laugh at this.

Henry went on. "Mrs. Waterford and Tex Lawrie were a different matter, I imagine," Henry said, on a slight note of interrogation.

Myrtle said, "I didn't know any of these people, Mr. Tibbett. I had the idea for the first Tex Lawrie book because I was bored and had time on my hands."

"And you were longing for excitement—even at second hand?"

"I suppose so. Anyhow, I submitted it to Oppenshaw and Trilby, and they took it—on the understanding that I changed to a masculine pen name."

"Good," said Henry. "Just as I expected. Now we come right

up to date, to a fact that is certainly known to the Oppenshaws, and maybe to others of you as well."

"What fact is that?" demanded Fred Coe.

"The fact," said Henry, "that Vandike, under his own name, was writing a history of the publishing house of Oppenshaw and Trilby, with emphasis on the career in the eighteenth century of the pioneer publisher Richard Trilby. However, towards the end of the book, he wanted to pay tribute to his friend Sir Robert, and so described how the firm was saved from near-failure after World War II, and was reborn as Oppenshaw and Trilby. Vandike had a young man doing research for him, the undergraduate with whom he was spending a holiday when he died. I have spoken to this young man. He tells me that in the course of his research, he looked up Mr. Francis Warfield's will and got a copy of it for Vandike.

"Now we come back to that impish sense of humor. Impish and unkind. Peter Turnberry, whom Vandike knew very well to be adopted, had won his way to Oxford and become one of Professor Vandike's favorite pupils. In the meantime, the Turnberrys had moved to the Isle of Wight, quite close to Carnworth. Vandike worked out the scenario for a practical joke, with his usual mixture of wit and cruelty. He told Peter Turnberry that he was, in fact, the illegitimate son of Jeannie Warfield, and so the rightful owner of Carnworth and the entire inheritance. But, Vandike explained, his own lips were sealed. As a lawyer, he could not make this knowledge public. Under present law, as you are probably aware, an adopted child is entitled to know the identity of his real parents. But that was not the case when Harold Vandike quite improperly told Peter Turnberry who he was. Left to himself, Peter would never even have known that he was adopted, for Mr. and Mrs. Turnberry had decided never to tell him. Vandike, however, supplied Peter with some spurious documents, intended to support his claim. He also suggested that in the event that he failed to make the claim stick legally, Peter could always marry Barbara, and thus come into his inheritance by the back door, as it were."

Barbara looked up, her eyes blazing. "I knew it!" she said.

"That was the only reason he ever proposed to me. And that's why I chucked him."

"Chucked him?" exclaimed Mrs. Turnberry, suddenly sitting upright.

"Yes. The evening before his accident, I broke the engagement. Mother knew all about it, didn't you, Mother?"

Pamela nodded sadly. "I was hoping it was just a lovers' tiff, and that it would blow over. But then poor Peter was killed, and there seemed no point in . . ."

"The crossword puzzle," Henry went on, "was, of course, Vandike's idea. He knew I was coming here as guest speaker, and the notion of sending me a classic murder puzzle was too tempting to resist. He had it all worked out in his mind—how Barbara had drowned her stepsister, even though she was only six. How Peter was the true heir. He was hoping that I would unravel not just the crossword and the other foolish red herrings, but the heart of this manufactured mystery. Peter was a sort of protégé of Vandike's, and naturally knew all about the crossword. What he did not know was that Vandike was playing a cruel joke on him. He really believed himself to be the Carnworth heir.

"Of course, Vandike forbade him to produce the spurious papers he had prepared, on the grounds that it would ruin him—Vandike—if it was known that he had shown them to anybody in the days when it was illegal to do so. So Peter, more and more frustrated, decided to take the second suggested course, and proposed marriage to Barbara. It seemed a reasonable arrangement. They both loved horses, and seemed on the surface to be an ideal couple. However, Miss Oppenshaw is a very sensitive and intelligent young lady, and she soon began to realize that Peter Turnberry was more in love with her inheritance than with her."

Henry turned to James and Nora Turnberry. "I'm very sorry to have to say this, Mrs. Turnberry, but I'm afraid it's true."

James Turnberry started to mutter something angrily, but his wife restrained him with a gentle hand on his arm. She said, "I know it's true, Mr. Tibbett. It made me very unhappy. Sometimes I felt that I didn't know Peter at all, especially after he went to Oxford and did so well. It was as though his life was one of those rock climbs he used to do, and he was determined to get to the top. He seemed to think Father and I were dragging him down. Of course, I didn't know anything about this inheritance business, but I don't mind telling you I never did think Professor Vandike was a good influence on the boy."

"You were quite right, Mrs. Turnberry," said Henry seriously. "In any case, Peter began to have a shrewd suspicion that Barbara was going to break the engagement—so he had an idea of his own. He came to Carnworth for the Guess Who week and went around to the various authors, trying to peddle Vandike's story in a slightly fictionalized form, as an idea for a plot. I suppose he had some sort of a Hamlet-like notion—'The book's the thing in which I'll catch the conscience of . . .' Well, never mind. Nobody bought his plot, although I understand Fred Coe did consider it.

"On that Friday evening, Barbara broke her engagement. Peter was then staking everything on my interpretation of the crossword, with its very explicit clues—'Peter holds the keys,' 'Hope Barbara has an alibi,' and so forth. I'm afraid I let him down. I solved the puzzle all right, and I guessed your pen names correctly. As far as I was concerned, the joke was over. It wasn't, however, for Peter, who wanted me to reveal him as the true heir to Carnworth, nor for Vandike, who wanted me to do the same, so that he could explode the whole balloon and make both Peter and me look extremely foolish.

"So, after our meeting here, as you all remember, Peter made an appointment to see me privately at five, skipped lunch, and rode as fast as he could on Melisande to his parents' house."

"Why on earth didn't he take one of the cars?" Sir Robert was genuinely astonished. "He only had to ask—"

"Because," said Henry, "he'd had his license suspended for speeding. He had to go on horseback. He rode posthaste to St. Lawrence, barely said hello to his parents, ran up to his room, and collected something—something small enough to put in his pocket. Obviously the papers purporting to prove that he was

Jeannie Warfield's child." Henry paused. "They were not found on his body. That made me suspicious for a start.

"Then there was the question of why the mare, Melisande, took so long to get home. Peter was hurrying his ride along the cliff path to get back here by five, and according to his parents he left their house in time to do so. That means the accident took place well before five, and yet Melisande didn't get home till nearly half past six. I was intrigued, and went to the stables to have a word with Mr. Timmond, the groom." Henry turned to Sir Robert. "Would you mind?"

"Certainly," Sir Robert said. He got up, went over to an electric bell near the fireplace, and rang it.

In a few seconds Timmond came in, cap in hand and awkward away from his own surroundings. He stood by the door, saying nothing. Henry gave him a big smile, and got a ghost of a grin in return.

"Mr. Timmond," said Henry, "I won't keep you for more than a minute. You remember the day Mr. Turnberry died?"

"Very well indeed, sir."

"Then would you tell these good people about the conversation you had with me that evening?"

Timmond looked briefly at Sir Robert, who nodded. He said, "You came around to the stables, sir, at about seven o'clock in the evening. I was still giving Melly her rubdown. In a proper state, she was. I told you, Mr. Tibbett, sir, that I didn't believe the girth had broken—she'd come home without her saddle, see? I also showed you a piece of frayed old rope attached to her bridle. It was my belief that somebody had tied her up after Mr. Peter fell, and that it had taken her an hour or more of plunging and rearing to break the rope and get away. That's why she were all of a lather."

"And the next morning?" Henry prompted.

"The next morning, sir, I went out with Sir Robert to ride the cliff path and try to find out what had happened. Well, there was the saddle, with the girth broken, right on the edge of the cliff—and though there were trees on the other side of the path, there wasn't any broken rope-end tied to any of them. So I reckoned I'd been wrong after all."

"Thank you very much, Mr. Timmond," said Henry. "That's all."

Timmond tugged at his forelock and took his leave.

Henry said, "I got up very early next morning, and visited the site of the accident myself. When I got there, about five-thirty, the saddle was lying under the trees, not at the edge of the cliff—and there was a piece of old rope, which seemed to match the one on Melisande's bridle, tied to one of the trees. I didn't touch anything. I simply came away. But clearly somebody else visited the spot between the time I was there and the time Sir Robert and Timmond arrived, because by then the rope had gone and the saddle had been moved. I may add that I was under the impression that the girth had been cut and ripped."

A murmur of surprise ran around the room, a little interrogatory buzz. Henry went on, "I reported all this to the local police, but apparently Sergeant Hemming is all for a quiet life. He didn't call me to give evidence at the inquest. Everything went like clockwork. Accidental death. But I'm afraid I'm a stubborn character. I couldn't let the thing alone. So I started bothering you people.

"I learned a lot of interesting things. About Francis Warfield's will, and about Peter's adoption having been arranged by Vandike. I also had an absorbing conversation with Harry Vandike the day he died."

There was dead silence. Everybody seemed to be holding their breath.

Henry continued, "He told his young friend that he was going for a solitary climb, and left his hotel early, in climbing gear. Actually he cycled to the nearest town, where he had hired a car the day before, and drove to London, stopping at Myrtle Waterford's house on the way to change into the city clothes that he had in his rucksack. He lunched with me, early, and then drove back, stopping again at Myrtle's to resume his climbing clothes."

"Then how did he die?" demanded Sir Robert. "A motor smash? No—the police would have—"

Henry said, "I admit I'm guessing now, but I think he died just as everybody thinks—by a fall from the Devil's Chimney, which he climbed after he got back, at dusk, and when he was tired. I'm told that you can drive—or bicycle—to a spot very near the start of the climb."

"Had the hired car been turned in?" demanded Dr. Cartwright.

"Yes. So he must have cycled. Whether his fall was accidental or not, we'll never know. However, he knew that I was very close behind him by then."

"Close behind him? What do you mean?" Fred Coe asked brusquely.

"I let him know indirectly," said Henry, "that I knew he was responsible for Peter Turnberry's death."

"Harry was?" Myrtle sounded incredulous.

"Yes. You see, he heard, as you all did, Peter making that appointment to see me. He also knew that Peter then went riding breakneck to St. Lawrence. It could only mean that he had gone to collect the so-called evidence, which Vandike knew was false. He couldn't afford to have those papers seen by a policeman. So he decided to intercept Peter on the cliff path during his ride back."

Pamela Oppenshaw said, frowning, "But if I remember rightly, Harry was out sailing that afternoon."

"Quite correct," said Henry. "Emmy and I were on the beach, and saw him. Sir Robert had asked him to stay inside the bay, but he didn't. The last we saw of him, he was rounding the point in the direction of Smuggler's Cove and the old path up the cliff. He could easily have beached the boat there—even the big lifeboat can get in—and the climb would have been nothing to him. He told me himself he had done it before."

"So what do you think happened then?" Dr. Cartwright was leaning forward, immensely interested.

"I think," he said, "that he stationed himself under the trees and waited. When he heard Melisande's hooves approaching, he came out and stood on the path. Peter would naturally have reined in the horse and asked what he wanted.

"Harry must then have demanded the papers, and I imagine Peter refused to give them up. Vandike was a great athlete and very strong. I expect he actually manhandled Turnberry off the

216

horse, and there was a fight. Of course, we'll never know the details, but Peter must have slipped and gone over the cliff to his death.

"Vandike had to cover up. He slit the girth and ripped it, hiding under the trees to do so. The rope must have come from the boat. Melisande wouldn't have galloped for home while there was somebody she knew around. It would have been easy enough to tether her—with a rope he knew would part quite soon. Then back down the cliff to extract the precious papers from Turnberry's body, and quickly up sails and away to establish his alibi.

"I think Peter's death probably *was* an accident, although a court might not agree. Sometime during the night, Vandike must have remembered the rope-end, and that the saddle was in the wrong place. He got up early—but I beat him to it. Emmy heard a car starting up and leaving by the back gate sometime after I'd gone—didn't you, Emmy?"

"Yes, I did," said Emmy.

"Vandike didn't have his own car with him," Henry added, "so he must have borrowed one. He drove as near as he could to the cliff path, walked to the scene of the accident, removed the rope, and put the saddle on the cliff edge, ready for Sir Robert and Timmond to find."

Henry looked around the circle of faces. "Well, ladies and gentlemen, that's it. That's my conclusion. Since the verdicts on both Peter Turnberry and Harold Vandike are basically correct—wrong only in matters of detail—I see no reason to interfere with them. The case—which has never been a case—is closed."

Immediately a babble of conversation broke out. It was abundantly clear that a great weight had been lifted from everybody's shoulders, and the mood was one of joyful and mutual congratulation.

Only the Turnberrys did not share it. James Turnberry, his head bowed, was muttering to himself, "The professor. Who'd ever have thought that the professor—"

Henry went up to him and put a hand on his shoulder. "I'm sorry," he said. "I thought you should know." He gave the shoulder a little pat.

Nora Turnberry said, "Come along, Father. Best be getting home." And to Pamela, "Thank you for having us, Lady Oppenshaw."

Later, in the privacy of their room, Emmy said to Henry, "That wasn't true, was it? What you said down in the drawing room?"

"No, not all of it. Some of it."

"And some of them know it wasn't true."

"That was my idea," Henry admitted.

"Also," Emmy remarked, "I don't seem to have played my role yet."

"Your role," said Henry, "comes tomorrow. Pray for fine weather."

19

Henry's prayers were answered. The next morning dawned dewy and slightly hazy, promising heat to come.

At breakfast, with all the guests assembled over eggs and coffee, Henry said, "I've got just one more thing I'd like to show you, before we go our separate ways."

"To show us? Whatever do you mean?" Myrtle spoke with a forkful of fried egg and toast halfway to her mouth.

Henry smiled. "Just to demonstrate that my theory is correct."

"Well, what do you want us to do?" Fred Coe sounded mildly amused. He was making a hearty breakfast, trotting to and from the sideboard, lifting silver covers to find yet more goodies.

Henry said, "It's nothing at all complicated. As you can see, it's a beautiful day. Emmy and I are going down to the beach and I'd like to make a party of it. I spoke to Sir Robert last night, and he's having a hamper of snacks and drinks delivered down there."

"What an extraordinary request," said Bill Cartwright. He looked a little uneasy. "What is supposed to happen on the beach?"

"Nothing really," said Henry. "Just a small demonstration."

"Oh, well," said Myrtle, "we've gone along with you so far, I suppose we'll have to say yes."

"Personally," said Coe, "I can't think of anything nicer. I'd been thinking of a swim anyway, and the idea of food and drink makes it even more attractive. We can talk over that Miss Twinkley idea you were roughing out last night, eh, Bill?"

"I suppose so," said Cartwright, with little enthusiasm.

Barbara Oppenshaw was sitting silently; the plate of food that she had just brought to the table lay untasted.

Henry said cheerfully, "Good. That's settled, then. Sir Robert can't come himself, but Lady Oppenshaw is to come by car with the chaps who are delivering the food. The road passes quite close to the beach, you know, although many people don't realize it. There's a right-of-way down, which hardly anybody uses." Henry paused. "Shall we say eleven o'clock at the beach, then?"

There was a general murmur of consent, in which Barbara Oppenshaw did not join.

Pleasantly, Henry said, "You'll be there, won't you, Barbara?"

"I . . . no. I don't see why you need me."

"I need you very much," said Henry.

Barbara turned on him. "You know very well that I haven't been down there since—"

"I know," said Henry gently. "That's why it's so important, you see. To lay the ghosts, once and for all. Please, Barbara."

"Very well." The words were barely audible, as if whispered by a child. "Very well, I'll come."

After breakfast, the members of the party went about their various pursuits. Henry made a phone call to the Turnberrys. Dr. Cartwright wrote a letter. Fred Coe read a book and Myrtle went for a walk. Barbara sat silently in her old nursery, stroking the battered teddy bear as she gazed out the window at the path she had not taken for nearly twenty years. The path to the sea.

Henry and Emmy changed into swimsuits, with shorts and shirts as cover-ups, and armed themselves with bath towels. As they came downstairs, they met Dr. Cartwright going up.

"What about the Turnberrys?" he asked. "Are they joining your beach party, Tibbett?"

"No," said Henry. "I've just spoken to Nora Turnberry. They always go to church on Sunday morning, and there didn't seem any reason to upset their routine."

220

Emmy thought Cartwright looked a little relieved. However, all he said was, "Going down already? You're early."

"Thought we might have a quiet swim," Henry said cheerfully.

"Mysteries, mysteries," said Dr. Cartwright. "I think you've been reading too many sensational stories, Tibbett."

"In my profession, I don't have the time," answered Henry with a smile, and he and Emmy went on their way.

On the pathway down to the beach, Henry explained to Emmy what he wanted her to do.

"Is that all?" she asked, surprised. "That's nothing at all."

Henry hesitated, then said, "Look, darling, I'm only going to tell you this. Whatever happens, you'll be in no danger. Do you understand? No danger at all, so don't panic. I know what I'm doing."

The path to the sea ran down through a dense copse, so that it was with a shock of surprise, like coming out of a dim room into sunlight, that one found oneself suddenly on the beach. At the far end of the crescent of sand, the right-of-way from the road debouched in the same way—but it was considerably more overgrown and less used than the path from Carnworth Manor.

Henry and Emmy stripped down to swimsuits and took a leisurely swim in the quietly rippling water. Only small waves broke onto the sheltered beach, and the water temperature was pleasant. Henry noted and pointed out to Emmy that the water remained quite shallow—about waist-high—for some fifty yards out; after that, there was a sudden steep drop off that took them both out of their depth by some feet.

As the Tibbetts waded back to the beach, other members of the party began to gather. Fred and Bill came together, in close conversation. Myrtle came alone, carrying a large beach bag from which she extracted a towel, a tube of anti-sunburn cream, and a women's magazine. She put on dark glasses, sat down on the towel, and began to read. It was obvious that she had no intention of swimming, for she wore the same flowered cotton dress as at breakfast time.

It occurred to Emmy that every time they had seen Myrtle, she had been alone, either physically so, in her own house, or

221

palpably isolated from the rest of the group, as at Carnworth. Presumably Mr. Waterford, the bank manager, did exist and did come home in the evenings, but Myrtle remained in Emmy's mind as essentially a solitary person.

Fred Coe and Bill Cartwright went in for a quick, brisk swim and came out of the water still talking earnestly. They settled down to sunbathe some distance from both Myrtle and the Tibbetts.

The next arrival was Pamela Oppenshaw, who came down the right-of-way path, pushing aside trailing branches and thick undergrowth to get to the beach. She was followed by two men, the Carnworth chauffeur and presumably a gardener. Between them they carried a big hamper and an even bigger ice chest. Everybody scrambled to their feet and made suitable noises of welcome and gratitude. The chauffeur then returned to the car for a folding table, and then, having set it up reasonably steadily, helped the gardener hoist the ice chest and hamper onto it. The helpers then withdrew.

Pamela Oppenshaw was certainly dressed for a beach party. Her beautifully preserved figure was showed to great advantage in a black and white striped swimsuit, over which she wore a frothy white lace and nylon cover-up. Her beach towel was enormous and jet black, with HERS monogrammed in white, and long white fringes. She seemed to be outfitted for the Riviera, Sardinia, or the Caribbean, rather than for the more austere waters of the English Channel. However, it was a lovely day, and the sea for once was reflecting the blue of a cloudless sky, so by a hairsbreadth Lady Oppenshaw avoided looking ridiculous.

"You must all come and have a drink," she cried, "and I believe Cook has made us some snacks. Let's see what we have. Fred, you open up the ice chest. Henry, see what's in the hamper. And I'll—" She broke off suddenly. "What's that?"

"What's what?" asked Fred, who was struggling with the complicated clamps holding the cover on the ice chest.

"Up there in the woods . . . there's somebody up there!"

Henry said, "I expect it's Barbara, Lady Oppenshaw."

"Barbara!"

"Yes," said Henry. "There she is. Come on, Barbara. You're just in time for a drink."

Barbara Oppenshaw was standing in the shadow of the trees, just short of the beach. It was as though she could not bring herself to take the final step out into the sunshine.

"Wonders will never cease," remarked Lady Oppenshaw. "Well, come on, Barbara, or don't. You can't just stand there all day."

Fred Coe had got the top off the ice chest, and was taking orders for drinks. The chest held cold white wine, beer, and various pre-mixed cocktails in plastic containers. Disposable plastic glasses had also been provided.

Henry and Emmy took wine, Pamela and Bill Cartwright a Bloody Mary apiece, and Fred a beer. Myrtle asked a little ostentatiously for "anything non-alcoholic—orange juice, preferably," and was told that there was no such thing, unless she waited for some ice to melt and drank the water. Having made her gesture, however, she accepted a large glass of Pimm's No. 1, and contrived to make it appear a sacrifice to do so.

Barbara, meanwhile, still hovered on the edge of the woods. Pamela Oppenshaw called again, impatiently, "For heaven's sake, Baba, come on and have a drink. You're behaving like a baby."

The predictable result was to drive Barbara farther back into the shadows. Henry filled a glass with the Bloody Mary mixture, and carried it over to where she stood. He was reminded of coaxing a small and very scared cat down from a tree. The others, meanwhile, were merrily exploring the contents of the hamper, where Cook had given of her bounty in the way of cheese straws and caviar canapés.

Henry held out the glass and said, "I know this is difficult for you, Barbara."

"You shouldn't have made me come." It was the same child-ish whisper as at the breakfast table.

"You had to come," Henry said. "You know that. You can't go through life with things you can never face. Take a drink, and come on out."

Tentatively she took the glass. Then, with a sudden gesture, she drained it and stepped forward onto the sand.

Once she had joined the party, Barbara seemed to get over her inhibitions and behave quite normally. Food and drink were handed around, and talk was general. Nobody mentioned Henry's promised demonstration; indeed, it seemed to have been forgotten. After some time, Henry glanced at his watch—which fortunately was waterproof, as he had, as usual, forgotten to take it off while swimming. Half past eleven. For just a moment he hesitated, hating what he was about to do, but knowing it must be done. Then he looked at Emmy and gave a tiny nod.

Very casually, Emmy detached herself from Fred Coe, who had been expounding, as authors will, on the general unfairness of contracts and the rapacity of publishers and printers. In her plain dark blue swimsuit, she sauntered down to the sea and into the calm water. She stood for a moment, and then seemed about to start swimming.

At that moment, the figure of a man in a black wetsuit and wearing a snorkel mask darted out of the trees near the right-of-way path. He flung himself into the sea and made for Emmy. The rest of the party had stopped eating and drinking, and were watching in amazed silence. Only Emmy, her face buried in the water as she swam out, was unaware that anything was happening. Then the man grabbed Emmy and began pulling her out into the deep water, at the same time pushing her under.

Two screams came simultaneously. One from Emmy, who had been taken entirely by surprise. The second, a wail of utter anguish from Barbara.

Running for the shelter of the trees, she screamed, "Daddy! Daddy, don't! Jeannie . . . please, Daddy, don't! Don't!"

Pamela Oppenshaw was standing on the beach in her ridiculously elaborate outfit, looking as if she had been hit in the face. The mysterious man released Emmy, who surfaced spluttering. Quite slowly and very deliberately, the man pushed back the snorkel mask to reveal his face. Even without the beard, there was no doubt. It was Harold Vandike.

Pamela Oppenshaw came to life. She whirled to face Henry.

"You devil," she said quietly. "I could kill you."

"I hope," said Henry, "that there'll be no more killing now."

She did not answer him, but ran up into the woods, following the path toward the house that Barbara had taken. Fred Coe seemed about to follow her, but Henry put a restraining hand on his arm.

"No," he said. "Let them go. It's their affair."

Meanwhile, Harry Vandike was wading out of the water, one arm supporting Emmy, who was still choking. With difficulty, she said to Henry, "You might have warned me—"

Henry said, "I told you, darling. If you'd known in advance, your reactions wouldn't have been natural. I'm sorry you had a fright, but you were never in any danger, and this had to be done. I didn't enjoy it any more than you did."

"Perhaps somebody will now do some explaining," said Fred Coe. "By God, Harry, I'm glad to see you. We all thought you were at the bottom of some ravine in Wales. Have a drink."

"I could use one," said Vandike with a sardonic smile. He began stripping off the wetsuit, to reveal ordinary swimming trunks underneath. "Returning from the dead not once, but twice, is quite an effort."

Dr. Cartwright said, "But yesterday, Tibbett told us that you—"

"I knew he wasn't dead," said Myrtle. "I told you so, Mr. Tibbett, and you wouldn't listen."

Henry said, "After yesterday's little charade, Mrs. Waterford, I thought that you might come and confide a little more in me. But you didn't."

"I had promised Harry," said Myrtle. "I'm a woman of my word, I hope."

"What had you promised Harry?" demanded Fred Coe, handing Vandike a large Bloody Mary.

"He came to see me last Tuesday," said Myrtle. "He was driving a hired car. He was all dressed for climbing, and he wanted to change at my house on the way to London. He told me he would come back in the afternoon and return to Wales. He also said he suspected he might be in danger, and he had decided to disappear for a few days. He said I shouldn't be alarmed at any reports of his death, and that I was to tell nobody that he was actually alive and well and in hiding. I did my best; Harry and I have always been friends. But when Chief Superintendent Tibbett convinced me that he had proof that Harry had been to see me, well, what could I do? I told half the truth."

Henry said, "Emmy remarked to me yesterday, after my little talk, that parts of it were not true, and that some of you must know it. We have just heard from Myrtle. What about you, Dr. Cartwright?"

Cartwright had gone very pale. "I've nothing to tell," he said icily.

"Oh, yes, you have," said Henry. "A great deal. You were staying here when Jeannie was drowned. You knew that her death was not accidental. You were almost certainly deputed to keep Barbara out of the way during the actual murder."

"I—" Cartwright began.

"Anyway," Henry went on, "now that she has recovered her memory of the incident, she'll probably be able to tell us. You also knew that Jeannie had had an illegitimate son, and you were instrumental in handing the baby over to Harold Vandike for adoption. Yes, Harry?"

"Certainly he was," said Vandike. He waggled a reproachful finger at Cartwright. "Really, Bill, you should have come clean. After all, it wasn't against the law."

"All this," said Henry, "was before Pamela Warfield married Robert Oppenshaw. In fact, Jeannie's baby must have been born shortly after Warfield's death. The only explanation of that will is that Francis Warfield knew that his fifteen-year-old daughter was pregnant. I don't think he would have wanted an adoption, but by the time the child was born, he had no say in the matter, and a teenage daughter with an illegitimate baby would have been highly inconvenient to the widowed Mrs. Warfield—the more so since the child would have done her out of her inheritance. Jeannie herself couldn't have known the provision her father's will made for her child—and Pamela certainly must have drilled into her that a baby was the last thing a young, pretty, and eligible girl needed." Henry looked around at the others. "Well? Correct so far?"

"To the best of my knowledge," said Cartwright stiffly. "But if you are accusing me—"

"I'm not accusing you, Dr. Cartwright. I am merely speculating. Lady Oppenshaw obviously had a very strong hold over you, or she could not have made you give her the drug that was intended to knock Harry out before his murder."

Cartwright began to protest, but Henry held up his hand. "All right, Doctor. I told you I was guessing, and the police do not take action on guesses. Nevertheless, there is a very obvious explanation of the hold that the Oppenshaws have over you. You were the father of Jeannie's baby."

Dr. Cartwright said nothing. Henry went on, "Jeannie was a minor. You were a young doctor. If the truth got out, your career would have been ruined before it started. Ever since, you've been at the mercy of the Oppenshaws."

"Not the Oppenshaws." Cartwright was as precise as ever. "Pamela only. Robert knew nothing about the baby, and still doesn't."

Henry turned to Vandike. "And you? Did you know whose child it was?"

Vandike hesitated. "Well, I—"

"Of course you did," said Henry. "You told the Turnberrys that both parents were healthy and of good family."

Vandike did not reply, but Fred Coe said, "That wasn't true. Pamela told us this morning about Jeannie's illness—"

"There wasn't anything the matter with Jeannie," said Henry. "Vandike knew it, and so did Cartwright. Pamela lied to her husband to make him feel better about drowning her stepdaughter. Because, you see, Robert Oppenshaw had to have that money then and there, or he'd have lost his chance to buy the firm. It's obvious that Pamela only told him after they were married that the money wasn't hers except for a life interest, and that only Jeannie's death could enable her to inherit outright. When Pamela married Oppenshaw, she knew she must get rid of Jeannie before her twenty-first birthday. In a way,

Robert's financial position was a godsend to her.'

In a shaking voice, Dr. Cartwright said, "The Turnberrys? You mean—Peter was my son?"

"Yes, Doctor."

"Oh, my God. And to think that I—" He stopped abruptly.

Henry said to Vandike, "I was explaining this morning that neither the natural nor the adoptive *parents* knew one another's identity. But Pamela Oppenshaw knew, didn't she?"

"She insisted," said Vandike. "I was able to assure her that the Turnberrys were a thoroughly suitable couple. Good solid business people who would give the boy a decent start in life."

Henry said, "Of course, you didn't know the provisions of Francis Warfield's will until quite recently, when Roger Talbot got a copy of it during research for your book."

Vandike's face darkened. "No, I did not. And I can tell you, Tibbett, that when I read that will, I was appalled. I saw at once that Pamela had had him adopted to do him out of his inheritance. The fact that she then remarried, and that Jeannie was drowned before her twenty-first birthday—well, it had to make one think. But what could I do? I had compromised myself by telling Peter that he was adopted and disclosing his mother's identity. Law or no law, a lawyer was never entitled to do that. I had also shown him the documents."

"Shown? Not given?"

"Of course not. I only discovered during the Carnworth week that Peter had gone back to my chambers and persuaded the clerk to let him take the papers out for another look. Since the clerk knew he had seen them with me, he saw no harm in it. Just for a few minutes. Long enough to get them photocopied. Peter told me that week that he had photocopies at his home in St. Lawrence, and that he was prepared to produce them, if necessary. He also told Pamela Oppenshaw that he knew his true identity and that if Barbara didn't marry him, he had evidence to prove that Carnworth should be his."

"It was quite a coincidence," said Henry, "that the Turnberrys should leave London and come to live so close to Carnworth."

Harry raised his eyebrows slightly and smiled. "Not really," he said. "Peter was one of my pupils at Oxford, and naturally I took an interest in him. He told me his father was planning to semiretire to the country. I knew that the St. Lawrence house was for sale, and I thought it would be nice for Peter to spend some years in the part of the world that had been his mother's home. I plead guilty—the suggestion came from me. In all innocence."

"I'll have to accept that," said Henry. "You told Peter who he really was some years ago, but you only recently realized the implications, when you read the will. You told him about that too, of course, and you were determined to get the young man his lawful inheritance, if you could. You suggested the cross-word puzzle lark, and compiled it in such a way as to throw all the attention on Jean Warfield's death, hoping I would solve the whole thing. I fear I let you down." He paused. "I'm afraid Peter let you down too."

"What do you mean?"

"You know what I mean. He was ambitious, grasping, and not very scrupulous. You were fond of him, and inclined to be indulgent about his faults—but you've just told me that he cheated you over the documents. You know that he proposed to Barbara simply to get hold of Carnworth, one way or the other. When she broke the engagement, he was desperate. When he went riding to his parents' house that day, you knew very well what he was going to fetch. You couldn't risk your career and reputation by letting me see those documents. So you determined to intercept Peter on his way home, and get the papers back. You took out the day-sailer, beached her in Smugglers' Cove, and were prepared to climb the cliff to the path. But you were too late, weren't you?"

Slowly, Harold Vandike nodded. "He was already dead, lying on the rocks. I went through his pockets, but the papers weren't there. So I got back into the boat and finished my day's sail."

Emmy broke in, "Why on earth didn't you raise the alarm then?"

Vandike said, "There was nothing I could do for Peter. Somebody had killed him and taken the papers. It didn't take much reasoning to decide that it was the Oppenshaws—probably Pamela. The fact that she had those papers gave her a stranglehold over me. I decided to keep out of the whole thing. I didn't even go to see Peter's parents the next day. I simply couldn't face them, knowing that Peter must have been murdered. With Peter dead, the Oppenshaws had nothing to fear—unless I made a fuss. So I didn't make a fuss."

"Just a minute," said Emmy. She turned to Henry. "The Oppenshaws couldn't have killed Peter. They both had perfect alibis—you told me that yourself."

Henry said, "I know I did, and I believed it at the time. As you all know, the Oppenshaws were at a large tea party given by Lady Whitstable, and my inspector found a witness to swear that their car never left the house. Well, Sir Robert's alibi is indeed foolproof, for he was talking to that witness throughout the crucial time. However, as soon as I heard that Dr. Cartwright had taken his car out that afternoon, I knew that Pamela Oppenshaw's alibi wasn't unbreakable after all. That's what you meant, wasn't it, Dr. Cartwright, when you began to say just now 'to think that I—'? You were under orders, but you never dreamt that you would be instrumental in killing your own son."

"It seemed such a little thing," protested Cartwright miserably. "Pamela Oppenshaw simply asked me to be at the back entrance to Lady Whitstable's house at a quarter past four. To leave my car with the keys in it and go for a walk. Come back at five and drive it back to Carnworth. I'd no idea—"

"Never mind that for now," said Henry. "It's easy enough for a guest at a big party to slip out the back way; so long as she's not gone too long nobody will notice. However, Pamela had to get her timing just right. She could calculate just when Peter would arrive at the one point where the cliff path passes close to the road. Incidentally, her one bad mistake was to tell me that the road never went near the path.

"Anyhow, she was in a desperate hurry. She had to knock Peter out—with a tire iron, I suspect—search his pockets for the papers, which she found, rip the girth and tether Melly—"

"If she had an alibi for the actual time of the murder," said Emmy, "why did she tie the horse up?"

"That's easy," said Henry. "She didn't want the alarm raised too soon, because she was determined that her husband should be the first person to ride out and look for Peter. She knew that she had some things to tidy up at the murder site the next morning, and she didn't want any strangers getting there first. She must have taken the car and driven up there as soon as Sir Robert and Timmond left the Manor at seven. They had a forty-minute ride to get there, so she could easily have fixed the evidence and been on her way home by then."

He turned again to Vandike. "You thought you could keep out of trouble by not making a fuss. You were wrong. Pamela Oppenshaw killed Peter and found the papers—but they were photocopies. You still had the originals, and you knew the truth. If you had really died, what would have happened to those originals?"

Vandike said, "Those relating to the Turnberrys would have been returned to them. Jeannie was dead, and the father was not named, at Jeannie's request. So those papers would have been sent to the next of kin."

"To Pamela Oppenshaw?"

"That's right."

"So," said Henry, "you see why you had to be disposed of. It must have been quite a shock when she telephoned you in Wales and suggested a meeting at Myrtle's house."

"Lady Oppenshaw!" exclaimed Myrtle. "I'd no idea—"

Ignoring her, Vandike said, "Yes, she telephoned. But it was I who suggested Myrtle's house as a rendezvous. Her idea was that I should come up to Reading by train, where she'd meet me, and we could discuss various matters. I wanted to know what she was up to, and I realized I might be in danger, so I was determined that a couple of people, at least, should know what had really happened. Especially when she suggested that I tell people at Aberpriddy that I was going out for a solitary climb. She said she'd drive me back there after we'd had our little talk. That's why I hired a car and came to town to see you, Tibbett. I was damned if I was going to be set up for murder so easily. Pamela wasn't too pleased with the idea of meeting at Myrtle's place, but I said it would be more private, and that I'd make

231

sure Myrtle was typing away at the new Jack Harvey mystery when I met the Bentley in the driveway."

"You told me," said Myrtle, with outraged dignity, "that you were driving to Great Middleford to change, and then on to London for some clandestine appointment. You said you would come back the same way, and advised me to stick to my typewriter and not to worry if I heard you'd disappeared."

"Correct, Myrtle," said Vandike with a sardonic smile. "I certainly didn't want you to worry. Actually, Pamela turned up a little late, and was surprised to see me in my city suit, with my climbing gear packed in the rucksack. However, as she had no intention of letting me get back to Wales anyway, she didn't bother. She was in a rush to be off, and said we could talk in the car. I felt pretty sure she'd got hold of some sort of drug to knock me out—"

Henry interrupted, "Dr. Cartwright, I presume?"

Cartwright, who was sitting with his head in his hands, just nodded.

"Well," Vandike went on, "when she offered me a sweet—the top one of an open packet, of course—I pretended to take it, but actually I palmed it rather neatly and threw it out the window. Professional magic has always interested me, and I've dabbled a little in it. It comes in handy when I play my celebrated jokes on people.

"Anyhow, pretty soon I pretended to pass out. I wasn't in the least surprised when, as soon as she thought I was unconscious, she turned off the westward road and headed south towards Southampton. I had just time to register that before she pulled off the highway at a deserted spot and bundled me and my rucksack down on the floor of the car, next to the driver's seat, and put a blanket over me. There's room for that in a Bentley. I was glad of the rucksack. I reckoned if it came to the worst, I could put up a fight with a piton."

"And where did she meet Sir Robert?" Henry asked.

"Don't ask me. Some little deserted creek off Southampton Water. He was there in a biggish motorboat. Between them they got me aboard, and then began to discuss the best way to dispose of me. It's an interesting experience," Vandike added, "lying under a blanket pretending to be drugged and listening to the disposal plan."

Emmy shivered in the sunshine. "You were very brave," she said.

"I had no choice, dear lady. I'd managed to extract a piton from the rucksack, but otherwise I was completely unarmed. Finally it was agreed that Pamela should drive to the ferry and back to Carnworth, while Robert dropped me and my rucksack overboard from the boat. He had thoughtfully brought a lot of heavy stones to weigh me down. Robert was adamant that they shouldn't tie me up. I had a feeling all along that he hated the whole business, and wanted at least to give me a chance, which was a relief. Anyhow, he simply loaded my jacket pockets with rocks, and Pamela made sure it was buttoned tight. The rucksack was heavy enough to sink on its own. In the unlikely event that my body somehow floated out of the jacket and was washed up—well, it would be another of those mysteries. Nothing to connect it with Carnworth.

"So far, so good. I'm a strong swimmer, and I can stay underwater for quite a time. It would be easy enough to get out of the jacket. So long as Oppenshaw didn't take me too far out before he jettisoned me, all would be well. Happily, he didn't. He was only too keen to be rid of me. Personally, I don't think he'd have gone along with the scheme at all, if he hadn't had Lady Macbeth on his heels."

"Lady Macbeth?" said Myrtle.

"Lady Oppenshaw, I should say. It was obviously the same with Jeannie's murder. My lady is the driving force, but she makes sure the old man does the dirty work. Ever since Jeannie's death, she's had him where she wants him.

"Anyhow, to get back to that eventful evening—Oppenshaw motored the boat down the creek and into Southampton Water. He knows those parts well, but luckily so do I. He aimed for the nearest deep water, and over the side I went. By the time I'd got out of that bloody jacket and surfaced, there was nothing to be seen of the boat but a couple of lights disappearing hell-for-leather towards the Solent.

"I took it easy for a while, then swam ashore to where I could see some lights—it was only about a mile. By then, I wasn't in what you'd call good shape. Sopping wet, exhausted, no jacket and no money, except for a few pence in my trouser pocket.

"I found a telephone box and put through a collect call to the Turnberrys. James just had time to catch the last car ferry from Yarmouth, together with some dry clothes. He found me, we put up at some small hotel for the night, and went back to the island early the next morning."

"I had a hunch you'd be there," Henry said.

"I hope," said Vandike, "that James put on a good show of grief, arousing pity and terror, at your exposition yesterday."

Henry grinned. "He was threatening to turn into a reincarnation of Sir Henry Irving. I had to give him a sharp slap between the shoulder blades, or he'd have started on 'The Bells.' However, Nora took him home safely. And they certainly seem to have conveyed my instructions to you efficiently this morning. By the way," he added, "why didn't you just get on to me at the Yard?"

"Because I could see how thin my story sounded, and I had a good motive for killing Peter. The Oppenshaws had apparently impeccable alibis, and they are powerful people." He appealed to Henry. "You know very well that you had to stage this whole charade to smoke them out."

Henry sighed. "Yes," he said. "I owe all you people an apology. The whole thing hinged on Barbara's amnesia about Jeannie's murder. I had to shock her back into remembering."

"So," said Fred Coe, "what happens now?"

As if in answer to his question, there came two sharp reports from the direction of the house. Two gunshots.

Henry jumped to his feet. "Stay here, all of you. I'll go."

20

Henry was just emerging from the shelter of the trees and into the open green of the park when he saw Barbara coming out of the French windows that led from the drawing room to the terrace. He also saw that she had a shotgun in her hands. He began to run.

"Barbara!" he called.

She stopped and looked at him blankly. Then she said, "They're both dead."

"What are you doing with that gun?" Henry demanded harshly.

"I shot—"

"You didn't shoot them. Barbara, listen to me. You didn't shoot them."

There was a long silence. Then Barbara said, "I went straight to the old nursery. I couldn't face anybody, not after I remembered. Then, a bit later, I heard voices from the drawing room. Father and Mother. Mother sounded hysterical. I came out onto the terrace and watched through the window. I saw Father's shotgun in there. I knew I had to kill Father, and then of course I'd have to kill her too, because she'd be a witness."

Henry said, "Where did you get that gun?"

"I went in and picked it up. They didn't even notice me. I wonder why. So I shot them."

"Give it to me."

Listlessly, Barbara held out the shotgun. Henry pulled a handkerchief out of his pocket and carefully took the gun by the barrel. He said again, "You didn't kill either of them." Raising his voice, he called, "Mr. Timmond!"

With suspicious speed, Timmond appeared from around the corner of the house.

Henry said, "You were watching, as I asked?"

"Yes, sir. And I'm afraid there's been a dreadful accident, sir. Still, I didn't come until you called, like you said. There was nothing I could do for the poor souls, in any case."

"Tell me what happened, Mr. Timmond."

"Well, sir, Sir Robert was in the drawing room. He had his shotgun that he goes after rabbits and such with, and he was cleaning it. I thought that was odd, because the drawing room's no place to clean a gun. Then Miss Barbara came running up from the sea path, looking proper put out, and headed for the old nursery. Next thing, Lady Oppenshaw came along."

"Did she seem upset?" Henry asked.

Timmond considered. "Agitated, I'd say, sir. More angry than upset, really. She went into the drawing room. I was keeping watch, like you said. I couldn't hear the words, but I could tell there was some big row going on. Lady Oppenshaw was very worked up then, sir, I could see. Sir Robert was very calm and sort of . . . well, detached, sir. He'd got the gun together again, and then—well, it happened so quick, sir—but it must have gone off accidental. Next thing, there's a scream and Lady Oppenshaw's down on the floor. Sir Robert just stood there, looking at her. I came closer, to where there's an open window. I didn't know what to do, and that's the truth, sir. Then Sir Robert said a funny thing. To himself, like. He said, 'Yes, Tibbett. All over. What a relief.' And, quite calm, he put the barrel of the gun in his mouth and . . well, that was it. They're both in there."

"And what about Miss Barbara?"

"When she heard the shots, she came running into the drawing room from inside the house—the old nursery's just on the other side of it, see? And she stood there looking, and then she

236

took the gun out of her father's hand and came out onto the terrace and met you, sir."

Henry turned to Barbara. He said, "You see? Luckily for you, I'd arranged to have someone watching them. Now, as your poor father said, it's all over."

Suddenly Barbara began to cry with utter desperation. Henry said, "Mr. Timmond, will you take Miss Barbara to the kitchen and ask Cook to give her a nice cup of tea? I'm going to phone the police."

When all the formalities had been sorted out, Henry had a quiet talk with Detective Sergeant Hemming. The police contention at the inquest would be that Sir Robert had accidentally shot his wife while cleaning his gun, and in an agony of remorse had then killed himself.

Hemming was convinced that this was the truth, and that the jury would accept it. The verdict on Peter Turnberry was not even mentioned. The miraculous return from the dead of Professor Harold Vandike would be put down to one of his well-known malicious pranks. He was prepared to issue an apology to the members of the search parties who had been scouring the Devil's Chimney area for him and to make a sizable donation to their cause.

When Hemming and his men had gone, Henry had a long and private talk with Barbara Oppenshaw. Her recollection of Jeannie's death was now perfectly clear.

"We went down to swim," she said, "and after a bit I came out of the water while Jeannie stayed in, doing some proper swimming instead of trying to teach me.

"Then I saw Dr. Cartwright coming down the path, and he called me. I went to see what he wanted, but I never really liked him much, and I wanted to get back to the beach. He was trying to show me toadstools and things in the woods—but I slipped away from him. That was when I saw Daddy He was on the beach in one of those frogman suits. I just had time to see his face before he put on his snorkel mask. Then he went into the water, making for Jeannie. I thought it was some sort of game. I called, but he didn't hear me. Jeannie saw him coming and waved, and then . . ." Barbara covered her eyes. "It was horrible. He just grabbed her and held her under. I think I screamed, but I don't think any noise came out. I was sort of numb. I remembered going back to Dr. Cartwright and asking him quite calmly about toadstools. He'd not seen anything, and he had no idea that I had.

"I said I wanted to go back to the house, so he took me, and Mother said in a funny sort of voice, 'Where's Jeannie?' And I remember now that I thought, I'm not going to tell *you*, so I just said, 'She's having a swim on her own.' Mother said I should go and lie down, and she gave me a drink and a pill and I went to sleep. When I woke up, I couldn't remember anything after leaving the house with Jeannie in the morning. Later on, they told me Jeannie had drowned—and I was just miserable, but the memory of what really happened had gone.

"It's funny, though. There must have been a subconscious memory, because I never felt the same way about Mother or Father again. All I wanted to do was to get away from here—first to boarding school and college, then to my own flat in London. I always felt guilty about it, because they were both so sweet and kind to me. I suppose that helped to make me . . . sort of mixed up. I never guessed the real reason."

Henry said, "You've had a frightful experience, my dear, and I'm desperately sorry. But you're young, and now that it's all out in the open, you'll get over it. Just as you'll get over the moment when you thought you'd shot your parents, even though they were already dead when you went into the drawing room."

Managing a sort of half-smile, Barbara said, "Since today seems to be my moment of truth, you'd better tell me about Peter too. I think you've guessed already that I was very deeply in love with him. It was only when I realized that he didn't care about me, but only about my money, that . . . well, something snapped. I'm afraid I behaved very badly. I was awfully rude to Emmy at your apartment that evening. Please apologize to her for me."

"You have nothing to apologize for, Barbara," said Henry

"You've been through several kinds of hell, and you've come out of them intact. Now you must get on with your life and your work."

"But Father killed Peter, didn't he?"

"No, Barbara. He didn't. Pamela did." After Henry explained that Peter was Jeannie's illegitimate son and told her how he had been murdered, he hoped that she would ask no more questions. Fortunately she did not.

When Henry and Emmy returned to their room to pack, there was a respectful knock on the door. It was Sowerby, the butler. He carried a silver tray, on which there was a letter addressed to Henry.

"Dr. Cartwright has just left the Manor," said Sowerby, with the blend of respect and mourning required by the situation. "He asked me to hand you this, sir."

The letter was undated, but was on Carnworth Manor stationery and marked "2:00 P.M."

Dear Mr. Tibbett,

If, as I suspect, the whole truth comes to light this afternoon, I am asking Sowerby to give this to you. I freely admit that I was the father of Jeannie Warfield's child. I freely admit that, at Pamela's request, I arranged for him to be adopted through Harold Vandike. I had no idea that he was Peter Turnberry.

I also had no idea that Robert Oppenshaw intended to drown Jeannie when he asked me to keep Baba away from the beach that afternoon. I had no idea that in complying with Pamela's apparently harmless request about the car, I was conspiring in the death of my son.

I freely admit that I gave her the drug which—although I did not know for what purpose she would use it—would render Harry Vandike insensible.

Of course, after Jeannie's death, I realized what must have happened, and that Pamela had tricked me into being an accessory. As for her other requests—I was utterly in the dark. I thought perhaps she might be cheating on Robert with some other man. Anyway, what I thought or didn't think has little relevance. I had no choice but to comply.

In view of all this, it is obviously impossible for me to continue in practice as I have done, even if no charges are made against me. I therefore propose to volunteer to serve in a mission hospital abroad, one I have supported financially for some time. I feel it would be a pity to waste what medical skill I possess.

W. Cartwright.

Some months later, Henry and Emmy Tibbett were having a pleasant lunch in London with Barbara Oppenshaw, Harry Vandike, and Fred Coe. This was their first reunion since the Carnworth tragedy.

Carnworth Manor had been sold, and was now a private school for young ladies of ample means. A new Miss Twinkley novel was in the bookstores and the public libraries. It was to be the last of the collaborative series. Fred had found, to his satisfaction, that he could produce plots as well as write the adventures of that intrepid lady. However, he did correspond on medical points with Dr. Cartwright at an address in Bolivia.

Barbara, to everyone's surprise, had assumed full control of Oppenshaw and Trilby, which was doing very well. The Lydia Drake books, Henry had noticed with some amusement, were now being published by another firm, and new titles appeared less frequently.

He said, "You're a very honest person, Barbara. I suppose it *would* be nepotism to publish your own books. But surely your new publishers must know who you are?"

Barbara grinned. "Can you keep a secret?"

"You should know I can."

"Well, poor old Myrtle was really running out of ideas, and for some reason she seems to have gone off the idea of violence."

Henry avoided meeting Vandike's amused eye.

"So," Barbara went on, "we've retired Jack Harvey—he has

given up writing and gone to live in the south of France. And Myrtle has taken over the Lydia Drake books."

"But—"

"Oh, I write them, of course. But she submits them to the publishers, and gets the royalties. I don't need the money, I write just for fun—and it means that she can keep that nice house of hers."

"And she still qualifies as a member of the Guess Who club," said Henry. "When's the next meeting?"

"We've dissolved the club," said Barbara easily. "After what happened, it seemed macabre to go on." Suddenly she looked across the table at Harry Vandike. "I've been longing to ask you for months, Harry. Where on earth were you when we all thought you'd been killed in Wales?"

With no trace of hesitation, Vandike said, "Oh, here and there. I spent some time with Henry, and some with Myrtle. Then, when I heard they were sending out search parties, I thought it was time to reappear. I'd had my fun by then, and scored off my victims."

"I see," said Barbara. "Another of your typically cruel practical jokes."

"That's right," said Harry Vandike.